D0211415

"Look, you're starting to weird me out," I said.

As much as I wanted to find out what had really gone down last night, I had a pretty good idea by now, and the thought of spending more time with my one-night stand was proving to be a huge mistake. "So while it's been swell, I really must be going—"

His hand clamped over mine again. "You're staying."

I was? Every fiber in my being protested that notion, yet I found that I could not disobey him. Weirdest thing. "Right. I'm staying."

I sat.

Noah's hand patted mine again. "I think we have a real problem on our hands."

"And why is that?"

He leaned in close and whispered in my ear. I leaned closer, too, my breasts pressing against the hard counter-top and my body tingling with excitement. Would he lick the shell of my ear? Would I burst into an instant orgasm if he did?

"I think you died last night."

Talk about killing the mood.

MORE PRAISE FOR JILL MYLES'S
TEMPTING DEBUT,

GENTLEMEN PREFER SUCCUBI

"Debut author Jill Myles just wowed me! She's written an outstanding first novel—I read *Gentlemen Prefer Succubi* in one breathless sitting. Want laugh-out-loud scenes, scorching eroticism, and pulse-pounding adventure? Don't miss this book!"

—Kresley Cole, *New York Times* bestselling author of *Kiss of a Demon King*

"Witty, sexy, and wickedly fun. Jill Myles is a captivating new voice, and I can't wait to see what she writes next."

—Ilona Andrews, *New York Times* bestselling author of *Magic Strikes*

"A fabulous rollercoaster ride filled with sex, adventure, humor, and just enough darkness to keep the reader guessing. A combination of old myths and brand-new interpretations blend together seamlessly in this erotic and fast-paced romantic urban fantasy. Jill Myles made me wish I had written this book! Hot, delicious, and witty, the hottest new star in the genre has just landed."

—Kathryn Smith, *USA Today* bestselling author of *Night After Night*

Gentlemen Prefer Succubi

Jill Myles

Pocket **Star** Books
New York   London   Toronto   Sydney

Pocket Star Books
A Division of Simon & Schuster, Inc.
1230 Avenue of the Americas
New York, NY 10020

This book is a work of fiction. Names, characters, places, and incidents either are products of the author's imagination or are used fictitiously. Any resemblance to actual events or locales or persons, living or dead, is entirely coincidental.

First Pocket Star Books paperback edition January 2010

POCKET STAR BOOKS and colophon are registered trademarks of Simon & Schuster, Inc.

For information about special discounts for bulk purchases, please contact Simon & Schuster Special Sales at 1-866-506-1949 or business@simonandschuster.com.

The Simon & Schuster Speakers Bureau can bring authors to your live event. For more information or to book an event contact the Simon & Schuster Speakers Bureau at 1-866-248-3049 or visit our website at www.simonspeakers.com.

Designed by Julie Adams

Manufactured in the United States of America

10 9 8 7 6 5 4 3 2 1

ISBN 978-1-4165-7282-4
ISBN 978-1-4165-8814-6 (eBook)

Acknowledgments

I wrote this book in 2005. In the five years between now and then, this list has grown exponentially and continues to grow every day. Getting a book published has truly been one of the most thrilling experiences of my life, and so many people have helped me or supported me along the way. I'd say that it takes a village to publish a book, but I'm pretty sure everyone uses that phrase.

Thanks to my Pocket team—my brilliant editor, Micki Nuding, who wields an editing pencil of greatness, and her fabulous assistant, Danielle Poiesz—I cannot gush enough about how wonderful it is to work with both of you. There should be some sort of national holiday involved to celebrate your combined awesomeness.

Thank you to the art team for the beautiful cover art that quite possibly made me stand up and prance around, waving my hands and squealing at the sight of it. The bellybutton sweat on the model nearly did me in.

Thank you to Carolyn and Ashley Grayson for finding this book a home. And to Holly Root, who preserves my sanity on a daily basis—you rock, you really do.

Mega-thanks to Jane Litte and Vernieda Vergara, because we have sent enough emails between us to make servers tremble. You guys keep me sane. Thank you to Meljean Brook, Roxanne St. Claire, and Kasey Mackenzie, who constantly let me bounce questions off them, even the weird ones. And to Ilona Andrews—I couldn't have done it without you. Or I might have, but there probably would have been a lot more panic attacks along the way. You're a great friend, and I'm going to stop teasing you about the mustard paper . . . someday.

Thank you to the pfriends (no typo) who are some of the best cheerleaders around—Jodi Meadows, Holly Mcdowell, Rae Carson Finlay, and Heather Marshall. Also, a thank you to my Purgie people—the Purgatory thread over on Absolute Write. I've never met a more supportive group! And a special shout-out to Gretchen McNeil, who is the fastest reader in the west.

To my Mom and Dad. You are the best supporters ever and I love you both. Please understand if I come to your house and rip out all the sex scenes in my books, though. And to my sister Jennifer, who is my biggest fan (you can keep the sex scenes in your copies, you dirty bird). To my cousin Betsy, who once said I could take a book from her shelves and I ended up sneaking away with a suitcase-full. You and several dozen paperback romances started me down this road.

And finally, I'd like to thank the Greek historian Herodotus. Because you wrote two paragraphs about an obscure Egyptian queen named Nitocris, and that was enough to set my mind on fire with a story.

To my husband, who allows me to be the world's worst wife. You're my hero.

Gentlemen Prefer Succubi

CHAPTER ONE

It had obviously been one hell of a night if I couldn't recall why I was waking up in a Dumpster.

I blinked a few times, staring at the sky overhead. *A Dumpster?* Surely not. But between the flies, the stench, and the garbage bags surrounding me, I didn't know what else it could be. My left hand rested on something clammy and wet, and I hoped that it was an old newspaper and not something more sinister. I didn't even want to think about what was tickling my bare toes.

I sat up, cradling my throbbing head and trying to think. What the hell had happened? I didn't normally find myself comatose and drooling amid piles of garbage.

Shit. My boss was going to be sooo totally pissed at me.

Something itched against my breast and I reached up to scratch, finding a hard plastic card shoved into the side of my bra.

A room key for a hotel. The Grand National here in New City, Wyoming.

My mind regurgitated a series of drunken memories from my bender last night. I'd met a man at the bar of the swanky hotel just as the sun was cresting into dawn and I was polishing off my latest martini. He'd walked into the bar and, since the place was deserted, headed straight for me and bought me another drink. I'd let him. I mean, hell, free alcohol.

He was even hot to boot, which was a nice change from the creeps that normally tried to pick me up. I vaguely remembered an amazing body, a voice that could stop traffic, and the bluest eyes I'd ever seen.

That wasn't the only thing I remembered. My brain flashed another image into my head, of a rather large part of my date's anatomy. Which I'd seen in close detail.

"Ohmigod. I'm a slut," I moaned, burying my face in my hands.

I'd never had a one-night stand before, but by the time I'd met my Blue-Eyed Casanova, I was eight or twelve martinis into an all-nighter and three sheets to the wind. I couldn't remember a darn thing except those eyes and that smile. And his dick.

That bothered me on levels I didn't even want to think about. I sighed and brushed a wet wad of trash off my hand and straightened my thick, smudged glasses on my face. At least they hadn't been wrecked in my night in the garbage.

"Who's there?" a warbling voice called, and I clambered through the trash to the edge of the Dumpster, peering over the metal side.

A bearded older man—homeless, if the stocking cap and reek of whiskey were any indication—stared up at me in surprise. A familiar cute black-and-pink handbag was tucked under his left arm.

"Hey, that's mine." I pointed a grimy finger at the purse. "Give it back."

Much to my surprise, he handed it up to me with a wide-eyed expression. "I thought you were dead. Sorry."

What an odd statement. I frowned down at him. "Sorry, no. Do you have anything else of mine I might be needing?" My legs were devoid of pantyhose, and my bare toes wiggled between the garbage. My shoes were nowhere to be seen, and I wasn't even sure I still had panties on—all of which was making me extremely nervous. Resisting the urge to cry, I swallowed hard.

"I didn't take them. I didn't take anything else." The bum sounded rather miffed that I had the gall to accuse him of stealing.

I ignored him and began to dig through the garbage, trying not to think too hard about what I was touching. Sure enough, my favorite pink-and-black Steve Madden pumps were there underneath a pizza box. I shook them out to be safe.

With my belongings in hand, I swung a leg over the side of the Dumpster and began to climb out. I'd probably given the bum a flash of panties (if I still had them), but I didn't care.

He took a swig from his brown-bag-covered bottle. "You were dead, you know," he pointed out. "You weren't breathing."

I slid down onto the pavement with a thump, losing a few strands of chow mein that had stuck to my skirt. "Um, what exactly makes you say that?" I asked as I put on my shoes.

"I'm serious," he protested. "I checked. You weren't breathing. I even saw your boyfriend dump you here. I wouldn't take a purse from a live girl."

I looked up from picking a noodle off my shoe. "You did? Blond guy? Blue eyes?" *Big package?*

The bum shook his head and took another swig of alcohol. "Naw. Black-haired. Real tall. Nice coat. He kissed your cheek and dumped you in there."

I didn't recall Bachelor No. 2. Good lord, what *had* I done last night? My date had definitely been blond. An image flashed through my mind—a memory?—of us in the shower, my arms twined around his neck while he lifted my bare leg to fit around his hips . . .

I wanted to cry. I didn't know if I was upset that I'd slept with a stranger, or that he was hot and I couldn't remember very much. I sighed and rubbed my neck. A sharp pain shot through my skin, like I'd rubbed it raw during my sleep. I touched the spot with careful fingers and found it sticky. Yet another gift from the garbage. Ugh. I looked over at my drunken companion. "What time is it?"

The bum checked his plastic wristwatch. "It's eleven a.m. Tuesday," he announced.

"No, it's not. Today's Monday." I remembered it, because we were scheduled to be short a docent at the museum today. Monday.

"It's Tuesday," he repeated. "You've been in that garbage since yesterday. Dead."

His story was getting pretty tiresome. I decided to change the subject. "Say, do you have any napkins, old man? Clean ones?" I touched the sore spot on my neck again and winced.

"I do. Cost ya five dollars."

I glared at him. "How about you give me the napkins and I don't call the police?"

He shrugged. "They give me three square meals a day and a bed to sleep in. Go ahead and call 'em."

Obviously I wasn't going to win this one. I sighed and pulled my wallet out of my purse. All the money was in place, crumpled dollars sandwiched between a few receipts, my ID intact. That was a good sign, and my spirits perked up a little. I held a five-dollar bill out to him. "Here. Trade you."

He held out a stack of Burger King napkins in return and took the money. "Thank you kindly, miss."

"Don't mention it," I said, swabbing at my neck and sizing up the alley as I tried to discern my location. It looked to be downtown New City, still outside the bar I'd found. The alley was strewn with garbage, murky puddles splotched the pavement, and mine was but one of many Dumpsters. Still, it looked like the entertainment district that I remembered being in before my memory blanked out, so that was comforting. I tossed down the napkin and stopped short when I saw the smear of dark red.

Blood?

I ran my hands along my neck in alarm. Nothing but smooth skin met my fingers—no cuts, no scratches, nothing. Maybe someone had spilled a daiquiri on me—I gave my neck another quick touch just to make sure there were no open wounds. Nothing.

"Well, it's been fun, but I should be running along," I announced to the bum, wiggling my fingers at him in farewell. "Thanks for the napkins."

"Anytime, dead girl." He took another swig, eyeing me as if I'd bite him.

I stumbled away, wobbling in my high heels. First, coffee. Then a bus home and a hot shower.

I turned the corner and saw two unexpected things: First, my alley wasn't behind the bar at all, but behind the rather large, sumptuous hotel that I sure as heck couldn't afford on a museum salary (but had a key to in my bra). And second, I ran smack-dab into Blue Eyes, dressed in a suit, a cup of Starbucks in his hand.

He stopped and stared at me in shock.

I did the same.

He broke the silence first. "Jackie?"

"Yes?" I felt stupid for responding with that, but my memory was full of holes. All I could remember were random, naked parts of his body. My eyes flicked down to his crotch. Yep, he was my guy.

"You're still here?"

I wasn't sure whether to laugh at his comment or cry. Boy, talk about uncomfortable moments. "Am I not supposed to be?"

He smiled, and my legs turned to Jell-O. Lord, he was gorgeous. "It's just a surprise to see you again. You left in quite a hurry." He stared at my hair with a look of surprise.

My date seemed . . . different somehow. I studied him, trying to decide what it was. It wasn't just the clothing— I seemed to recall a lot of his bare, tanned chest pressed against my pale, fleshy one. It was his eyes. They weren't the same beautiful shade of blue as I remembered from last night—or yesterday, whatever—but more of a washed-out silver. It was disappointing to see him in the daylight and realize that he'd had beer beauty. Sure, he was still a gorgeous hunk, but there'd been something utterly . . . carnal about him that my drunken self had been unable to resist. My brain flashed other images— his fingers digging into my waist, my breasts bouncing in the air. I straddled him, rocking my hips atop his as he drove his hard cock deep inside me . . .

I buried my face in my hands, trying to stop the onslaught of memories.

"You have noodles in your curls." He reached out to touch a filthy hank of my hair.

"I do?" I felt around the mess myself. Sure enough, a long spaghetti noodle had entangled itself in my reddish-brown hair. "I think I fell asleep in someone's dinner. You know, when you left me in the *Dumpster*?"

"When I awoke, you were gone." He touched my cheek in a tender gesture, his fingertips brushing against my thick glasses. "I thought you were mad at me. That you regretted what happened between us."

At the smile, my heart thudded in my breast and my nipples tightened. I remembered that slow, sweet grin. He'd flashed it at me just before he'd lowered me to the hotel bed. He'd sucked on my nipples through my plain white bra, teasing them through the cheap fabric. The tips of my breasts hardened with the memory and I crossed my arms over my chest.

Oh my God, I *was* a slut. He was hot as hell, but I never slept with a guy on the first date. Never. *It wasn't even a date*, I reminded myself with horror. *He picked you up in the bar. Drunk. Easy.*

I scowled at him and batted his hand away. "I don't know why you get your kicks from leaving girls in the garbage, but getting me a cab and saying that you'd call me would have done the trick if you didn't want to see me again."

He gave me another heart-meltingly puzzled look. "What are you talking about? I woke up and you weren't there." He pulled my hand into his free one, rubbing his thumb across my dirty skin. "I wanted to find out your full name, Jackie."

We were only on a first-name basis? Talk about a slam to the ego. "Jackie Brighton," I blurted out.

He smiled at me as if I were delicious, and a low heat started throbbing between my legs. "Nice to meet you, Ms. Brighton. I'm glad we got to see each other again."

I pulled my hand out of his before I could jump his bones again. Wild sluts like me were capable of anything, after all. "What's today?"

The smile became puzzled. "It's the seventeenth. Tuesday."

Either he was in cahoots with the homeless guy or something really weird was going on. I frowned and pulled my cell phone out of my purse, staring at the date on the screen. Sure enough, the seventeenth. My phone had been on for so long that one lonely power bar remained at the top corner. "I seem to have lost a day somehow."

"You look exhausted." He touched my cheek again, and that awful, wonderful melting feeling started in my belly again. "Would you like to grab a bite to eat? It's about lunchtime. We can catch up on things."

"Lunchtime?" My stomach rumbled in response, reminding me that I hadn't had much to eat before my martini bender. Which, according to everyone but me, was *two* nights ago. "I hadn't really given it much thought."

"Come on," he said, taking my hand in his. "You look like you're having a rough day. I'll buy."

As soon as his warm hand closed over mine, the world rocked and desire exploded through me. My clothes itched and I suddenly yearned to throw them off and drag him into the nearest alley and ride him.

I settled for snatching my hand out of his. "Don't touch me."

He seemed nonplussed by my standoffish attitude. "I'm buying you lunch."

"Fine." As soon as I said it, I regretted it. Why was this guy so hard to resist? The lure of coffee was tempting, but not quite so much as the urge to find out what exactly happened the other night. And somehow, I just couldn't say no to him. "Coffee is fine, but no funny business, mister."

His mouth slid up in a gorgeous smile, and a pulse of attraction shot straight through me. Definitely the same guy, blue eyes or not. How embarrassing that I was still attracted to him.

How embarrassing that I didn't remember his name.

"Noah," he offered. "Noah Gideon."

"Fine," I repeated, trying not to think of his package or the wonderful things he'd done to me with it. "Coffee, and you can fill me in on the details, Noah."

"I would love for you to have coffee with me," he said, lifting my hand and kissing the knuckles, garbage smell and all.

Dumpster, I reminded myself. *He left you in a Dumpster!*

Now someone tell my throbbing loins that.

CHAPTER TWO

" Two coffees," he ordered, indicating that I should sit. The waitress looked shell-shocked at the sight of my gorgeous date and nodded, hurrying away. I could understand how she felt.

I sat down at the booth, determined not to be won over by the sexy smile he was beaming in my direction. "Nice place," I commented uneasily, unwrapping the silverware and placing the napkin in my lap. "Hope the fact that I'm covered in garbage doesn't bother you."

"Well, I was hoping you'd wash your hands." He winked at me.

I nearly melted into a puddle right there. God, those lips. They'd tugged on my flesh in countless naughty ways, and my brain seemed determined to feed those moments at the most inappropriate of times. A memory of his face between my parted thighs made me bolt to my feet, flushed and bothered. "Be right back."

I washed my face and hands in the bathroom, then returned to my impromptu date. The eatery was more of a small, trendy café than a full-service restaurant, but I cringed at the looks some of the other patrons were giving me and my wrinkled, dirty clothes. Or that brown smear that wouldn't go away on my sleeve, no matter how hard I'd scrubbed with the hand soap.

The blinding white smile on Noah's face could have melted an iceberg. "I like the atmosphere here, don't you?" He nudged a menu toward me as I slid into the booth. "Order something. You look like you had a rough night."

I nearly swallowed my tongue. Biting back a retort, I smiled sweetly at him and pushed the menu away. "I'll just have a salad. I'm not that hungry."

Actually, I was ravenous, but I couldn't eat a burger in front of such a gorgeous man. He'd probably wonder why my size-fourteen self was merrily chowing down when I should be dieting. At his incredulous look, I didn't know whether to be offended or cheered. "Salad sounds just lovely," I said, and refolded my napkin on my lap. "Now, about last night . . ."

I broke off the conversation starter when the waitress returned to take our orders. To my credit, I didn't bat an eye when my date ordered a triple-meat cheeseburger with extra mustard and onions. Instead, I concentrated on opening one Sweet'N Low packet and very carefully pouring half into my coffee.

"Miss?" The waitress looked at me, her pen poised above her notepad.

"Salad," I said, trying to remain pleasant.

She raised an eyebrow at me. "You—"

"Can I just get a damn salad?" I bit off before she could embarrass me further. Was it so hard to believe that a fat girl wanted a salad?

She scribbled something on her notepad. "I was going to tell you that you have a noodle in your hair."

Oh, of course. I picked the offending noodle out and wadded it into a napkin, holding it out to her. "Could you . . . ?"

When the waitress took it and stomped off, Noah sighed after her. "You realize she's going to spit in my burger now."

"Guess you should be a bit more discerning when it comes to your dates," I said, wrapping my hands around the coffee cup and blowing on it. "Which brings me to why I'm here."

"It's not for the pleasure of my company?" His voice was low, husky.

The simple words sent a bolt of desire straight through me again, a rather unnerving feeling in itself, much less when experienced in the middle of a crowded café. My mind dragged itself back into the gutter as he picked up his glass of water, and I found myself fixated on his long, tanned fingers. Those fingers had trailed all over my skin like hot feathers, stroking and brushing against my most sensitive areas. I remember how he'd looked into my eyes with his deep blues as he'd stroked at my clit. I had come against his fingers so hard that I'd screamed.

A flush crept over my entire body.

"Um." I fanned myself with my hand. What were we talking about again? Oh, yes. "That's just the thing. I don't *remember* the pleasure of your company. And seeing as how I woke up in a Dumpster *sans* pantyhose—or panties—I think enlightening me would be great." I did my best to sip my coffee with a bland expression on my face. *Must not be overwhelmed by his sexy voice. Or those lips. Or those broad, yummy shoulders.*

Noah leaned in close, smiling. "So does this mean you're not wearing any panties right now?"

I broke out in a nervous sweat. "Just answer the question."

He leaned back and his hand went to his thick blond hair, ruffling it. "Well, ah. We met at the hotel bar. You'd been there all night from the look of things, and I offered to call you a cab. The next thing I knew, you were climbing into my lap. I took it as an invitation—a very nice one, if I do say so." He looked over at me, and I could have sworn his eyes had a hint of blue to them. "You can do really amazing things with your mouth."

I spat coffee all over the table. Good lord, that didn't sound like me at all.

He took a sip of his own coffee, unbothered by my strangled noises. "You mentioned a disappointment at work just before . . . you know." Pale eyes gleamed as he scanned my appearance. "Something about getting passed over for a promotion? Does that ring a bell?"

I'd told him about that? "Exhibit coordinator at the museum. Much better than a lowly docent."

"A what?"

"A docent." No one ever knew what a docent was. "We give tours and point out the paintings."

"Ah." He paused, sipping his coffee. "Exhibit coordinator is much better, then?"

Much better was putting it mildly. I'd finally get to work with the ancient artifacts, bringing me a step closer to my real love, archaeology. I'd had my eye on the exhibit coordinator job since I first began as an intern at the New City Museum of Art. I'd worked my butt off for the last two years, but when it came down to it, the job had been given to someone with fewer degrees and bigger boobs. It was enough to drive anyone to drink, even a prude like me.

"I was upset." I shrugged, trying not to show how much it bothered me, even as I blinked back frustrated tears. "I went out for a few drinks at Escapes." Escapes was a lousy dive on the far end of town from my place, but the cheese fries were good.

"Isn't that in the south part of the city?"

I drank my coffee, hoping it would quell the growling of my stomach. "It is."

"So what are you doing here in downtown now?"

"I was hoping you could tell me." I blew on my coffee, trying to distract myself from looking into his beautiful eyes like some lovesick fool. Again. "To be honest," I said, "it's all a blur after the mugging." A big, sex-filled blur.

Funny, I hadn't even remembered the mugging until a few moments ago.

"Mugging?"

"Yeah." I shot a glance over at him. He was watching my mouth with a strange fixation, as if he'd remembered all the things that drunken-slut me had done to him with my "talented" mouth. I blushed and recrossed my legs. Man, it was warm in here.

"Weirdest thing," I said, trying not to reach across the table and do naughty things to him. "I remember this guy grabbing me on the way out of Escapes and grabbing my purse. Only I didn't let go of it."

I didn't want to add the *because I was drunk* part. "I seem to recall an alley, and"—I rubbed the side of my neck—"I think he *bit* me. I don't remember much after that, except passing out in the back of a cab and sharing a few drinks with you." The memory of the biting-mugging bothered me. My fingers touched my neck again, and I had to swallow hard.

The sexy, reach-across-the-table-and-fuck-me look was gone from his face. In fact, he looked rather green. "Did you say you were bitten?"

I nodded, looking mournfully down at my empty coffee mug. Noah wasn't looking at me like he wanted to eat me anymore. No coffee, and the waitress was probably slipping a hair or two in my salad. "Like I said, it's all pretty much a haze."

Noah reached over the table and grabbed my hand in his. "Jackie, this is very important. What was he wearing?"

I tried to jerk my hand from his and found that a rather useless action. "Let go of me or I'm going to start screaming."

"What was he wearing?" His voice was deadly low.

I rolled my eyes, trying to seem casual. "A black trench coat, I think. In August—go figure. Can I have my hand back now?"

Noah paled and released my hand at once. It was almost amusing—except he looked like he'd just been told he was about to be a father. "Bloody hell."

"Problem?" I inquired, tilting my head. "I don't see

why this guy's coat is so important. I mean, I was the one molested by him and you don't see me freaking out." I paused. "Which, come to think of it, is kinda weird in itself."

"He *bit* you, Jackie. He drained some of your blood and brought you to this side of town to throw off your trail." Noah rubbed a hand down his face. "And to put you right in my path. Bloody, bloody hell." His mouth set in a grim line, he looked back at me. "Tell me about the last day you remember. Your timeline. Everything you did."

"Look, you're starting to weird me out," I said. As much as I wanted to find out what had really gone down, spending more time with my one-night stand was proving to be a huge mistake. "So while it's been swell, I really must be going . . ."

His hand clamped over mine again. "You're staying."

Every fiber of my being protested that notion, yet I found that I could not disobey him. Weirdest thing. "Right. I'm staying."

I sat.

Noah's hand patted mine again. "I think we have a real problem on our hands."

"And why is that?"

He leaned in close. I leaned closer, too, my breasts pressing against the countertop and my body tingling with excitement. Would he lick the shell of my ear? Would I burst into an instant orgasm if he did?

"I think you died," he whispered.

Talk about killing the mood.

CHAPTER THREE

"Not you too?" I slammed up from the booth, tipping over coffee cups and causing several people to turn around. I didn't care—all of my dislike was focused squarely on Noah. "I've had enough of this. Go to hell!"

Did everyone around here have some sort of sick obsession with death?

Noah stood too, and his strong hand clamped my upper arm. "You'll sit down, and you'll be quiet." His voice remained low and calm.

To my surprise, I did just that, slouching back down in my seat and blinking at him. Noah sat as well, regarding me quietly as the waitress hurried over and cleaned up the spilled coffee. A few silent moments later, our cups were refilled and we were alone again. "Now sit and drink," he commanded.

"Why is it that whenever you say something, I feel like I have to obey you?" I picked up my mug, bewildered by my own actions.

He sighed. "I was afraid of that. Are you going to sit and listen to what I have to say, or do I have to force you to remain in place?"

I didn't suppose that it mattered either way, so I gave him a fake smile. "I'm all ears. Go ahead." Noah was the second person who thought I had died. And skeptic though I was, the hairs on the back of my neck were starting to prickle.

He raked a hand through his hair, looking rather distressed—until the waitress dropped his double cheeseburger in front of him. Then he just looked pleased.

My salad looked unexciting, but at least it wouldn't gravitate immediately to my hips. I took my fork and began picking out cucumber chunks and moving them to the side of my plate as I waited for him to begin speaking again.

"You're not taking this seriously enough," Noah began, between bites of his extremely greasy, extremely sloppy hamburger. It amazed me that he managed not to get any on his shirt, but remained neat and tidy. His tongue darted out to clean his lips, and I salivated.

What the hell was wrong with me?

Annoyed at myself, I tossed a napkin at him. "It's hard to take a man seriously when he's got mustard dripping down his chin," I lied.

I wanted to lick his lips for him.

Noah took the napkin and swished at his chin. "Sorry." He put the burger down and gave me a grave look. "I'm going to explain, and I don't want you to interrupt until I'm done."

I opened my mouth to protest, but nothing would come out. Crap! Another one of his mind-control techniques. What was it with this guy? And why wasn't I scared of a man who could force me to do whatever he wanted?

Actually, it turned me on. I crossed my legs again, hoping I'd hit that magic spot where the incessant pulsing would vanish.

It might be the whole utterly gorgeous thing he had going on. I'd never seen a better-looking man than him, like *ever*. Brad Pitt held nothing to this guy. His hair was dark blond, thick and curly. Longish, too—it scraped the collar of his well-made starched shirt. High cheekbones graced his face, accentuated by a perfect nose and chiseled mouth. He looked like he was heading to a business meeting in slacks and a pressed white shirt, but without the tie. Broad shoulders and big hands. Big everything. I flushed and shifted in my seat again.

He was almost too pretty for a man, all chiseled lines and aquiline features, topped off by those beautiful silvery eyes. When they were blue, like before, they had been stunning. Did he have colored contacts?

"You're quiet."

I stopped studying him through my thick glasses and gave him an annoyed look. When he merely blinked at me, I pointed at my mouth.

"Oh, right. Sorry, I'm a bit new to the whole 'controlling' thing. See . . . I'm . . ." He paused, thinking hard and staring at me like I was the enemy. "This is a bit difficult for me to explain." He rolled up his sleeve, then extended his arm toward me. A tiny set of archaic symbols was tattooed on his wrist. It didn't resemble anything I'd ever seen before, and I gave him a blank stare.

"Right. You don't know what that is. I forgot how ignorant modern society is."

What was he talking about?

He pointed at his wrist, glancing around to make sure nobody was listening in. "This is a symbol from the angelic alphabet." When I continued to quirk an eyebrow at him, he added, "I'm an angel."

Apparently I could still snort in disbelief.

"I'm serious," he protested. "You may not believe me, but that's not important right now. The point is, I'm one of the fallen—the Serim—and why I'm here is not that important. It's what happened between us that's important."

What a shame, I thought as I stared up at him with longing. Gorgeous and totally loony. I was dying to retort, but all I could do was chew my salad.

He looked rather tormented by my skepticism, and I began to feel bad. I waved my fork for him to continue.

"The problem is . . . I think you were bitten by a vampire before we met."

Oh, for Pete's sake. Sex with an angel, now this.

"See, vampires are related to the Serim, in a fashion, but their curse is different. They crave the blood, a darker, deeper hunger than that of the Serim, who simply crave the flesh. They traded for that, long ago."

I was almost done with my salad and stole a french fry

off his plate. Noah was still talking, and I forced myself to listen.

". . . a vampire's bite is an unnatural thing," he was saying. "It does something to the mind of the victim—it clouds the mind so that memories and inhibitions are fogged. It also fills the victim with intense desire and longing for the next few hours. Those who are heavily drained are the most intensely affected, before they drop dead a few hours later. Like you."

I paused, another purloined fry midway to my mouth. A feeling of dread slid into my stomach, and the fries no longer looked appetizing. My disbelief had boiled away, leaving only an uncomfortable feeling prickling at the back of my neck. It made sense—the clouded memory, the sexual demon I had been instead of my normal nerdy, inhibited self.

But that didn't explain why I had awakened in a Dumpster. I picked another piece of garbage out of my hair, pointing at it.

"I don't know why you were in the garbage. Moreover, I don't know why you were fed on to the point of sexual madness."

I blushed at his frankness. My glasses were sliding off the end of my nose and I shoved them back up violently. *Right, sexual madness. Sounds just like me.*

"Most vampires take only a little from their victims. Think of it as an aphrodisiac, but the memory is clouded just enough so that the victim can't remember the evening. You, however, were drained to the point of insatiability, and, er, that's when I met you."

Oh boy, here we go.

Noah raked his fingers through his hair again, an obvious nervous habit. "The Serim feed off the desire of others. It was time for me to feed, and you were willing—very willing." His eyes flickered blue again.

I put my napkin down, feeling sick.

"And I think that because of what happened between us, you got up later, maybe to answer the call of your vampire master. He finished the job, then left you in the Dumpster. And since you've awakened, I can only assume one thing, given the . . . nature of your desires." His silver eyes searched my face, and I averted my gaze. I couldn't look him in the face.

"You've risen again as a succubus."

What? That was the best he could come up with? He'd actually had me going there for a while. I crossed my arms over my chest and glared.

"I'm serious," he said, defending himself. "You won't notice anything at first, but you'll see some changes start to happen, and I don't want you to be alarmed."

Alarmed?

All I wanted was to get out of there.

"You're not saying anything. What do you think?"

I straightened my glasses and opened my mouth to speak, testing out my vocal cords by clearing my throat. That worked. He must be done, then. "What do I think? I think you're crazy, that's what I think."

He looked disappointed, and I felt almost like I'd just kicked a puppy. "You don't believe me," he said.

"Let me get this straight. You've just told me that I was

bitten by a vampire, had sex with an angel, then I died, but I've risen again as a succubus. And you're wondering why I don't believe you?"

"I see your point."

"Darn right. What is a succubus, anyway?" I had my suspicions, but I wanted to hear him say it.

"An immortal creature that feeds off sexual desire. The object of sexual fantasy." He sighed. "I'm afraid you're one of us now."

I waved a hand, cutting him off. "Save it for the chicks in the bar. I'm out of here." I stood up again, hoping that he wouldn't stop me.

He didn't. I was out of my seat and nearly to the door when he spoke again. "Wait. Before you go . . ."

I felt my feet slide to an involuntary halt and I turned. "*What?* What now?"

He merely held a business card out to me. "Put this in your purse. If you notice anything odd going on, give me a call. I can help you with everything that's going to happen. Believe me."

My fingers stretched out and took the card of their own accord and I put it into my purse, just as he'd directed me. "I wouldn't hold your breath if I were you."

"Just call me if you need help, okay? And don't call the police. They'll just make a mess of things."

Real comforting words. I stomped out of the diner without a backward glance.

The streets were crowded with pedestrians, the skies bright with midday sunshine, and the wind crisp and biting. My head immediately began to feel clearer now that I was out of Noah's vicinity.

I raised a hand in the air and hailed a taxi. I just wanted to go home and take a nice long shower and forget that this experience had ever happened. I'd get into my pajamas, curl up in bed, and not think about sexy hot men that I'd slept with—or their big packages.

Or which one of us was the crazy one.

Chapter Four

Somewhere between 3:00 and 4:00 a.m., I decided that having no dreams was worse than having dreams about Noah. I hadn't slept a wink in hours of tossing and turning. I chalked it up to the weird day I'd had, and dragged myself out of bed and into the shower for a third time. Showering always helped me think.

The hot water did a lot to rejuvenate me, and I decided to head to work early and catch up on some paperwork. Maybe one of the higher-ups would notice that I was putting my nose to the grindstone and I'd get considered for the next promotion.

Fat chance, but I didn't have anything better to do with myself.

I did, however, encounter a bit of a problem when I dressed. As I was putting on my bra, I noticed something awful. I had gained weight again. My boobs were spilling over the top of my bra in a rather distressing way. You know, when you put on a bra that's way too tight and you end up with the quadra-boob? I glared at my four breasts in the mirror, vowed to eat more salad, and tried on another bra. And another. And another. But even my "fat and bloated" bra felt like a tourniquet. Mind you,

this wasn't a bad thing for a B-cup like me, just depressing. I put on my elastic-waist "fat" pants, struggled into
a formerly loose-fitting shirt, threw a jacket over the
ensemble, then took a quick look in the mirror. No wonder I only attracted the psychos. I yanked my wet hair
into a ponytail and headed for the bus stop, determined
not to dwell on that depressing thought.

The busses of New City are nice and clean, nothing
like New York. Then again, New City was way Midwest,
and I think that had a lot to do with it. At any rate, I got
to work early and began to sort through my in-box, overflowing thanks to my unexpected absence.

My boss came in a shade after 7:00 a.m. and stopped
by my desk immediately.

"Hi," I said, looking up from the folder on my desk
and pasting a fake smile on my lips.

Julianna took one look at me and gave a haughty sniff.
"Did you dye your hair?"

That was an odd conversation starter. I touched my
hair curiously. "Er, no. Does it look darker?"

She shook her head at me and took a sip of her latte.
"It's a perfectly garish shade of red, if you ask me. But I
suppose you didn't, did you?" Julianna gave me a tight-
lipped smile and turned away. "Do remember that this is
a museum and not a brothel."

Insulted, I made a quick run to the restroom to check
it out. Huh. It did look a little brighter than usual, and
shiny as could be. I was rather pleased. Maybe the new
shampoo I'd bought was working wonders on my lack-
luster mane.

At nine, the morning crowds began filing in, and I went to stand at the museum entrance and greet the school groups. The museum was the biggest in the state, and always busy at the beginning of the school year. I think the teachers were trying to break the kids into class with ease and started the year out with a lot of field trips. Then, when the kids were good and trapped, throw the monotonous crap on them.

We had a good showing, so I put on my best docent smile and straightened my glasses. My eyes watered and a massive headache pounded between my eyebrows. I was tempted to fling the glasses off—I could do the Pre-Raphaelite spiel by heart now and wouldn't need sight to lead the tour.

I wimped out and left the glasses on. Nudging them up the bridge of my nose, I headed for the first adult I saw, who had a strained look on his face. The middle-aged man had to be a teacher, judging by the sweater vest. "Good morning. I'm Jackie Brighton, the tour docent. Are you read—"

I had to break off because the man was staring at me with the most unnerving look on his face.

"Hi," he whispered after a rather long, uncomfortable moment.

"Um, hi." *There's always one weirdo,* I thought with irritation. "I'll be the docent for your trip through our museum. Think you could gather your students around so we can get started, Mr. . . . ?" I waited patiently for a name.

He put his left hand in his pocket as I spoke, and

when it emerged it was ringless, with a nice white tan line where a wedding band should go.

Real cute.

"I'm Jackson. Jack Jackson." Instead of shaking my hand, he kissed the back of it, reverence in his eyes. "You must be beautiful—I mean, Ms. Brighton."

I pried my hand out of his, ignoring the way it made my hormones flutter. "Yep, that's what I said just thirty seconds ago. Shall we get started?"

"Do you want to go to dinner sometime?"

"Not really."

"No?" He looked absolutely crushed. "Are you sure?"

Positive, I thought but forced a fake smile to my face. "It's sweet of you to ask, but perhaps you should take your wife out instead." It was amusing to think that a guy had a crush on me. That didn't happen often. Like, ever.

Yet now this teacher was staring at my breasts (all four of them) with disconcerting fascination. I waved a hand in his face. "Remember me?"

"Boy, do I." He sounded awed.

How can you not love that? Creepy or not, I was warming up to him. "Shall we move on to the tour? Please?"

"Of course." He followed me reverently to my docent stand, where I passed out brochures.

The museum had three wings, and my tour went through two of them in detail. The adoring teacher was pleasant and well behaved for the rest of the tour, to my relief. He was actually the most attentive guest I'd ever had. When I pointed to a Waterhouse painting that was a particular favorite of mine, he made the appropriate awed noises, and I was touched. I could forgive a little boob staring, I suppose. My breasts *did* look rather odd, even to me, and I saw them every morning.

The disturbing thing was that by the end of the tour, most of the students had wandered away and I had a tour group full of male teachers, all as reverent and adoring as the first.

Was there some sort of joke I wasn't in on? If so, it wasn't funny.

It wasn't funny to my boss, either. Julianna was glaring at me from a distance, so I excused myself from my group and hurried over.

"What is going on, Jackie?" Julianna crossed her arms over her chest and peered down at me.

"I swear that I don't know, Ms. Cliver." I tried my best to look contrite and apologetic, when what I really wanted to do was cram a pencil up her beaky nose. "I think someone's playing a prank on me. Look at how they're acting."

She gave a sniff of distaste and looked down her long nose at me. "They do seem to be rather adoring. You're right. It must be a prank of some sort." She fixed her sharp gaze on me. "Fix it."

Fix it? How do you fix having a mob of men following you around?

I "fixed" it by hiding in the women's restroom for the next two hours. Just call me courageous.

Chapter Five

The end of the workday couldn't come soon enough. In fact, it didn't, so I took off early. To be on the safe side, I slid out of the receiving doors in the back and took the long way to the bus station.

Julianna must have sniffed something odd with that nose of hers, because she came running after me in the parking lot. "Just where are you going, Jackie?" Her nasal whine made me shudder. "We have two more tours scheduled to come through this afternoon and I'm short a docent as it is."

"I came in early this morning, so I thought I'd leave early," I began, then stopped myself. I didn't have to explain anything to Julianna. "I'm sorry, but I can't stay." I turned to face her, putting on my best poker face. I suck at lying, but desperate times call for desperate measures. The men in the museum unnerved me. "Something's come up." Like my stress level.

She fixed her baleful gaze on me. "You can't stay for the rest of the day? One more hour? We need you here, Jackie. What am I supposed to do without two of my docents?"

I didn't think it'd be a life-or-death situation to let a

class or two wander the museum unaccompanied, but of course I didn't say that. I opened my mouth to protest and was cut short by the rip of fabric and a snapping sound.

"What was that?" Julianna asked.

"I think it was . . . my bra." My breasts suddenly felt rather loose and fancy-free. Sure enough, the clasp dropped to my feet, looking like it'd been through a war zone. Mortified, I pulled my jacket closer and buttoned it up the front, which didn't work so well, because it gaped in all the wrong places. "I *really* can't stay now, Ms. Cliver."

She sniffed and avoided looking at me. "I guess not. Be sure and be in tomorrow, then."

"But—"

"You'll be in tomorrow if you want to keep your job, Jackie."

"Fine," I said sullenly, thinking with longing of the nine days of sick time I had accrued.

"And make sure that you wear clothes that fit you." With that, she turned on her heel and pranced back to the museum. "For a change," she called back over her shoulder in a nasty voice.

Sometimes I hated my job. Mostly due to my boss, who made a boring job completely unlikable.

The bus ride home was one of the longest I've ever had. I kept my arms crossed over my breasts to keep them from bouncing and kept my jacket clutched tight to me, but I still got a lot of ogling. I was never so glad to get off a bus in my life, and I half-expected the man sitting next to me to follow me home. To my relief, no one did.

I ran straight for my apartment once I got to my building, without stopping to check my mail or say hi to the doorman like I always do. He gave me a curious look as I rushed past and I raced up the stairs two at a time, then slammed my door behind me. Lack of sleep had made me paranoid.

I needed new clothes, since I'd outgrown my old ones. It was a depressing thought, and I resigned myself to salads for the next six weeks. I slid out of my work clothes and picked up one of my discarded bras. Double-boob or not, I had to wear something.

My body froze when I pulled off my shirt and looked down at my naked chest. "Holy shit," I breathed, wondering if I was seeing things. I rubbed the lenses of my glasses and looked down at my breasts again.

They were enormous. As in Pamela Anderson enormous, and all natural. Alarmed, I grabbed them in my hands and jiggled, testing for sensitivity. They didn't hurt; what could have caused this bloating? Food allergy? I squeezed into a bra, wincing when the straps cut into my skin. It'd have to do for a few hours. Then I tossed on a sweatshirt and some sweatpants. To my surprise, the sweatpants were falling off my waist. I had to use a hand to keep them up. What was going on?

My doorbell rang. I went to the door and peered in the peephole. It was the doorman, his back turned to me. Had I dropped something on my rush in? I opened the door. "Hi, Bobby. Something wrong?" I never got visits from the staff.

The doorman turned and revealed a huge bouquet of red roses, giving me a sheepish grin. He wasn't more than nineteen or twenty, and skinny as hell. *So* not my type. "Hi, Miss Brighton. You're looking lovely today." He thrust the roses out at me.

"For me?" A flush of pleasure rushed through my body, and I extended a hand for them. Suspicious though I may be, I have a weakness for flowers. "Who are they from?"

"They're from me." Again the blush covered his cheeks. I smiled, a hot, pulsing feeling of warmth coursing through me. He looked adorable. Good enough to eat, or at least nibble on for a while.

"I just thought you looked lovely today," he continued. "I was wondering if you were busy later?"

He was asking me out? How sweet. The flush of pleasure grew stronger, and the blood rushing through my veins began to throb in some surprising places. I crossed my arms over my chest, hoping that it hid my sudden headlights. I'd never paid any attention to Bobby before, but he was looking rather good at the moment. "Why, thank you. I . . . I'm busy later."

"I see." He licked his lips and turned away.

At the sight of his tongue, I don't know what came over me. The next thing I knew, I tore off my glasses and tossed the roses down. I grabbed him by the collar and hauled him into my apartment. He came in without a word of protest, and before I had the time to think about what I was doing, my mouth was on his, and his hands were on my ass, and it felt *good*.

"Miss Brighton," he breathed, and I stopped any protests he might have by sliding my mouth over his again and biting his lower lip.

"Do me a favor," I whispered, pressing him against the wall. "Don't talk."

I pressed my body against his, and I could feel the hardness inside his slacks. The feeling excited the hell out of me, and I ground my hips against his with a tremor of delight.

He didn't need much encouraging. His hands were all over my backside, pulling it against his cock. He rubbed my pelvis against his own, his tongue mimicking a thrust as it dove in and out of my mouth. Sensations shot through me on overload, overwhelming my mind and making all rational thought disappear.

"God, you have the most gorgeous blue eyes," he moaned, just as my hands were reaching into his waistband to free his erection.

That stopped me cold. "What?" I jerked away. "What did you say?"

He gave me a dazed look, rubbing my behind like some sort of horny masseuse. "Your eyes. They're so beautiful. Did you get contacts?"

I darted for the bathroom mirror, and one look nearly sent me into shock. "Oh no," I moaned, putting a hand to my face. I *hoped* it was my face. They were my features, but somehow different. My cheekbones were defined, my lips as full as if they'd been shot full of collagen, and my hair rippled down my shoulders in a glorious red mass that framed my glowing blue eyes.

Blue, not brown, like they'd been ever since I was born.

And glowing the way I remembered Noah's had.

Oh, boy.

From behind, Bobby grabbed my hips and ground his hips against my own. "Miss Brighton?"

I nearly doubled over from the unnatural wave of pleasure. Either this kid was talented, or there was something seriously wrong with me.

"Uh . . . hmm?" I was having difficulty forming coherent thoughts with his erection pressing against my backside. I wanted nothing more than to shuck my sweatpants, fling him down on the floor, and make sweet monkey love to him.

Something was *definitely* wrong with me.

"Did you want me to leave?" His voice was husky, his hands gripping my hips in the most heavenly way. He knew very well I didn't want him to leave.

"Yes," I managed to squeak out, surprising myself.

"What?" Bobby pulled away from me, and I could see his sexual tension turn to confusion.

Without his body pressed against mine the haze of desire cleared a little, and I turned on the faucet and began to splash water on my face. "Leave, Bobby. Please leave."

"But . . . but . . . can I come see you later?"

I forced myself to shake my head no. "Maybe some other time." Poor kid. He was probably confused as hell.

He wasn't the only one.

"Oh. I guess . . . let me know if you need anything."

I didn't have to be a mind reader to read horny longing and hurt feelings shooting off him like sparks. The door shut a few moments later, and I found myself alone.

What on earth was wrong with me? I never approached men, and I sure wouldn't have attacked a nineteen-year-old doorman. I was twenty-seven, for crying out loud, and I didn't like them young. Yet when I'd seen him standing there, licking his lips, I'd wanted nothing more than to maul him, and I had.

Flashes of my conversation with Noah floated through my mind.

"You won't notice anything at first, but you'll see some changes start to happen, and I don't want you to be alarmed," he had said, looking as serious as can be, handing me his business card. At the time I had blown him off, thinking him arrogant and crazy as hell.

Not anymore.

I raced for my purse and tore out my wallet. Sure enough, there was his business card. It was simple, with just the name "Noah Gideon" on it and a cell phone number. Oh, and his little "angelic alphabet" design was in the top right corner. I'd give the man some credit—when he came up with a story, he really went all out.

Unless . . . it wasn't a story after all.

I dialed the number with trembling fingers, and put my ear to the receiver. Three rings, then voicemail.

Drat. I wasn't about to leave a message. What would I say? *Hi, my boobs grew overnight and my eyes are blue; call me?*

I hung up and sat down next to the phone, deciding to wait it out. He had to pick up at some point. I flipped on the TV. I wasn't tired in the least, and too agitated to sleep anyhow. So I called. All night. And watched TV in between calls.

Okay, so I watched porn. I couldn't help myself. In fact, I stayed up all night watching porn. There was something about the flesh licking and uninhibited responses that I found riveting. Between movies, I kept trying Noah's line.

Shortly after sunrise I finally got an answer. The phone rang twice, then "Yes?"

No "hi" or "hello" for this guy.

"Noah, it's me. Jackie."

"Jackie?" His voice was questioning.

Annoyance shot through me. Was he such a ladies' man that he couldn't remember who the hell I was? "Yeah, Jackie. Dumpster girl, remember?"

"Ah, Jackie." His voice was a soft caress, sending a distress signal straight to my groin.

"I was hoping you weren't going to call." He sounded disappointed, which only made me even more annoyed.

"You and me both. Listen, I have a real problem—"

"Does it involve having blue eyes?"

Stunned, I was silent for a few moments, then nodded.

"Hello? Are you still there?"

Duh. He couldn't see me nod. "Yeah, I'm still here. My eyes are blue, yeah. And something else is wrong with me—well, a lot of other things. What is going on?" My voice squeaked with alarm.

"It's probably best if we meet up again. Say, six-thirty at St. Anthony's cathedral? That's a half hour from now. Do you know where that is?"

I blinked in surprise. A cathedral at the crack of dawn on a Wednesday? "Are they even open this early?"

"The doors of the church are always open." He sounded amused at my naïveté.

"Uh, okay. Why so early?"

"I'm unavailable during evening hours." Before I could say anything about that weird comment, he continued. "I need a few minutes to round up a friend. And be calm. Everything will be fine."

Easy for you to say. I sighed. "Okay, I'll meet you there. I'll be the one with the clothes that don't fit." *Dry humping the pews.*

"Sounds like when we met the other day." He chuckled, sending twin bolts of desire and rage through me.

I wanted to hang up on him, but I forced myself to end the call politely. Help was on the way, though I was terrified of what he was going to tell me. I hadn't paid much attention to his earlier nonsense—something about a succubus. Now I wished I had.

Tense and moody, I wandered into my closet to see if I had any pants that would stay around my waist and a shirt that wouldn't outline my overly excited nipples.

I hoped Noah had a good explanation for what was going on, because so far? this sucked.

Chapter Six

He took his damn sweet time getting to the cathedral. I'd been checking my watch every thirty seconds since the clock struck seven, and still no sign of Noah or his friend. When seven-thirty crawled around, I decided that Noah had been yanking my chain. This was just another joke in the long line of misfortunes that had been my life lately.

Of course, just as I stood up from the pew, Noah walked through the double doors, sending my hormones through the roof. At the sight of his broad shoulders, my insides quivered and I felt a flush sweep over my body and centralize between my thighs.

Then I noticed what appeared to be a supermodel following close behind him, and distaste flared as well. How dare that jerk make me wait because he was on a date? Self-consciously, I smoothed my hair and hoped my Notre Dame sweatshirt didn't have any stains on it.

Noah looked as delicious as ever. His wavy dark blond hair was pushed off his face in tousled bed-head fashion, and he wore a cool gray jacket and dark gray slacks. His shirt was a dark garnet color, which I wouldn't think would go well with a business suit, but he made it work.

No tie again, and his collar gaped slightly, revealing a smooth, tanned chest.

"Hi," I choked out, trying to control myself. The urge to dive onto him and kiss him madly was tough to resist. "Thank God you're here."

The supermodel took off her sunglasses, revealing pale blue eyes. "Wow, she's got it bad, Noah. Check out her eyes."

"I see them." His gray ones stared into my own. "Are you all right, Jackie?"

"I don't think so," I said, unable to keep the whine out of my voice as I sized up the competition. The girl behind Noah was utterly gorgeous, tall and dusky. She must have been Indian or Arabian or something along those bloodlines. Her hair was a smooth black curtain rippling down her shoulders, and she was built like a Barbie doll. Her light-colored eyes were striking, and her skin was the most delicious shade of deep olive I had ever seen. A short, tight minidress revealed impossibly long legs and a svelte figure that had likely never seen a Slim-Fast shake in its life. I was pretty sure I'd seen her before somewhere—like on the cover of *Sports Illustrated.*

"Why'd you bring *her*?" The petulant words slipped out of my mouth before I could stop myself.

Supermodel took one look at me and began to laugh. She nudged Noah forward. "Didn't you explain *anything*? Good lord, man. Her panties must be soaked at this point, and here you show up with a date."

I blinked at her crude words. "I beg your pardon?"

Noah put his hands on my shoulders, and my entire body began to tingle. God, he smelled good. I grew dazed at the thick, masculine scent; he smelled like leather and cinnamon. I leaned closer, admiring the hard angle of his jaw. If I moved in close enough, I could tuck my head under it and be enveloped in his arms, held against that broad, delicious chest.

"Are you okay, Jackie?"

"Not really. Something's wrong with me, Noah." I reached for him, dying to touch him, then pulled my hands back at the last moment. Maybe I was being too forward.

Noah sat down on the pew, and I sat next to him so close that I was practically in his lap, and stared into his eyes.

"Do you believe me now?" he asked.

"About?" I said, distracted by his nearness.

"You've been turned into a succubus." His hands clasped my own.

"Right . . ." My skin began to itch, and I wanted to rip the jacket off his shoulders. I was having a hard time concentrating. If he moved his finger just slightly, he'd rub against my palms. My thighs quivered at the thought. "And what exactly does a succubus do, again?"

"It's a long story," Noah's friend explained. I'd almost forgotten she was there, like a buzzing fly. "I doubt it'll sink in until we take care of your Itch."

"My itch?" I echoed. How had she managed to put her finger on the exact word for what I was feeling? I was itching, all right. My whole body was pulsing, and the feeling was centralized in my pelvis. Noah's proximity didn't help, either. I shifted a little closer, my thigh brushing up against his.

"The first time's always the worst," she said cheerfully.

I barely heard her; my entire being was focused on that leg so close to mine. Noah had very large thighs, I noticed.

Noah must have sensed what I was telegraphing. He picked me up off the bench and slid me into his lap, and my nerves thrilled at the contact. My mind swam from the sudden rush of blood, my senses fogged, and all nerve endings focused entirely on the small of my back where his hands rested.

"I guess we'd better find someplace to take care of this." I heard his voice from far away, through the roaring of blood in my ears. I wrapped my arms around his neck and pressed my breasts against him as he glanced around the room.

The supermodel snorted as I buried my face in Noah's neck and began to lick his skin. "Yeah, it must be a real chore for you, Noah. I'll sit here in the back and wait for you two to finish, 'kay?"

Noah stood with my legs locked around his waist. The juncture of my thighs pressed against his groin and I could feel the hardness in his pants. Thank God it wasn't just me.

"The confessional," he murmured, and headed for the side where the wooden booths were set up, near the long row of unlit prayer candles.

"The confessional?" I lifted my head to look at him.

Bad idea—this close up, he looked even more perfect and delectable. There was a hint of a dimple in one cheek and I wanted to touch my tongue to it. "We're in a church," I said faintly. "I'm pretty sure that's against the rules."

He pushed the door to the confessional open and slid me against the wall of the booth. I breathed a sigh of delight when he gently bit my earlobe. "You can say a few Hail Marys after we're done." His eyes had flicked to bright blue and now blazed into my own.

Warm hands slid under my sweatshirt and his mouth hovered just above mine. His hands paused when he discovered I wasn't wearing a bra, then his mouth crushed against mine in renewed excitement. My moan of pleasure was swallowed by his mouth, and I returned the kiss with fervor. God, the man could kiss! His tongue did things to me that I didn't think were possible.

My hands were busy ripping off his jacket and shirt. A button popped off and he chuckled. "Slow down, Jackie. Pace yourself."

"I can't," I whimpered, sliding my hands against his chest. "Something's wrong with me. I can't help myself."

He sensed my frustration and pressed a tender kiss against my forehead. "Shhh. It'll be all right. I'll make it better for you. I'll protect you."

It was a weird word choice for a guy I was getting busy with in a confessional, but for some reason I was comforted. I slid my hands into his hair and tangled them there, anchoring him against me.

Noah held my face between his hands. "Are you okay with this, Jackie?" He pressed up against me again, his cock hard and hot against my thighs. "I won't touch you if you don't want me to."

Of course I was okay with it. I wanted him inside me, all over me, poured into me. My body was on fire and I saw only one way to ease it. "Please, *yes*, Noah." Searching for his mouth with my own, I brushed my nipples against his chest in an unspoken invitation.

"Good," he said against my mouth, and I tasted cinnamon mixed with the taste of his lips. "Because I really want to touch you right now. And I think you want to touch me." In the darkness of the booth, his eyes shone bright blue, and before I could comment on that, he grabbed my hips.

His pelvis ground against my own again, and I slammed hard against the wall of the booth. My groan was one of pleasure, and I gave an un-Jackie-like squeal of delight when he slid me down the wall and began easing my sweatpants down my legs.

They were off within seconds, along with my panties and shoes, leaving only my fuzzy socks. His hands kneaded my hips and he groaned into my hair. "You smell amazing."

"That's just what I was thinking about you," I said, then bit at his lip again. The man was heavenly, all hot and warm and hard all over. My fingers slid down his taut abdomen and unbuckled his pants, and within moments his hard cock was free. It was huge, too, and thick, and my brain flashed back to scenes of the night I'd forgotten. Noah leaning over me in bed, thrusting into me, his blue eyes fixed on my face. Him breathing my name over and over again in litany. Me screaming out his.

Breathless with the memory, my hands wrapped around his cock and gave it a gentle squeeze. "I remember this."

The next thing I knew, he was shoving me up against the wall again and murmuring in my ear, "Give me your leg, Jackie."

Obediently, I lifted one leg, and his fingers stroked my wet folds. I thought I was going to die right then and there, and it must have sounded like it from the moans I was emitting. Noah's mouth covered my own as he shushed me, his fingers sliding against my clit and circling against it. Feathery-light at first, his motions grew bolder when my body gave an involuntary shudder in response. He circled my clit with the pad of his thumb again, hard.

Overwhelmed with sensation, I gave a soft cry of longing, my body aching to be filled. I needed him *inside* me. "Noah," I whispered against his mouth. "This is really great and all, but I'd really like you to fuck me right now. *Hard*. I'm itching like crazy."

He groaned against my mouth, grabbing my other leg in his hands and hiking me up against the wall until I was straddling him, pinned between the confessional wall and his glorious hot body. The head of his cock slid against my sex, teasing and rubbing against me for a mere breath of time. I barely had a chance to say how much I liked that when he was sliding that hard length inside of me in one sharp thrust. My legs clenched around him, and my muscles spasmed as I had the strongest orgasm of my entire life.

My moan of pleasure echoed through the booth, and he tried to kiss me again to silence me, but it wasn't working. His groan matched my own in volume as I locked my ankles behind his waist and buried my head against his neck, riding out the wave of pleasure with him.

"Oh God, Noah!"

"Don't say that," he murmured against my skin, his teeth gritted. "Not here. Just hold on to me, Jackie." With that breath, he stroked into me again. I hadn't even had a chance to come down from the last orgasm as he hammered into my flesh, over and over again. Within moments I bit his shoulder, trying desperately to keep myself from screaming my pleasure.

I clung to him and held on for dear life as he pounded into me with long, measured strokes, enjoying every sweaty second of it.

Just before I slipped over the edge again, Noah groaned and shuddered, releasing inside me. As he gently rocked me on his cock and tried to control his breathing, I tried not to be disappointed that I'd only come once. But I must have given him some sort of hint couldn't be all the wiggling I was doing—because he slid a hand between us and reached for my clit again. "One more for the road," he whispered against my mouth, and within a few moments, I clenched and shuddered my orgasm all over again.

A few minutes later, reality began to sink in: our sweaty bodies, pressed against each other, inside the church confessional.

The church *confessional*.

"Oh God," I murmured, shock coursing through me. "I'm going to Hell for this for sure."

Noah pressed a kiss against my sweaty brow and disentangled his body from my own, not an easy feat in the tiny booth. "God will understand. Some things just can't wait. You were in a bad way."

I slid down to pick up my clothes and tried not to feel raging embarrassment. "I can't believe what we just did. I can't believe I was mauling you like that."

"Remy calls it the Itch. I'm sure she can sympathize with you."

I felt immensely relieved, like a huge itch had been scratched. Maybe the name was appropriate, after all. "Remy—is that the girl out there?"

I could hear his clothing rustle in the dark booth as he straightened his clothes. "Yes," he said. "I wanted you to meet her—she's the only other succubus I know."

"She's a succubus?" I was surprised. "Really?"

He laughed. "You sound relieved. Did you think she was my girlfriend?"

If I could have found his arm in the darkness, I would have socked it a good one. "Don't laugh at me." I threw the rest of my clothes on and hoped like mad that the booth didn't smell *too* much like sex. "Are you decent yet?"

"Yes." He sounded amused.

"Good." I slammed the door open and stomped out, trying to straighten my hair. I had a rat's nest on the back of my head from the ride against the wall; I was lucky I didn't have splinters in my you-know-what.

Remy sat quietly in the back of the cathedral, looking angelic and innocent. She smiled at the sight of us and pulled a pair of earbuds out of her ears. "Looks like we're back to normal now, I see?" She pulled out a compact from her purse and handed it to me. "Take a look."

I looked. My cheeks were flushed with high color and my forehead shone with a hint of sweat. I even spotted a hickey on my neck. "Right," I said, blushing. "What am I supposed to be looking for?"

"Your eyes aren't blue anymore. That means the Itch is gone for now."

Sure enough, pale silver eyes stared back at me in the mirror. "Wow. You're right. The two are connected?"

Remy nodded. "The bluer your eyes are, the closer you are to feeding." Her pale blue eyes sparkled. "I'm due tomorrow, in case you were wondering."

"I wasn't going to ask." A thought occurred to me. "So, uh, do you get the Itch pretty often? As an, um, succubus?" The thought that I was one took a little getting used to, but the wave of abject horniness was gone and now I could think a bit more reasonably. Since being completely sex starved and having a crazy libido were not normally part of my day, I assumed that was part of the kit and caboodle.

"About once a week," she said. "We're stuck between the two races. Hasn't Noah explained to you? The Fallen—that's the Serim, Noah's kind—they crave sex as part of their curse. The Serim must bring pleasure to their partner—not themselves—or they get as wild as we do. They're affected about once a month, usually near a full moon. Vamps must feed more frequently, and feed on blood. We're some sort of bizarre blend in the middle, since we come from both." She offered me a hairbrush without batting an eyelash. "We have the addiction to sex, like the angels—except ours is a more selfish version—and we have the feeding frenzy of vampires."

"You're kidding me." I gaped at her. "I'm going to turn into a raving nymphomaniac because of angels and vampires?"

"It's a really long story, and one better told over breakfast." Remy cast a glare at Noah. "I can't believe you didn't explain any of this to her before. What were you thinking?"

It was Noah's turn to look embarrassed. He tugged at his collar, straightening it, and I was secretly delighted to notice the sheen of sweat on his skin, sweat that *I* had caused. "She wasn't listening the last time we talked."

That was true; I hadn't listened to a word he was saying. "Breakfast sounds good to me," I said.

Noah glanced down at his watch. "I'm afraid I can't go with you. I have to meet someone."

Of all the embarrassing things, I felt tears prick my eyes. "You're leaving me? Now? But we just got here." He'd just screwed my brains out in the confessional and now was too busy to stick around? I swallowed past the humiliated knot in my throat.

He shook his head at me and gave my forehead a gentle kiss, his eyes bleached silver once more. "I wish I could stay." His eyes stared into mine for a moment, his thumb caressing my cheek. "I'll catch up with both of you tomorrow. Remy will take good care of you."

"Promise?" Lord, I sounded needy.

Remy rolled her eyes at the two of us and grabbed me by the arm. "Save the foreplay for sex. We've got a lot to do, and I don't feel like hanging around here and waiting for one of the you-know-who to find her." She pointed at the ceiling and gave Noah a pointed look.

"One of what?" I stared up at the ceiling. "Roofers?"

This time, two snorts of laughter met my ears. "Come on." Remy tugged at my arm. "Let's get you something to eat. We can catch up with Noah some other time."

"But . . ." I protested as she dragged me toward the thick wooden doors. I felt odd leaving the man I had just waited hours for. "I thought . . ." Hell, I didn't know what I thought anymore. I just felt abandoned, used.

At least I did until Remy flashed me a brilliant white smile. "I've waited *forever* to have another Suck around. This is going to be *so* much fun!"

"Excuse me?"

She blew a kiss at Noah, who was pulling out a cell phone. "Suck, succubus, whatever you want to call it. I was the only one in New City before, and I'm glad that you're here now." She flashed me a wicked, exotic grin. "We're going to paint this town red."

"Great," I echoed unenthusiastically, sparing a longing look back at Noah. He was whispering into his phone and a spurt of irritation flared through me. If I felt used, it was because he was acting like I was some sort of discarded piece of trash.

Remy was chatting my ear off as we left the cathedral. "First things first, girl. We have got to get you some serious clothes. You look like a bag lady."

"Don't we have more pressing matters to worry about?"

Remy gave me an incredulous look. "Nothing's more important than appearances, sweetheart. Bite your tongue."

Maybe this was Hell, after all.

CHAPTER SEVEN

R emy leaned against her car window and peered
at the drive-thru menu. "You want a burger or a
shake or something?"

I shook my head, feeling too self-conscious to think
about food. Much. "No thanks."

"I need a triple cheeseburger with fries," Remy
shouted at the speaker box. "Extra mayo, extra cheese,
and a chocolate shake. Oh, and a side order of chicken
nuggets. And an apple pie." She looked over and grinned
at me. "A snack."

Good lord.

We rolled around to the front of the drive-thru and
Remy handed her money over, taking the bags of food
back from the pimply boy at the window. "So, did Noah
tell you *anything*? I want to make sure I'm not recapping
anything you've already heard."

"He said he was an angel, and that I got bit by a vampire, but he skipped a few details," I said dryly.

Remy turned a corner, sipping her shake, and pulled
into an empty parking lot. "Okay, then I'll start from the
beginning. Have you ever heard of Enoch?"

My mouth watered as I watched her take a huge bite

of her burger. It looked delicious. I hoped my stomach wouldn't growl and embarrass me. "Enoch . . . isn't he in the Bible?"

"He's in Genesis, but the rest isn't included anymore. Lost book of the Bible, I believe. Anyhow, if you read the Book of Enoch, it explains how the angels fell from Heaven." She took another enormous bite of her burger.

"It does? I didn't know that."

She nodded, wiping her mouth with a napkin. "Yep, they fell in love with mortal women and had sex with them. God said that was a big no-no and told 'em to stop, but they didn't, so he cast them out. When the Big Cheese speaks, it's generally a good idea to listen," she intoned sagely, then ruined it by cramming some fries into her mouth. "Sure you don't want any?"

I shook my head. "So Noah's been cast out from Heaven?"

"Him and a few thousand other guys, yeah. Gabriel and the rest that stayed behind were really angry, too, so they cursed the Serim. Since they were so hot for female flesh, they were cursed to crave it and to indulge themselves every full moon. Not so bad, you would think— but then the Archangels went and killed all their women and they were left with nothing. It's a sad story, really. Some of the Serim turned to evil as a result, and that's why we have vampires. They wanted their wings back, no matter the cost. Lucifer was willing to give them wings, but they had to sell their souls. At least, that's the rumor. All you need to remember is that the Serim can only go out in the daytime, and the vamps can only go out at night. That's what happens when you mess with the big guns."

My eyes widened. "Jeezus, that's a terrible story. All of their loved ones died?"

She shrugged. "Die now, die later; they're all still screwed. All the women were mortal, so it's not like they were going to have a really long life together. French fry?"

Disgusted by her callous attitude, I turned and stared out the window, hoping that the conversation would steer to more pleasant matters.

"You're not much of a talker," she complained. When I offered no rebuttal, she gave up and started the car again, the burger clutched against the steering wheel. "Come on, then. Let's go to the mall!"

I stared up at the neon sign over the mall entrance with trepidation and wondered for the ninth time why I was heading to a shopping mecca with a supermodel. I must be sick.

Remy pulled into the parking lot in her tiny BMW and beamed at me. "Ready for some fun?"

I was actually ready for a bite to eat, but since I'd declined to eat at our pit stop, it seemed silly to ask for food now.

Ignoring my rumbling stomach, I asked, "What sort of fun are we going to have, exactly?"

"We're going shopping, of course." She got out of the car and moved around to my side, since I hadn't budged.

I rolled down my window a crack and peered up at

her. "It's been a weird couple of days; I just had sex in a church not long ago; I haven't slept in two days. Not to mention my job's probably wondering where I'm at."

I was trying not to think about work. Julianna would be furious that I had another unexcused absence. "I'm not exactly having a great streak here. Can we do this some other time?"

Undeterred, Remy opened my door and waited for me to get out. "That's the beauty of a twenty-four-hour mall, my friend. All shopping, all the time, and enough time to get it all in. If you smell bad, we can stop by a bathroom first and you can mop up anything that Noah left behind."

Ouch. She had a potty mouth. I flinched and got out of the car, albeit very reluctantly. "I'm really tired," I tried.

"Horseshit," Remy announced in a singsong voice. "We don't get tired."

"We don't?"

She shook her head and dragged me by the arm toward the glass double doors in the distance. "Sucks don't need to sleep. Vamps do, Serim do, but we don't sleep a wink. It's odd at first, but you get used to it."

I was horrified. "We don't sleep? At all?"

"I haven't slept a wink in four hundred years."

This was a nightmare of vast proportions. I *loved* sleeping. There's nothing better than diving under the sheets and snuggling into some dreams of yourself and your favorite actor.

"This just keeps getting worse and worse," I complained as we stepped into the brightly lit mall. I squinted at the light and turned to look at Remy. "Anything else you want to tell me? Do I turn into a hooker at the full moon? Should I avoid people with garlic around their necks? Or—wait—since we're succubuses, should we avoid people with birth control?"

Remy giggled at my ranting. "You're quite the funny girl, you know that? I'm so glad you're one of us." She patted my hand and threaded my arm through hers as if we'd been best friends since grade school. "Like I said, I've been the only Suck in New City for quite some time, so it does get a bit lonely."

She'd avoided my question, but I decided not to press the issue. If she was laughing at my concerns, maybe it wasn't as bad as I thought. "So why don't you move, if you don't like New City?"

She shook her head. "Can't. My masters are here. Both of 'em. So here I stay."

I eyed the Gap with longing as she steered me away from it, an expression of distaste on her striking features. I hitched my sweatpants up around my waist again. "Masters? Kind of like an I-Dream-of-Jeannie thing?" I wasn't too keen on that idea. "I'm not real good with being all submissive and stuff."

Remy shrugged and led me toward Frederick's of Hollywood, which sank my spirits almost as much as her next words. "It's just the roll of the dice, I'm afraid. Since you were created by a vampire and a Serim, you have to answer to both." She gave me an odd look. "Didn't you notice that you couldn't contradict anything that Noah told you?"

I had noticed that. My spirits plummeted. "I have to do *everything* he tells me to?" Then visions of handcuffs and kinky sex games rolled through my mind, and sweat beaded on my forehead.

"'Fraid so, but you're lucky. Noah's a good guy. He won't abuse you or anything."

"And the other guy? The vampire?"

"Who can say?"

At my stricken look, she patted my hand. "Don't worry. If the vamp turns out to be an unsavory sort, you just avoid him. He can't tell you what to do if he can't find you, right?"

"Right," I echoed. "Is that what you do? Avoid yours?"

She shrugged and began to flip through a rack of clothing in the back of the store. Frederick's of Hollywood was crammed full of lacy undergarments in all shades of red, pink, and black, and I'd never noticed that they carried clothing, too. I'd never been shopping in here before—no sense in sticking a bikini on a sausage.

The store was empty this early in the day, except for one yawning salesgirl who flipped through a magazine at the counter, Jamba Juice in hand.

"Sometimes I avoid them," Remy was saying, pulling out a bright blue top with some fuzzy crap around the collar.

I had to think back to what she meant. Oh yes, masters.

"Most of the time, though, we just have an understanding." She held the top against my chest and nodded. "You should definitely dress in brighter colors. Gray is so blah. And sweats? Burn them, girl. Only fat slobs wear sweats."

I flinched at that and tried to hand the fluffy top back to her. "You're not going to find anything in my size here, Remy. We should go somewhere else." This was going to be downright humiliating, once she realized I was one of the fat, sweats-wearing slobs.

Remy just started piling miniskirts and slinky bodysuits into my arms. "You're wrong. I'm a pretty good judge of flesh." She winked at me. "And you're a size six, I'd say."

"Uh, you meant to put a one in front of that number, didn't you?" Okay, so I was closer to a 14, but I could border into unfriendly territory during certain times of the month.

"Nope." She shoved me toward the dressing room. "Go try this stuff on. If you're going out with me tomorrow, you have to dress appropriately."

"I'm going out with you tomorrow?" Who the heck agreed to that one?

"Don't try to change the subject. Get dressed." She flung a few hangers of lacy panties at me and ignored my question. "What bra size are you?"

"Remy—" I began.

She cut me off. "Do you like these panties?" They were crotchless.

I cringed. "You want me to try on underpants?"

"No, dummy. Just put on one pair and we'll buy the rest." She snorted and tossed more undergarments my way. "Rube."

"Remy!" I repeated, standing there clutching my pants around my waist. "I'm not trying these on."

Remy rolled her eyes. "I suppose I'm going to have to do everything for you. You look pretty pathetic right now, you know that?" She turned away and waved to the salesgirl. "Excuse me, but my friend here needs to be measured for a bra. Her tits are overflowing."

Her voice was loud enough to carry into the mall. I wanted to die right then and there. Instead, I slammed the dressing room door shut and wondered if there was a way to escape before she forced me to try the clothes on.

There was a hesitant knock at the door. "Um, miss? I need to measure you for a bra." There was some whispering on the other side, and the salesgirl paused, then added, "Your friend says I have to, or she's going to bring Noah back."

Visions of having mad sex in a dressing room crowded through my mind. Horrified at the thought, I edged the door open a crack, glaring at Remy. "You don't play fair."

"I know." She grinned.

I took my sweatshirt off and allowed the girl to measure me, my eyes shut so I couldn't see disgust cross her face as she saw my unsightly flab exposed to the world.

"34 double-D" the salesgirl announced, then exited the room.

"Huh?"

Remy snorted and shut the door, leaving me alone with the mirror. "I'll give you a minute to dress."

I stood there in dumbfounded surprise until a bra

smacked me in the forehead. Another flew over the door, and then another, a veritable rainbow of bras—all 34DD.

I picked one up and stared at it in shock. "This is a mistake, Remy. I'm a B. I have been since puberty."

"Not anymore," she called out cheerfully. "Sucks have a few perks, one of which is being the object of every man's fantasy. Which comes with nice boobs, I might add."

I'll say. I was staring at the mirror in shock at my naked chest. *Speaking of perks.* They were perky, all right. We're talking plastic-surgery bounce and fullness, but without the fakeness. Not a stretch mark, not a flaw, not even a hint of sag.

My waist was amazing, too, curving in more than I'd thought possible. I was shocked I even *had* a waist. I blinked and poked the mirror, wondering if it was a trick of the light. When I passed my hand in front of it several times and it looked normal, I began examining the rest of my body with delight.

The face was the first to hit scrutiny. It didn't look that different, except a bit more sensual. My brows were perfect, my lips full and pink, and my eyes were a striking shade of silver. My hair looked like something out of a Pantene commercial, shiny, bright red, and bouncing in thick waves across my shoulders. I turned and let my sweatpants fall to my ankles.

Holy crap, I had an ass.

Which is not to say I didn't have one before, but it was flat and wide and had little cellulite dimples. The new butt in the mirror was perfect, rounded, and nary a hint of cottage cheese.

Remy knocked on the door. "It got quiet in there. You okay?"

"I don't look like *me* anymore," I said, turning in the mirror.

"Yeah, I know. Like I said, there's a few perks with the job. I was as fat as a Christmas turkey before I changed." Remy sounded amused. "You get used to it, and then you start to enjoy it. Trust me."

I ran my hands down my new gorgeous body. I could almost live with the forced "sex every week" thing if this was the trade-off.

Almost.

CHAPTER EIGHT

Thirteen stores, ten hours, and several thousand dollars later, I wobbled out of Victoria's Secret in a pair of stilettos. "I can hardly walk in these things. What made you think dressing me up like this was a good idea?" They'd laugh me off the museum floor if I showed up in a pair of shoes composed of a few artful pink straps held together by a glittery butterfly.

"Because it is? And if you're going in to work with me tomorrow, you've got to be a little more stylish."

I wasn't sure how a snakeskin miniskirt and thigh-high leather boots were job-appropriate, but it was her money. Same went for the electric blue silk tank top barely covering my large, rather bouncy breasts.

I did have to admit that I looked hot as all get-out. Remy had shelled out thousands of dollars for the clothing we currently carried without a word of protest. And while it wasn't clothing that I would have bought in a million years, it looked pretty damn good on the new me.

I paused in front of my reflection and fluffed my flame-red hair again, still shocked that the gorgeous woman staring back was me.

Remy cleared her throat and turned to glare at me.

"Can you stop checking your reflection every window we walk past? It's getting a little old."

Mortified, I whirled around and nearly walked into a tall black-haired man in a trench coat. "Sorry," I said, and hurried over to Remy's side.

He nodded and flashed a bladelike smile in my direction, an inky lock of hair falling over his forehead. "Not a problem."

I glanced back at him as he continued on his way. "So," I said, changing the subject. "Why do I have to go to work with you tomorrow?"

We were passing the food court, and it smelled like Heaven. Granted, I might not see Heaven at this point, given my line of work, but if I did I imagine it'd smell like Cinnabon and Taco Bell.

To my immense relief, Remy made a beeline for the food court, her long black hair swinging as she walked. "Because I can't leave you alone by yourself. Who knows what kind of trouble you'll get yourself into?" When she glanced over at me, I noticed the startling blueness of her eyes. They'd gotten brighter over the past few hours, which meant that she was about to go into heat. "The first few days are crucial."

Seeing as how I knew nothing about succubuses, I was forced to believe her.

We threw our shopping bags down on a table, and I practically ran to Taco Bell. When I returned, I saw that Remy had not one, not two, but three cheeseburgers on her plate, and the biggest milkshake I'd ever seen. I'd tried to play it cool and get a taco salad, and at the sight of all her food I was totally jealous. "How can you eat that much and stay so skinny?"

She gave me an odd look. "You can eat whatever you want—your appearance isn't going to change. That's part of the whole package."

Heaven indeed! I was starting to think I'd be okay with this. "I'll be right back, then," I said, excitement in my voice, and headed back for a few more burritos.

To my surprise, the hot guy in the trench coat was in line and smiled at me as I stepped forward to order. He walked away as I ordered, and I grabbed my tray full of food, frowning. A stalker?

I hurried back to our table, where Remy was polishing off her first burger. "That's the second time I've seen that guy in the black coat," I told her, then took a huge bite out of my first burrito. It was better tasting than anything I'd had in weeks, and I closed my eyes in bliss. An Afterlife full of carbs couldn't be all that bad.

When I opened my eyes Remy was out of her seat, cheeseburger hanging from her mouth as she gathered up her bags again. I crammed as much of the burrito in my mouth as I could, not caring how ridiculous I looked. "Um, are we leaving?" A few beans trickled out of my mouth as I spoke. "Can we eat first?"

She shook her head and headed for the exit doors. "Leave. Now." Her words were muffled around her own cheeseburger, and I scooped up my clothing and burritos and trotted after her as best I could in my four-inch heels.

The hair prickled on the back of my neck as we ran

through the empty parking garage and back to her BMW. We had the doors locked within seconds, and Remy didn't even let me buckle my seat belt before ripping out of the parking lot like the end of the world was upon us.

My burrito smashed into the passenger window, spraying beans and hot sauce everywhere. I slid against the door, trying to stay in my seat and failing. "What the hell is wrong with you?" I shouted, glaring at her from the other side of the car. "You're going to get us killed!"

She ignored me, tossing her cheeseburger on the dashboard and putting both hands on the steering wheel to take the most frightening U-turn of my life. My body slammed against the car door again and I groaned. "Stop that!"

"Quit being a baby and buckle up. We have to get out of here ASAP unless you want to stick around and find out if your follower is a vamp or a dealer. Either one spells trouble."

I fumbled with the seat belt. "You think someone's after me?" Heck, I didn't even know what a dealer was, yet I'd managed to piss one off?

Remy ran a red light and cut through a side street. I closed my eyes so I couldn't see her driving anymore. "If the vamps suspect you were turned into a succubus—and I bet someone knows—they'll be looking for you." The car swerved hard to the right again, and Remy's long hair smacked me in the face as we cornered. "A succubus is the perfect tool for a vampire, since we can go places they can't. Throw in your vamp master, and you don't have the luxury of telling them 'no.'"

She paused for a long moment, the only sound the squealing of the tires and other cars as they honked at us. "Speaking of which, if your vamp master is an unscrupulous type—and most are—then it's a safe bet that he's going to try to use you for his own devices. I made a deal with my master, and you can do the same with yours, but they're generally not *good* deals to make. I had to give up two hundred years of my free will to get him off my back for the next two hundred. And when those finish, I have to answer to him again."

I thought of the Dumpster and what the homeless man had said: *Black-haired. Real tall. He kissed your cheek and then dumped you in there.*

"I think they know that I'm still alive," I admitted.

"I thought that might be the case," said Remy. "They seem to have their fingers in everything, and they're going to try to get to you before the dealers do."

"What are dealers?"

"Most of 'em are angels, but not the kind like Noah. These are the ones with access to Heaven. Most Sucks I know call them dealers because that's what they do. They offer you a deal, which turns out to be more like a hit of drugs for us undead types, and you end up addicted. You need to avoid dealers most of all, because they tend to offer things that you feel you can't pass up. It's best to never get involved."

Silence hovered between us.

"What are you thinking?" Remy's voice floated through the silent car.

"I'm thinking that the clothes, the new body, and the

food can't hide the fact that this is a major shit deal," I said, unable to keep the fear and anger out of my voice. I clung to the chicken bar in the car, keeping my eyes squeezed shut. "If I'm stuck between angels and vampires that want me to do their dirty work, and I have to have sex every seven days—"

"Two," Remy corrected.

My eyes flew open just in time to see her screech through a four-way stop, slamming on her horn as she cut off a Buick. "What did you say?"

"I lied to you earlier. It's actually sex every two days. I just didn't want you to get alarmed."

Alarmed?

Alarmed?

I wasn't alarmed, I was furious. "You're kidding me, right?"

She shook her head, put on her turn signal, and raced up a long driveway. "Nope. Two days."

"Before meeting Noah, I hadn't had sex in a year and a half. Or even *dated* in a year and a half."

Remy giggled girlishly. "Really? How funny."

"I'm not laughing," I snapped. "I don't go around getting into bed with every guy that I date, either. I only have sex in relationships."

She winked at me and reached for her cheeseburger off the dashboard. "That's not what I heard outside the confessional."

I gasped. "I think I hate you."

Remy laughed at my outrage. "No, you don't. Try to think of me as your new best friend. Trust me when I say you'll want to stick with me for the next few weeks. It's much safer that way."

Our frightening roller coaster of a ride had taken us to a sprawling mansion that should have been in Beverly Hills. Trimmed hedges adorned a perfectly sculpted lawn, the driveway was longer than the street I'd grown up on, and twinkling lanterns lined the path to the door. The very big, stained-glass door with a beautiful rose window above it could have been copied from the cathedral at Notre Dame. "Uh, is this your place?" I asked as Remy parked.

She nodded, grabbing her bags out of the back of the car. "Fully warded against all angels, vampires, and demons. Magical protection to keep them out. You can stay with me, until we establish your boundaries with all of the gang. Come on, I'll show you your room."

I wobbled after her on the cobblestones. "Did you just say *demons*?"

CHAPTER NINE

The room Remy graciously gave me for my personal use was bigger than my apartment on the far side of town. The angry part of me was disgusted, but the girly part of me wanted to frolic in the massive closet, the canopy bed, and the sunken bathtub with power jets. I let the frolic side win.

After I hung up all my new clothes, tested all the expensive shampoos and lotions on the vanity, and took an hour-long bubble bath, I poked through my new clothes. My mouth watered as the faint scent of breakfast hit my nostrils, and I decided to follow the scent of bacon downstairs. I dressed in my new silk pajamas—the most decent item of clothing I now owned—and searched through the mansion until I found Remy, my cell phone in hand.

My new roommate was in the kitchen, sitting at the marble breakfast bar with a cup of coffee. Her silky black hair hung in an elegant, smooth ponytail, and she was dressed in a beautiful lounge set of sky blue. She looked like an ad for *Elegant Living* magazine. "Back so soon?"

I thrust the phone at her. "First things first. If I call in sick to work again, I'll get fired for sure."

She gave me a curious look. "And? You don't need that job. You're with me now, and what I can't provide, Noah will."

"As swell as that sounds, I'd rather not be a kept woman, or kept succubus, or whatever I am now. Besides, I like my job." It wasn't much of a lie; I did like it most of the time. There were just aspects of it I hated—like my boss. "Just because I'm undead doesn't mean I have to totally change my life."

At least I hoped it didn't mean that.

Remy smiled and put down her coffee cup. "We're not undead. We're immortal."

"I'm immortal?"

"Essentially. There are only two ways for our kind to die."

"And how is that?"

"Usually by proxy. If both of your masters die, you die."

That sounded like a crappy catch. "And what happens then?"

She lifted her shoulders in a dainty shrug and avoided eye contact. "You cease to exist on this plane."

Gee. "Do I still exist in another plane?"

Another vague shrug. "I suppose. It's not something our kind likes to talk about."

I ignored the feeling of dread in my stomach. I wouldn't think about that now; I'd think about that later.

I shoved the phone under her nose again. "Regardless, I need you to call in to work for me." I wasn't budging on this. "Do you know how hard a good museum job is to come by in this city? And my boss will smell a scam a mile away, so you need to, like, be my doctor or something. Tell her I have something harmless, okay?" I took the phone from her fingers and dialed the number before she could protest.

Remy grinned at me and held the phone up to her ear, waiting. I assume someone picked up on the other end, for Remy cleared her throat and began in a businesslike tone, "Yes, I should like to speak to . . ." She paused to look at me.

"Ms. Cliver, museum director."

"A Ms. Cliver, if you please. She would be the supervisor of a Ms. Jacqueline Brighton." Gone was the playful, teasing Remy voice. In its place was a clipped British accent. She flashed me a wink while we waited. "Yes, Ms. Cliver? This is Dr. Summore. Jacqueline Brighton is a patient of mine, and she wanted me to let you know that she is having an adverse reaction to the anesthesia she received. I'm afraid we cannot release her from the hospital for several more days. She will remain under my care until then."

There was a pause in the conversation and Remy nodded, making a few "mm-hmm" noises of agreement. "It was a surgical procedure of a personal nature." Another pause. "Breast augmentation."

I gasped and tried to snatch the phone away from her. Remy sidestepped me easily and continued to talk into the phone. "I understand, Ms. Cliver," she responded, looking me straight in the eye and trying not to laugh. "Yes, I will tell her when she recovers consciousness. Yes,

yes, of course. Good day to you." She snapped the phone shut with a smug smile and handed it back to me. "All taken care of."

"What are you thinking?" I exploded. "My boss can't think I'm skipping work for a boob job!"

"If it makes you feel any better, she said she wasn't surprised. Besides, how else do you plan on explaining the new, improved you?"

As she spoke, a small elderly woman in an apron and powder-blue dress entered the kitchen and my protest died in my throat as I watched her prepare a plate of bacon, eggs, and sausage for Remy.

My stomach rumbled at the sight. Remy picked up a piece of bacon and nibbled on the end. "You hungry?"

"We just ate not too long ago." But I *was* hungry.

"Your metabolism's different now that you're immortal." She leaned in, whispering, "Besides, if I have the servants cook three meals a day for me, they think I'm normal."

"You have servants?"

Her brows creased together. "Uh, yeah. You didn't think I was the housework type, did you?"

Well, no. I leaned in, trying to keep my voice low. "But what about the whole undead thing? The vampires?"

She rolled her eyes and took another bite of bacon. I was tempted to steal it off her plate; it smelled amazing and I was starving. "First of all," she said, "quit saying that we're undead. It makes me think of zombies. Second of all, no vamps or any other weirdos can come here. I'm warded, remember? The best witches in town crawled all over this place. Priests too, so stop worrying about that part. Third of all, it's not like I do anything unusual except have a few male guests now and then." She shrugged once again. "Ethel just thinks I'm a bit of a loose woman." Remy took another bite of bacon and beamed at me. "So do you want breakfast?"

Of course, I did. I turned to Ethel. "I'll have what she's having, please."

Remy grinned at me. "Well, well, aren't we proper and polite? I bet you turned in your homework on time and made straight A's through school."

I ignored her and poured myself a cup of coffee.

Remy wouldn't be deterred. "Any boyfriends? Or did dating interfere with work? And how about sex partners? I'd be guessing fewer than three."

She'd be guessing two too many, if you didn't count Noah, but I wasn't letting her know that. I returned her ambiguous shrug and dug into the food Ethel placed in front of me.

"Oh, come on. Are you still mad about the job thing?" Remy gave me an incredulous look.

"I'm a little mad, yeah," I found myself saying. "Do you know how hard it is to find a decent docent position in this city?"

"A decent what?"

"A *docent*. Museum tour guide. It's a good job."

Remy's bright blue eyes looked over-bright in her honey-colored face. "Sounds boring as all hell. Don't worry, I imagine you'll still have a job in a few days—which gives you plenty of time to figure out what your situation is."

I stirred four cubes of sugar and some creamer into my coffee and slurped it. Delicious. "Uh, situation? What do you mean, other than the whole succubus thing?"

Remy polished off her breakfast with a few quick bites. "Well, you've got a lot of things on your plate right now: first and foremost being the fact that someone took the time to drain you dry and then left you in Noah's path. It could have been coincidence, but I'm not a big believer in that sort of thing. That means the vamps have an agenda, and we need them to make the first move so we can figure out what they're up to. Not to mention I'm still expecting one of the others to make an appearance. They usually do."

I took a bite of the most blissfully crisp bacon in my life and sighed with delight. As I ate a few more slices, Remy continued to stare at me. "Oh," I said, realizing she was waiting for me to respond. I had to think back to what she had said. "What 'others' do you mean?"

"Angels and the like. If we're unlucky, a demon or two."

I choked on my bacon. "Do we have to see all those?"

"I'm hoping not, but you never know—especially with a new succubus. You're like an ever-flowing goody bag to them, so they're drawn to our kind."

I wrinkled my nose at her. "So in other words, I'm now catnip to the scum of the world?"

"Scum of the Heavens is more like it." Remy jumped up and grabbed my plate as I was buttering a biscuit. "Come on, we've got to leave soon if we don't want to be late."

I crammed the biscuit into my mouth and watched longingly as she removed my plate. "Why is it," I muttered around a mouthful of food, "that we can't be late to *your* job? My boss thought I was out getting my boobs done."

Remy winked. "Trust me, all right?"

I sulked. "I hate it when you say that."

"That's why I say it. Now go and get dressed like a good little succubus."

I slammed out of my seat. "Fine. But we'd better be making a doughnut run on the way, or someone's going to be cranky."

Remy laughed as I trotted upstairs.

Since I didn't know what Remy did for a living, I didn't know what I should wear. Since she was dragging me against my will, I opted for casual and slid into the hot pink Juicy sweatsuit we'd picked up yesterday. It was comfortable, hugged my new body like a second skin, and bold printing across the fanny pronounced my ass was "Juicy" indeed. With my new looks and my new friend, it felt more like I was playing a role than being myself, and I decided to dress for the part. I stepped into some matching sneaker pumps and grabbed my purse.

Remy met me at the bottom of the staircase. I was relieved to see she was wearing something similar, except her jumpsuit was a dark blue and she wore a shirt under it that had a pink star across the chest. "Let's get going, shall we?"

She drove, naturally. I didn't own a car, and Remy didn't seem like the public transportation type. I had to admit that I didn't mind riding around in the posh little BMW.

The drive downtown was relatively short. Perhaps because it was so early in the morning, but the traffic was clear as could be. Remy was as wide awake as me, and since neither of us had slept in days, I supposed that the not-sleeping thing had some truth in it.

We pulled up in front of a nondescript building on the corner of Sixth and Main, in the business district. The windows were clean, the shades open, and I could see people moving around inside what seemed to be a busy office. Surprised, I turned to Remy. "You work in a corporate office?"

"Not exactly." She winked at me and slid out of the car.

The sight of two beautiful women walking into the office didn't cause even one head to turn. It bugged me; I knew how damn good I looked. But the suits sat in their desks, answered their phones, and ignored us. Bizarre.

Remy waved at the receptionist as she walked to one of the back rooms. "We're heading for the studio."

I followed close behind her, curious. "Is that why you looked so familiar to me? Are you an actress?"

"Something along those lines, yeah." She gave me a very blue-eyed look and I realized that Remy would need to feed her Itch, and soon, or we could have some problems.

She pushed through the double doors ahead of me and was immediately greeted by a man with a headset over his ear. "Remy baby, how are you?"

"Good morning, James. I'm lovely. How are you?" She gave him a kiss on the check, her hand sliding into his. "Is everything ready for the shoot?"

"Ready as they'll ever be." He gestured to the set in front of us, which looked like a bedroom in the final stages of preparation. Stage hands rushed everywhere, fluffing pillows and straightening the covers, and securing microphones in out-of-the-way locations. I watched with interest, wondering what they were taping. Soaps, maybe?

"Your costar's in his dressing room. I'll get him if you like, and we can begin whenever." He turned toward me and gave a low whistle of appreciation. "Who's your friend? Redheads are in right now."

Flattered, I gave him a faint smile and looked to Remy. She beamed and looped her arm through his, grinning. "This is my friend Jackie. She's a museum dough-spend."

"Docent," I corrected, offering James my hand, smiling graciously. "At least, if I still have my job."

"They'd be fools to fire you," he whispered against my hand, raising it to kiss. "Let me know if you'd ever like a job in the industry."

"The industry?"

Remy shook her head at me. "Trust me when I say I don't think it'd be your thing."

At first I bristled, but James's attention was definitely riveted on particular parts of my appendage. I extracted my hand from his. "I'll think about it," I lied.

Remy flashed me a smile and bounded away, bright blue eyes gleaming. "I've got to change into wardrobe. Have a seat; hopefully, this won't take too long."

I sat in the director's chair I'd been pointed to at the edge of the set. "How much time are we talking?"

"An hour or two. We just have to reshoot this one scene."

A male assistant came up to me and held out a tray of snacks and a variety of bottled waters, which improved my mood. "Fine," I said, picking up a finger sandwich or five. "I promise I'll be good while you're gone."

She trotted to the far end of the bustling studio and disappeared into a room with a star on the door, which I assumed was her dressing room. Cool. Her own dressing room. Maybe I should take her boss up on his job offer, since I was about to be unemployed. Being famous would be neat.

"So Remy's a big star, huh?" I glanced over at the assistant still holding the tray for me and took a cookie off his hands.

"Miss Summore is our biggest draw," he gushed, smiling down at me.

Or rather, smiling down at my boobs. I resisted the urge to zip my top up higher. "Great," I said, turning my attention to the stage. "So what are we filming here?

Commercials? Soaps? It'd be really cool if Remy was a soap star."

A strangled look crossed his face. "Soaps . . . ?"

He was saved from answering me as Remy entered the small stage flooded with lights. She sat on the edge of the bed in a filmy night robe—part of her costume, I guessed—and her blue eyes shone like beacons.

"Is Braddock behind the door?" the director boomed into his megaphone, and I watched all cameras position themselves on Remy's lovely face.

Someone gave the thumbs up, and the director nodded. "Action, then."

I leaned forward, nibbling on my sandwich. "How awesome is it to see a movie made from the front row?" I glanced over to the assistant, whose eyes were glued on the stage, and I turned my attention back there as well.

And nearly choked on my sandwich. Braddock had entered the room all right, naked as a jaybird. Remy was disrobing as well, and she had nothing on but a black garter belt and some stockings, and the highest spiked platform heels I'd ever seen.

Before I could spit out the piece of lettuce that was clogging my throat, they set upon each other like rabid wombats in mating season. And then I just *couldn't* look away. Her tongue was all over his face, and then she was throwing him down on the bed and making a beeline for what had to be the biggest schlong I'd ever seen.

"Um," I managed, covering my eyes. "Is she doing what I think she is?"

The sounds of slurping and moaning echoed through

the microphones on the set. "Oh yeah," the assistant breathed, his eyes riveted to the bed.

"Are they . . . supposed to be doing that?" I mean, Remy's eyes were blazing. Maybe her hormones went out of control and she was just nailing the first guy she'd run across.

The assistant looked at me in surprise. "Miss Summore is a huge adult film star, didn't you know?"

Aww hell. I'd probably seen her on cable the other night and not even realized it. That was why she looked so familiar. It would also explain the money, and how she managed to control her Itch.

It also explained the smarmy director, who'd given me a few creepy looks. I shuddered at the thought.

A low groan caught my ears and I couldn't help looking over at the bed again. Remy was locked onto the actor in a position I'd heard referred to as "reverse cowboy." She had her head thrown back, her black hair rippling down her back as she cried out in ecstasy. I wasn't sure if it was real or fake, but it was sending aftershocks directly to my groin. As I watched, she licked her fingertips and slid them down her body to finger herself. My body responded to the blatantly sensual move with a jolt, and I shifted in my seat, trying to accommodate the sudden throb of desire.

I *hated* being a succubus.

On a hunch, I jerked out my makeup compact and took a look at my eyes. Sure enough, they were brightening with every moment I spent watching Remy have wild porn-film sex like some horny voyeur.

That thought was a little too close to the mark.

When Remy cried out again and he grabbed her long hair, arching her backward over his body, my breath caught in my throat. I had to get out of here, or I was going to end up joining them on the bed.

I stood up abruptly and handed my sandwiches to the assistant. "I'm going to Remy's dressing room."

"Whatever," he breathed, eyes focused on the bed.

I bolted for the dressing room and slammed the door shut behind me, breathing hard as I leaned against it. My skin felt dewy with sweat and I fanned myself frantically, my pulse pounding in my ears. To think that my body could betray me so easily was appalling. I staggered into the room and my hand hit something soft on the table—a dildo the size of Manhattan.

Horrified, I stepped backward and took a good look around me. Remy's room was like something out of, well, a bad porno. Posters of close-up shots of Remy's face licking all kinds of anatomy adorned the walls, and there was a large bed with silk sheets in the center of the room. Mirrors covered the ceiling. Sex toys of all imaginable types were lined up on every inch of counter space, and her open closet door, revealed a ton of lingerie and spiked shoes. The dildo stared at me from across the table, along with a few other pieces of equipment that I did *not* want to guess the purpose of.

So much for a safe haven. I flew right back out and heard Remy's cries of "Oh yeah, baby, do me just like that!" and "Harder!" echoing in the room.

I had to get out of here.

I bolted out the first door I found, ignoring the buzzer that went off as I escaped through the emergency exit into the alley. I stumbled over to the main street, where I allowed the pedestrian traffic to swallow me. My brain was throbbing, my loins were throbbing, and all I could think was that I'd rather flip burgers for the next millennia than end up astride some guy for money like Remy.

I headed across the street to a small chapel that was sure to be deserted this early in the morning. Alone time was just what I needed.

The peace of the tiny church washed over me as soon as I stepped through the doorway, and I hesitated in the aisle. I felt like a hooker at a church social. I didn't belong here anymore, did I? Forcing those thoughts out of my mind, I moved to the back row of pews to sit down and focus my thoughts.

No sooner had I sat down than I felt a hand on my arm. Startled, I jerked away, only to find myself staring at the most singularly beautiful man I had ever seen. White-blond curls framed his pale face, and the biggest pair of dark blue eyes stared back at me. A faint smile touched his lips. He was dressed in flowing white robes, with a white fur cape tossed over his back.

Frightened at his sudden appearance, I jumped out of my seat, clutching my handbag. "You can't sit here. That seat's taken."

"It is a sin to lie in church, Jacqueline." He gave me a soft smile.

My jaw dropped; so did my purse. "How do you know my name?"

"I am sorry if I startled you." Again, the self-deprecating smile.

"Who are you?" I began to suspect my new friend wasn't your normal garden-variety churchgoer. "And why are you dressed like something from *Jesus Christ Superstar*?"

He laughed, a sweet, gentle sound. Weird or not, there was something appealing about his manner, and I relaxed. "Is that what you think, my dear Jacqueline? Look closer." He obligingly leaned forward to show me.

I gasped. What I had taken for a fluffy fur coat was actually feathery down: massive wings cascaded around his shoulderblades and swept down his back.

"Holy shit, you're an angel."

His smile faltered as he sat upright. "Please, your words."

I gasped and covered my mouth. "Ohmigod, I'm so sorry." When he flinched again, I winced. "Oh crap, I did it again, didn't I?"

"God understands the vagaries of human language, but I confess it is a bit hard on my ears."

I collapsed on the pew next to him again. "I'm so sorry," I repeated, not knowing what else to say. "What are you doing here? Are you cast out, like Noah?"

He looked a little green at the thought and shook his head. "No, no. I am not like your Noah."

I blinked hard. "You're still an angel, then. Like, a real one, not a Serim. Wow."

The angel gave me another softly sweet smile, and I immediately felt trampy and unworthy in my Juicy sweatsuit and overly bountiful new body.

"I am glad that you have come here. I wished for us to . . . talk a moment. My name is Uriel. I've heard of your plight."

Uriel—it even sounded angelic. I was in awe: a real live angel, here with me. My hand reached out to touch a ringlet of his white-blond hair to make sure that I wasn't dreaming, and it felt real and baby-fine. "I can't believe I'm meeting an angel. I never thought it would happen to me."

"Most likely it would not have. Only the deceased may gaze upon us, and we rarely exit Heaven. Humans with regular lives never see our kind." He cocked his head at me and took my hand in his. "But that was stolen from you, was it not? A regular life?"

To hear someone else state it like that made me pause, uncomfortable. "I guess so. The succubus thing is a little hard to get used to, but it could have been worse." I pried my hand out of his—not that I didn't love touching him—but my hormones were keeling toward overdrive and I didn't want to think nasty thoughts about the beautifully pure man before me. It seemed . . . wrong. "Remy's been really great, though," I defended. "Noah, too. I'm lucky that I have them to fall back on."

He gave me another knowing, pitying look and clasped my hand in his. "Is that true?"

I slid my hand back out of his once more. I liked his

touch way too much for my own good. "Look, I'm feeling a bit under the weather right now, so I'd prefer that you don't touch me, if it's all the same to you."

His brows drew together in a faintly puzzled look, then acknowledgment dawned, and he shied away from me like I had a wad of snot hanging off my nose. "Ah."

"Yeah." I blew my bangs up off my face in frustration. "It's the downside to the whole shebang—the constant maniac sex drive." I dug through my purse for some aspirin for the throbbing that was bound to turn into a headache soon.

"Don't forget eternal damnation."

I choked on the aspirin that I had just flung into the back of my throat. "What?"

"Eternal damnation," Uriel repeated and turned innocent eyes on me. "Did your new friends not explain *that* to you?"

I spat out one of the aspirin, my throat suddenly dry as a bone. The other had lodged itself to the roof of my mouth and I had to fish it out with a finger. "No one menshioned efernal damnashion," I said around my finger.

He gave a knowing nod. "I thought not. Their kind prefers to gloss over the negative details of their hedonistic lifestyle." Uriel had a hand to his heart, a sad look on his face. "I seek to help you return to your normal, mortal life. Don't you fear what paths you will take if you follow your friend Remy's lead?"

"Her lead?"

A line formed between his brows. "I refer to the After-life."

Now that threw me for a loop. "Uh, I thought I already died?" I looked around. Yep, still New City. I could smell the smog even from inside the church. "It's not exactly what I pictured, but it could be worse."

He shook his head, white-blond curls moving in a symphony that made me long to reach out and touch them again. I picked up my purse and clasped my hands around it to keep from reaching out. "This is not your Afterlife. You were scheduled for greater things, had not you been forcibly detained upon this earth."

He had my interest all right. "Forcibly detained?"

Uriel arched a delicate eyebrow at me. "Do you mean to tell me that you planned this?"

Well, no, I hadn't exactly. "Er . . ."

He nodded, as if that was the answer he had been expecting. "Precisely. It is lucky for you, Jacqueline, that I have decided not to hold your current status—or the company you keep—against you. Most of my brethren would not be so enlightened."

My feelings hurt, I resorted to the oldest of defense mechanisms: sarcasm. "So what makes you so special?"

Uriel's lips thinned, a sure sign I was irritating him. "I see I must get straight to the point with you. Very well, then. I need a favor."

"From me?" There was a squeak in my voice, despite my best efforts. "What could Heaven possibly want with me?"

"Not Heaven itself," he corrected me. "Just me. Uriel." He sent me a smile so warm, I thought I would melt right there in my seat. "Your friend."

"Oh," I breathed, scooting closer to him. He had the most beautiful face. Even Noah's amazing looks didn't compare with Uriel's perfect, sculpted beauty.

"Watch the wings," he reminded me in a gentle voice.

I shied back in embarrassment. "Sorry."

He touched my cheek, and I felt my knees go weak. "It is all right. I know you do not want to harm me."

"Oh, I don't," I said, breathing hard.

"I know," he repeated, the smile looking a little more . . . forced at my adoring gaze. "Especially when I have heard of your situation and decided to help you."

"Help me? How?" My ardor turned to puzzlement. How in the world could an angel help me with my current situation? Unless . . . I slid a glance over to the confessional. "You mean . . . I thought angels didn't do that."

"And how is it that you think Noah got into his predicament?" Uriel tilted his head at me like an inquisitive bird.

"Sex?" I blanked for a moment. "Really?" Noah had mentioned that, come to think of it.

Uriel leaned in, his voice soft. "It is not my story to tell, but perhaps you should ask your friend the next time you see him."

I noticed that the angel scrupulously avoided Noah's name. I almost asked about it, then changed my mind. I didn't want to make him angry. He seemed so . . . sweet. Wholesome.

I wanted to do dirty, nasty things to the man. His scent was wonderful, like cookies and baby shampoo—an odd, but fresh combination. And he was leaning very close to me, his gaze intent on my face.

"You shouldn't lean in to me," I warned him, recognizing the signs. "I'm sort of . . ." There wasn't a delicate way to put it. In heat? About to tackle him in a fury of lust? I just pointed at my eyes, which I'm sure were bluer than his own. "You know . . . this."

He smiled and my heart melted. "It's why I'm here."

I straightened in my seat, surprised. "You're here for that? But you just said . . ." I frowned at the thought of helping an angel, well, *fall*. Word traveled fast in the Afterlife. "I'm not some sort of celestial hooker, thank you very much."

Uriel looked almost as offended as me. "You've misunderstood me." He shook his head and put his fingers on my chin, pulling me closer. "Let me show you."

At his touch, my whole body throbbed, and I leaned in to the embrace. Instead of my lips, though, he brushed my forehead with a chaste kiss, and I pulled away in surprise. "You came here to do that?"

The edges of his mouth pulled up in a faint smile. "You take too much at face value, Jacqueline. Tell me, do you feel any different?"

I sat for a minute, thinking. My fingertips tingled, but that could be due to the fact that I was clenching my purse against my body. I set it down gently on the pew before me. "Am I supposed to feel different?"

"No urges?"

Gasp!

He was right. The obnoxious throbbing between my legs that told me that I was about to go sex crazy again had stopped. Ceased. Gone. My breasts didn't feel heavy and aching with need, and I could think clearly. I shot him a look of disbelief and jerked my purse open, rummaging through it for a compact. Sure enough, a quick look in the mirror showed my eyes bleached to the pale silver of Remy's and Noah's.

I was cured!

CHAPTER TEN

Uriel's next words shattered my hopes.

"It's a temporary reprieve, I'm afraid. The effect should last about a week, but I think you'll enjoy it in the meantime."

"Hell, yeah," I enthused, wincing at his grimace. "Oh, sorry. I keep forgetting who I'm talking to." I stared at my forehead in the mirror. The spot where he'd kissed me glistened like it had been covered with glitter. I touched it, but it didn't rub off. "Gosh, I don't know how to thank you." It was true—grateful couldn't begin to describe how I felt at the moment. Not having to track down Noah in the next few hours sounded pretty darn great. Going to him for sex would have been humiliating, and I didn't have any other likely candidates.

"You could do me a favor."

Uriel's slightly wheedling tone made me look up from my mirror. I'll give him credit—his face was perfectly neutral, not showing a hint of any sort of interest, but I knew it was there, all right. I wasn't born yesterday. Reborn, like maybe two days ago, sure.

"A favor?" I was reluctant to ask, since I knew that I probably wasn't going to be too keen on the idea, but the tingle on my forehead reminded me that he'd already made a gesture of goodwill toward me. The least I could do was hear him out.

Uriel shook his head and smiled. "Nothing quite so dire as that, my dear Jacqueline. I promise."

I felt bad for doubting him. "Sorry. I've been a little touchy for the past few days, as I'm sure you know." I couldn't resist sneaking another peek into my mirror to look at my wonderfully washed-out eyes. "Ask away."

"I'm not sure how much Noah has told you about our kind. As an angel, I am bound to sacred grounds. I cannot go where the ground is not blessed, or is unhallowed."

"So you can't leave this church?" He nodded and I promptly stopped feeling jealous of his beauty. Wow, that really sucked.

"As one of the fallen Serim, Noah can visit both hallowed grounds such as this church, or 'neutral' territory like your city. He cannot visit unhallowed ground or someplace blessed by the darker side of nature. Do you understand what I am saying?"

Oh, I understood all right, and I was scared. "I'm thinking you want me to go visit some voodoo temple or some graveyard, and I'm not interested."

His lips thinned into a narrow line. "You exaggerate as to what I ask. What I meant to say before I was . . . interrupted"—he leveled his best "I'm an angel of God and you're not" look at me—"was that I need to know some information, and I cannot go where I need to find it."

Information? That didn't sound too bad. Besides, I

was starting to feel rather guilty with the kiss burning on my forehead and all. "What information is it?"

"There are vampires in this city—the more extreme version of your friend Noah—who have chosen a darker path. If you have not already encountered them, I suspect you will very shortly."

Vampires? Oh dear. Remy had mentioned we were supposed to avoid them. "I don't know . . ."

"Vampires are immoral creatures, as you can imagine, and they are stirring like a black horde through this city. They follow a queen, an unholy demoness who they adore and worship. I believe she is planning something foul against our kind, and I must find out what it is."

"Whoa there," I said, putting both hands in the air. "What the heck am I supposed to do against a flock of vampires and their demon queen?"

Angels have amazing poker faces, I must say. He didn't show any outward signs of annoyance with me other than a slight compression of his lips again, but I knew he was frustrated.

"You will not have to go to anywhere dangerous. The vampires you wish to question congregate at several nightclubs in the city. All you need to do is get the information I seek. Do this for me, and you will receive another kiss, a longer-lasting one. You would be free from your obligation for a month, possibly longer."

No wonder Remy called them dealers. "Visiting a few nightclubs doesn't sound too bad." Something about this deal bothered me, though I couldn't quite put my finger on it. "Don't vampires eat people?"

Uriel's lips slid into a faint smile. "Jacqueline, the vampires would *never* hurt you."

I doubted angels could lie. "What makes you say that?"

"Your kind fascinates them. You will not be harmed but welcomed."

Welcomed by vampires? Somehow, it didn't sound enticing. "While I'd love to help you, I don't know how I'd get the information you're looking for. I doubt the queen's going to confess her deep, dark secrets to me over a few martinis."

His soft smile became a bit strained. "A succubus has ways of getting information. You can find it in their dreams. That is the private territory of your kind alone."

"Dreams?"

"Yes, dreams. You need only to control the dreams of a sleeping being and you can manipulate their subconscious. Have you never heard the tales your kind tell of succubi?"

"You mean succubuses tell stories about other succubuses?" Jeez, my "kind" needed to get out more.

"No." I could hear his teeth grinding. "And the proper plural is succubi. I meant that humans tell stories of succubi—"

"But I'm not human anymore—"

Uriel put a hand to his forehead, as if being with me were the most stressful thing in the world. "Never mind. If you will not help me, I suppose we will not find what the evil in the city is up to until it is too late, and then the fate of all mankind will be upon your head, not mine."

Guilt shot through me like a cannonball. "What do

you mean? People are going to die?" I asked as he stood and I tugged on his hand. "Don't go. I want to help, I do."

"Do you truly?" He turned those brilliant blue eyes upon me again, his gaze the benevolent, yet ready-to-be-disappointed parent. "Do you wish to help us prevent a tragedy?"

I couldn't speak around the knot of anxiety in my throat, so I nodded.

He leaned in and pressed his cheek against mine in a surprisingly tender gesture. "Then go and return here when you can tell me what they seek."

Then he vanished as if he were never there. He didn't even leave behind a feather or a faint smell in the air. There was nothing to remind me that I had just spoken with—and irritated—an angel.

I sat in the pew for a moment, my thoughts boiling, and then flipped open my compact again. In the mirror, the faint gleam of the kiss still shone.

So it *did* happen. Now I just needed to go find some vampires.

CHAPTER ELEVEN

I managed to slink back into the studio just in time to see Remy wrap her silk robe around her body and head for her dressing room. I snagged a bottle of water off a nearby tray and followed her in, shoving my bangs down to cover the angel mark. Now to remember to be angry.

"So where'd you run off to? I looked up and you were gone." Remy's silver eyes gleamed in the dim yellow light of the dressing room. "Don't tell me you had to go to the bathroom in the middle of my big scene."

"Where do you get the nerve?" I began with that and immediately felt proud. It was a good start to standing up for myself.

"Nerve for what?" She looked genuinely puzzled.

"You're a porn star! How could you not tell me? Did you think I wouldn't notice?"

"Oh, come on. How could you not notice? Did you see my DVD collection at home? I'm in half of them. And the name? Remy Summore? Ram-me-some-more? Get it?"

"I thought your name was REM-me, not RAM-me."

She shrugged. "Remy is spelled prettier. Besides, it's

porn, not rocket science. Nobody cares how your name is spelled."

This whole conversation was just wrong on *so* many levels. I shook my head, words failing me.

"Oh, come on." She flopped down on the couch and tossed one of the tasseled pillows at me. "Don't tell me you're going to be a prude about this. You had sex in a confessional yesterday with a man you hardly know, so you can't judge me. Besides, it's a good way to make money and kill the Itch at the same time." She shrugged at me, her dark hair cascading over her shoulder, looking as relaxed as could be surrounded by black silk and sex toys.

My mouth opened and closed. She thought I was *prudish*? How could a succubus be prudish? I couldn't think of anything to say, so I just said, "When can we leave?"

"Right now, Miss Cranky-butt," Remy said. "But you'll disappoint James. He likes you, you know."

I shot her a dirty look.

Remy smirked. "You sure you don't want a souvenir DVD—"

"Forget it."

I spent the rest of the day pretending to sulk in my room. That was much easier than trying to explain to Remy—or to Noah, for that matter—where I was planning to head that night. So I ignored Noah's phone calls and Remy's attempts at getting back in my good graces.

Okay, so she didn't really *try* to get back into my good graces, inasmuch as she sent room service up to me in the form of Ethel with delicious snacks. I wasn't fooled, though. It was a peace offering, and I took the food but not the apology.

After all, Ethel made incredible cheesecake brownies. No sense in sending those back. The brownies weren't at fault.

I passed the day watching bad daytime TV, eating food that would have put ten pounds on my thighs if my thighs weren't supernatural, and picked through my wardrobe. What would be good for hanging out with vampires? I needed something that said I was at home there but didn't want any funny stuff. Something that said "look but don't touch."

I decided on a sweater set of pale pink that was somewhat low cut in the front and a pair of jeans. It was nice without being tarty, and it showed the right amount of cleavage. I brushed my hair for about an hour, admiring the way it curled and swept over my shoulders. It was fascinating and the most brilliant shade of red. Whether or not I cared for the whole succubus thing, I was shallow enough to admit that my new looks were stunning. I'd never been attractive before, and it was as interesting to me as it apparently was to the opposite sex.

Grabbing my purse, I tucked my high heels in my hand and headed for the grand staircase that swept through the foyer of Remy's ostentatiously huge house.

Of course, who should I meet at the bottom of the stairs but Remy herself, in slippers and clutching a pint of Häagen-Dazs. Her brows furrowed as she stared at me. "Where are you going?"

It figured that I'd get caught on the verge of making it out the door. Of course, I hadn't thought very far ahead in my plan; I had no way to get to the city once I got out to the driveway. I guess every plan has to have its fatal flaw. "Er, nowhere."

She snorted. "Do tell."

"I'm going to the museum," I lied. "To pick up my pay-check."

Remy approached me and poked me on my bare breastbone. "Dressed like that?" She scanned me with sharp eyes and began to circle like a vulture. "What look were you going for with this ensemble? Jeans, so something casual. Heels, which means there'll be men there. A sweater set, which means you're a dork." She studied me while eating a spoonful of ice cream. "Did you buy that with me? 'Cause I'm pretty sure something as nerdish as that never made it into the bags when I was looking—"

"Hey!"

"But at least it's low cut," she concluded, "which means wholesome but not unavailable." She took a big bite of ice cream and pondered. "Not too slutty, but just attractive enough to get some attention?" Remy gasped and flung her spoon at me. "You skank! You're going to a club and you didn't invite me!"

"I'm not going to a club," I protested, my voice weak. It probably would have been more believable if not for the look of shame on my face.

"Going to pick up men, without *me*. After all I've done for you," Remy wailed dramatically, putting a hand to her forehead. Then she cocked her head and studied me. "If you were picking up a guy for the Itch, you'd be dressed differently. Why aren't your eyes even the tiniest bit blue right now? You're due."

I blanched and panicked, spitting out the first lie that came to mind. "I met someone earlier today. Had sex in a public bathroom."

Her eyes were the color of flint. "Oh yeah?"

"Yeah."

"What was his name, then?" Remy tilted her head, regarding me.

"His name? Um, it was Bob."

She snorted. "You are a really bad liar, you know that?" Remy tossed the ice cream onto a nearby table and approached me like a lion that had just spotted prey. "Show me your forehead."

I backed away, sensing a trap. "Why?"

Within the space of one breath, Remy had me pinned to a wall and was pushing my bangs up, revealing my glittering angel hickey. "Oh shit, Jackie. What have you done now?" She released me and stomped away through the foyer.

That was not the reaction I was expecting. I certainly didn't expect Remy to be pleased, but I didn't expect her to walk away so I followed. "Where are you going?"

I turned the corner and saw Remy with a phone to her ear.

"Who are you calling?" I put my hands on my hips

and contemplated leaving for the club, but again, still no ride.

Remy gave me a cross look and ignored me pacing in front of her. Someone must have picked up on the other end, because her expression changed to one of relief. "Noah? It's Remy."

I groaned. "You had to bring Noah into this?"

"I have a problem," she said into the phone as if I weren't there. "Yeah, I know the sun's about to set. This won't take long, I promise. Our friend has been naughty—there's an angel mark on her forehead." She held the phone away from her ear, and I heard a loud, explosive curse come through the receiver.

Well, that certainly wasn't good. My feelings about Noah were mixed, but I sure didn't want him pissed off at me.

"Yeah, I know," Remy said, the phone cradled against her ear again. She pinched the bridge of her nose between two fingers, as if fighting off a headache. "It was my responsibility and she got away from me. I'm sorry. No, I know." Pause. "I *know*." Pause again. "Look, I got it already, okay?" Annoyance snapped through her voice, and she nodded a few more times in irritation, then handed the phone to me. "He wants to talk to you."

I took the phone, regarding it like I would a snake. I pressed my fingers over the mouthpiece and whispered to Remy, "What if I 'oops!' drop it and we get disconnected? Think he'll call back?"

She snorted at me and shook her head. "Trust me,

you don't want him any more pissed off at you than he already is."

I made a face at her and held the phone up to my ear, waiting for the explosion. It was silent on the other end, so I made my voice as cheerful as possible. "Hi, Noah," I chirped.

"You just find this all one big joke, don't you?" I couldn't tell how Noah was feeling from his voice. It was emotionless, like he was reading off a piece of paper.

"I don't understand what all the commotion is," I began, keeping my voice light. "What's the big deal if I made a new friend?"

"They're not your friends." Noah sounded exhausted, and I could hear him stifle a yawn.

"Gee, sorry if I'm boring you."

Noah sighed. "You're not boring me. Quit being so damn needy. The sun is down and I'm going to be passing out in approximately five minutes until the sun comes up again, so let's finish this, all right? Who was it that you met up with?"

Was I that needy? That obvious? I flushed at the thought. "He said his name was Uriel."

Noah began to swear a blue streak at the exact same time that Remy did.

"Uriel," Remy moaned, then headed toward the bar. "I need a drink."

On the other end of the phone, Noah was still cussing like a madman, and I began to get irritated. And a little scared. Okay, a lot scared. I watched Remy slug down a shot of whiskey, and sighed. "I did something bad, didn't I?"

There was quiet on the other end of the phone. After a moment, Noah cleared his throat. "It depends. Did you hunt him down or did he find you?"

"He found me."

"Interesting." Noah certainly sounded calmer, which I took to be a good sign. "And did you agree to do anything for him? Any favors of a sort?"

"Nothing big—"

I had to break off my sentence and hold the phone away from my ear because of the cursing that ensued. I looked over at Remy, who was downing her second shot of alcohol.

"Didn't we warn you?" Noah shouted. "Didn't we tell you to stay away from them? That they were bad news?"

I winced. "Yeah, but he's an angel. How can he be a bad guy?"

Another round of expletives. "Forget it. I can't stay awake any longer. Tell Remy that I said to stay put until sunrise, and I'll be there at the crack of dawn. Got that?"

"Got it," I echoed, and disconnected with a satisfying click. "Sheesh, what a jerk." I made a face at her. "He told me to tell you he'll be here at the crack of dawn." The words rolled out of my mouth, compelled by my Serim master.

"I can't believe you got tangled up with Uriel already, and it's only been two days," Remy moaned from across the room, shaking her head like I was on the verge of death. "Noah's going to have my head. What did he say to you?" She fixed intent gray eyes on me.

"Nothing special, just that he wanted to have a talk with me when he wakes up." I omitted the teensy part about how we weren't supposed to go anywhere. "So what's so bad about Uriel?"

Remy gave the whiskey bottle another longing look but stepped away from the bar. "Uriel is one of the head honchos upstairs. If he's taking an interest in you, it means big things are afoot."

"But I didn't do anything," I protested. "I went into a church and he was there."

She shook her head at my ignorance. "That didn't clue you in?"

I threw my hands up in the air. "Never mind. Just forget I said anything, all right?"

"So what did you promise to do for him?" Remy crossed her arms over her chest and cocked her head, regarding me. "Let me guess, just a little something small, right?"

I blinked. "Yeah, come to think of it. He just wants me to go hang out with a couple of vampires—"

Remy exploded at that. "Hang out with a couple of vampires? Why in all the nine hells is an angel sending you to rub shoulders with that lot?"

All this screaming and cussing was really getting annoying. You'd think I'd agreed to smuggle nuclear weapons into an orphanage, not just say hi to a few folks with questionable dentistry. "Look, if it gets your panties into a wad, I just won't go, all right?"

She shook her head at me. "You have to now. You promised."

"Well, then, I guess I lied. He'll get over it." I waved it off with a flick of my hand. "I've told worse lies."

"No, you don't understand." Remy was shaking her head with determination. "You *can't* take your word back once you give it to an angel. It's like lying to the IRS. That shit carries straight to the top, and if you ever terminate here on earth, you don't want to be heading downstairs, if you get my drift." She rubbed her face, looking rather tired and put-upon.

"Once you make a deal with an angel, you have to follow through—because they may be good guys, but they never forget if you wrong them. That's why our kind avoids them and Noah's kind calls them 'dealers.' They offer you a free hit to suck you in and bring your guard down. Then they ask for just a little favor, and you do it, because you promised. And they keep coming back to you with more and more little favors, until you find yourself trying to take down the whole vampire syndicate singlehanded because that's what Uriel or Gabriel or one of the bigwigs wants, and you're so far in you can't stop. Ever."

I ignored the uncomfortable feeling in the pit of my stomach. Uriel had seemed so nice, almost cuddly. "But he said he just wanted me to check things out. That's all." It sounded pretty lame even to my ears, and I sighed. "Maybe you're wrong. Maybe they don't do these kinds of things."

"Are you kidding?" She stared at me in amazement.

"I've known several succubi that have had their existence ended because of angel interference. And I'm pretty sure none of them went upstairs, despite all the gun-running they did for their angel pals." Remy hauled me back up the staircase behind her. "Face it, kid. When it comes to the major leagues, the best thing you can do is stick to the minors and keep your nose clean."

"Got it," I replied meekly, allowing her to drag me into my room. "What are we doing?"

She headed straight for my closet and thrust the doors open. "Dressing you for the part. If you're going to go 'hang out with a few vampires,' you'll need to dress in something sexier than a sweater set."

I sat down on the edge of my bed, watching her. "Um, I don't think I want to go anymore, if that's all right."

Remy shook her head. "I'm afraid you don't have a choice. You gave that up the moment you let that angel put his lips on you."

I scowled. "Well, don't pick out something super-slutty. If I'm going by myself, I want to at least be comfortable and somewhat normal seeming."

She tossed a glittery red corset top at me. "You'll wear what I give you, and who says I'll let you go in alone?"

My eyes widened. "But I thought you don't like hanging out with vampires. You have them warded and stuff."

She shrugged and pulled a hanger out of my closet. "Doesn't mean that I'll let you walk into the lions' den alone. Oh ew, why'd we buy these pants?" Remy tossed them to the floor. "Where are the leather skirts? We need something short and tight."

"Back of the closet," I said. "And thanks."

"Don't thank me yet. Thank me when we're done," she pronounced. "Now, let's get you all slutted up for the vamps. They like their women with a lot of skin showing. Lucky for you, we've got some mighty fine choices here. How do you feel about cutoffs?"

"I think I feel sick," I mumbled.

CHAPTER TWELVE

A short time later, I was fiddling with the knobs of the A/C in Remy's BMW and scowled at her. "I can't believe we're going out dressed like this."

"Believe it, girlfriend. What's wrong with what you're wearing? You look like a woman out to get a man, which is precisely our goal."

"I look like a streetwalker."

"Well, as long as you don't look like a librarian."

I was pretty sure that was a jab at my museum job, but I decided to take the high road and say nothing. I didn't want Remy to bail on me and leave me heading to the vampire club alone.

Remy sped down the expressway, bobbing her head in time to an old Duran Duran song. It was blissfully quiet for all of two minutes. Then she glanced over at me. "You weren't going to snag anyone's attention in your old getup."

She just couldn't let it drop, could she? I didn't care if she was right or not. I slouched lower in my seat, staring out the window. "Whatever." I tugged at the hem of my skirt as she crossed three lanes and exited. The corset wasn't so bad, but the skirt was really bugging me. "I think you can see my underwear when I sit down in this thing."

"You're wearing underwear? Who told you to do that?"

I smacked her arm. "Very funny."

"Hey," she protested. "Trying to turn into the parking lot here." She pointed at the long trail of cars streaming outside what looked to be a busy nightclub. There was a line outside the door that wrapped around the building, and I could hear the thumping bass from inside the car with the windows rolled up.

"Are you sure this is a good idea?" I'm not much of a club goer, and the thought of having to do some Scooby-Doo–style sleuthing in a club full of vampires scared the crap out of me.

"No, this is a terrible idea." Remy screeched to a halt in front of the valet parking. "But you started it, so we need to finish it."

"Great," I said, getting out of the car. "Next time I try to do the right thing, smack me in the head, will you?"

"I can do that." Remy grinned and slammed her door shut. She held the keys aloft and jiggled them to the waiting parking attendants. "Who wants to take extra-special care of my car for me?"

I watched in amazement as three guys leapt to take the keys from her. Remy smiled wickedly and held them out to a thin, slightly nerdish man with thick glasses. He gave her an adoring look. "We'll take great care of it, Miss Summore."

Either Remy was more famous than I thought, or she was on a familiar basis with the club employees. It bugged me either way. I trotted up to her and grabbed her arm.

"I thought you said you didn't associate with vampires?"

"I try not to, but it still happens." She gave a tiny shrug. "Hazard of the business. It's not working with them that's a problem. It's the whole 'double-agent' thing you're trying to pull." She put her hand through the crook of my arm and strolled to the door, past the line of people waiting to get in. "Now, do me a favor and keep quiet while we're in here. Let me do the talking, all right?"

"Got it." I glanced back at the line and wondered how long they'd been waiting. If I had been in that line and someone pushed to the front, I'd have raised hell. As it was, the women shot us dirty looks, but the men . . . well, they didn't seem to mind at all. I caught one checking out my ass in my short skirt and I gave it another tug with my free hand, positive that my thong was showing under the hem.

The bouncer was a giant of a man, his shaven head covered in complex barbed-wire tattoos. Earrings studded his ear all the way up; he wore an old Metallica T-shirt and the biggest pair of boots this side of Kentucky. He was easily a foot taller than me, and I was no shrimp at 5 foot 7.

He also lit up like a Christmas tree as soon as he set eyes on Remy. "Miss Summore," he said, awed. "What an unexpected treat. How are you?"

Remy walked up to the giant and patted him on the cheek. "Couldn't be better, Dingo. It's sweet of you to ask about me." She flashed him her best sultry gaze, laying the charm on thick.

Dingo unchained the velvet rope blocking off the door

and blushed crimson. "I could never forget you, Miss Summore. Do come in."

"Cover charge?" She tilted her head and looked at him expectantly.

"None for you. Never for you." His voice was openly worshipful. "Stamp?" He held up a stamp pad.

Remy nodded. "Tonight's one of those nights, I think. Stamp me and my friend here." She gestured to me.

I seemed to register on Dingo's radar for the first time, and his gaze darkened. "Miss Remy, she's not on the list. I can't stamp her without approv—"

"Dingo, darling," Remy chided. "She's an out-of-towner and a close friend of you-know-who's. Be a dear and let her in. I assure you, everything will be fine." She placed her hand on his arm in entreaty. "She's a good friend of mine. Isn't she pretty?"

I supposed that was my cue to turn on the charm. I smiled, thinking I probably looked more like a deer in headlights than a seductive babe. "Hi, Dingo," I squeaked. "I hate to impose—"

My words cut off in a yelp as Remy's heel stomped down on the toe of my shoe. Okay, bad route to go. I could see Dingo's eyes darkening even more, and he was starting to look like a rabid dog. A really huge one. I changed tactics. "I promise I won't leave Remy's side all night. Though I wouldn't mind getting to know you better, if you had a few minutes for me." I winked, laying it on thick, too.

Both Remy and Dingo looked at me in surprise, and I wondered if I'd said something wrong.

"Any friend of Miss Summore's is a friend of mine,"

Dingo said at last, unable to take his eyes off me. I was a little unnerved at that. Yeah, I'd probably gone and said the wrong thing again. I held out my hand for the stamp and tried to look confident.

The stamper pressed against the back of both of our hands, but nothing showed up on my skin when I looked at it. Remy winked at Dingo and wiggled her fingers at him. "See you later, darling, and thank you."

He nodded and bowed. "Of course, Miss Remy. You and your lovely friend have a good evening, and come out and see Dingo if you get bored." Lust-filled eyes followed me in the club.

I tugged at my skirt hem again as I followed Remy through the double doors and into the antechamber where coats were checked and people came out to lounge. Another bouncer stood at the door before us, and the music was even louder.

As soon as the door behind us slammed shut, I leaned in to Remy. "What did I say back there?"

She burst into laughter. "Usually when a girl offers to spend some solo time with a bouncer, it's a blowjob to get into the club."

My eyes nearly bugged out of my face.

"Midnight's a very exclusive club." She giggled. "And since you're already in the door, he must assume that you really like him."

I resisted the urge to punch her. "You should have told me. And what's with the name Dingo, anyway?"

She shrugged. "I never bothered to ask. Some things you just don't want to know."

Amen to that.

Remy led me past the second bouncer without stopping and then we were enveloped in the smoky, throbbing atmosphere of the club. Her hand grasped mine and she leaned in to shout in my ear, "Stick close to me. We're not staying in here."

"Sounds good to me." I had always found clubs obnoxious and overly boisterous, and Midnight was no exception. Tables were crammed into every dark corner of the room; the outskirts of the dance floor were cluttered with chairs and people drinking and talking. The dance floor was lit up with a multitude of colored lights, and bodies pulsed and writhed before the DJ booth, pressed against each other in a frenzied crush. The scent of sweat in the air touched my nostrils, and as I watched moist skin pressed against skin, I felt the kiss on my forehead flare.

Remy headed straight for the bar, which suited me just fine since I could use a drink or three, and dragged me to the last two bar stools. Two men sat in the seats already, but that didn't deter her in the slightest. She leaned in and tapped the man closest to her on the shoulder. "Excuse me."

The man turned, an ugly look on his face as if he was about to tear whoever it was behind him a new one for disturbing him. His expression changed the moment he laid eyes on Remy, clad in her leather bodysuit, her silky black hair tied into a waist-length ponytail. "Hey, gorgeous," he breathed. "What can I do you for?"

She rewarded him with a catlike smile. "You and

your friend can give us your seats at the bar. We'll talk about . . . favors . . . later."

His eyes slid over to me and bugged out. I'm sure we were quite a sight—two super babes slumming in a trashy bar, dressed like we were on the prowl. His gaze looked me up and down and then focused on my boobs, most likely due to the fact that the corset hiked them up to my chin. "Your friend is nice," he said to Remy, unable to look beyond my torso.

"Her friend has a face," I snapped.

Remy squeezed my hand painfully, reminding me that we were supposed to infiltrate the crowd. I forced a tight smile and managed a strangled "Cutie" at the end of my sentence.

By now we had his friend's interest, and he was as scary as the first guy. Both looked like they could bench press a bus.

"Are you sure this is a good idea, Remy?" I leaned close so the men couldn't hear our conversation. "I mean, they could be serial killers looking to pick up their newest victims. Or what if they're rapists? They could tackle us, drag us into an alley, and have their way with us, and you're flirting with them!"

Remy eyed the two men in a decidedly lascivious fashion. "It might suck, but it wouldn't be rape. You'd be willing after about one second."

I gasped, affronted. "Oh my God! You are such a bitch someti—"

She grabbed my face and planted her lips onto mine. I heard the men around us suck in their breaths moments before my hormones kicked into overtime.

It was weird, having a woman kiss me. I mean, Remy was a great kisser, but the entire thing was just . . . odd compared to a guy. Her lips were soft, her kiss more delicate than other ones I received. I could feel the Itch starting to blast through my body. My forehead blazed for a moment with a painfully bright flare, and then just like that, the Itch disappeared.

Pleased beyond words with that result, I was still speechless when Remy broke off the kiss and smiled to the two men. "So, what do you say? Can we have the seats or not?"

I've never seen men stumble out of their chairs so fast. One bar stool was knocked over in their haste and quickly straightened again.

Remy smiled at the two men, looking pleased as could be. "Thanks, boys." She put her hand around my waist and steered me toward the chair.

I sat, my forehead still throbbing. "What did you do that for?" I scowled and tugged at my skirt.

"For starters, it got the desired result, didn't it?" Remy looked unconcerned as she flagged down the bartender. "And it shut you up, which was an added bonus."

"You're a sick woman, you know that?"

"What's the old saying? Takes one to know one?"

She had me there. I decided to change the subject. "So aren't we supposed to be finding some vampires around here?"

Remy shot me a look that could kill. "Don't make me kiss you again."

I clamped my jaw shut and crossed my arms over my chest, doing my best to ignore the two creeps loitering behind us, waiting for either me or Remy to turn around.

The bartender came over, his face getting the same glazed look on it the moment he laid eyes on her. I'll say one thing for being a succubus: sex will get you everywhere.

"What can I get for you, miss?" He shot a look at me as well, his eyes resting on—you guessed it—my cleavage.

I sighed. I'd never thought the day would come when I hoped for a guy who *didn't* think I was sexy.

"A Bloody Mary for myself and my friend here." Remy smiled at the bartender and placed her hand on my arm.

Ugh. "Remy, I hate tomato juice—"

She gave me another dirty look. "Two Bloody Marys."

The bartender asked, "Got a stamp?"

Remy held the back of her hand out to him. "Of course."

To my surprise, he took her hand in his own and sniffed her skin gently, then released it. I wondered what they'd stamped us with. It seemed that I'd almost fucked up the super-secret code, but how was I supposed to know? I held my hand out as well. "Me, too."

He gave my hand a sniff, then nodded. "Be right back." The bartender walked to the far end of the bar, motioning over another bouncer and talking to him.

Remy turned in her bar stool and faced me. "You really suck at hints, you know that? Do me a favor and keep your mouth shut for five minutes, all right?"

Feeling rather sulky, I made a face at her. "Fine. I won't say anything at all."

Relief splashed across her face. "Perfect."

Oh, I was *so* going back to my apartment after this.

The bartender returned after a moment and placed two drinks before us. "As requested, your drinks." He cast a meaningful look at Remy, then walked away.

That was weird. I picked up my drink and sniffed it. It smelled like tomato juice. I hoped I wasn't supposed to drink it as part of the signal.

Behind me, someone tapped my shoulder. I turned around just as a large hand clamped over my bare shoulder. It was yet another bouncer, if the black T-shirt and huge arms were any indication. He had a unibrow that would have made a mobster jealous and shoulders that you could probably build a house on. "Come with me, ladies."

This whole process was starting to scare me. I gave Remy an uncertain look so she would know how nervous I was. She looked as cool as a cucumber.

"Of course," she said, and downed her drink in one long gulp. I heard a collective intake of breath behind her from the men.

I took her lead and choked mine down as well, gagging on the taste. "Ready here."

The bouncer escorted us through the crowd to the far end of the bar, where a door marked "Emergency Exit" was covered in bathroom graffiti. "Through here."

Since I'd been pushed to the front of our little pack, I opened the door and stepped into darkness.

I heard the door slam behind me, and the sound of the music was immediately muffled into a low throbbing. I felt Remy move next to me and I reached for her hand. She gave my fingers a reassuring squeeze and didn't move, so I stood still as well, my heart hammering in my throat.

A tiny flame lit up the room, and the end of a cigarette flared into life, bright orange in the choking darkness. "What brings you two ladies to Midnight?"

The voice was masculine, with an inflection that I couldn't put a name to. Urbane and smooth, it rolled across the darkness, and I felt the angel mark flare on my forehead again. Jeezus, he must have a *really* nice voice.

"We're interior decorators, looking for a few good contacts, and we were told this was the place to come." Remy's voice slid through the darkness.

"Sure you are, Remy," he said, his voice marginally closer than before. I heard the sound of a long pull on the cigarette and boots thumping on the floor as he walked. "Who's your friend?"

"Her name is Jackie."

"She doesn't have a tongue in her mouth?" The man's voice sounded amused. "That must be how she's managed to stay friends with you for so long."

I snorted. He seemed to know Remy and her bossy tendencies pretty well. Remy squeezed my hand again, and I remained quiet.

"I see," the man said, his voice thoughtful. "And the fact that she smells like one of your kind should be a hint as well. Should I tell Nitocris you're here, I wonder?"

"Zane," Remy said, her voice taking on a pleading edge. "If you tell her I'm here, she'll make both of our lives a living hell."

Whoa. I didn't know which was scarier—that Remy was afraid of this Nitocris person, or that she was reduced to pleading with this guy. I shivered in my platform heels and wondered if I was up to this.

My ears detected the sound of Zane taking another drag from the cigarette. "So what do you give me if I decide *not* to tell her that the resident succubus of New City has deigned to gift us with her presence again? Or that she has a friend in tow?"

"What do you want?" Remy's voice was resigned.

"It's not you, my dear. A trip on the town bicycle isn't nearly as fun when everyone's already run it roughshod."

I heard Remy's swift intake of breath and her hand clenched mine painfully. "You're such an asshole."

"Of course I am. Comes with the territory." The end of the cigarette brightened for a moment and swung toward me. "Your little friend here, though . . . what's her name? Colette?"

"Jackie," Remy reminded him, her voice grating as if butter wouldn't melt in her mouth.

"She's got quite the figure. Nice red hair, too."

I thought that was a pretty neat trick, seeing as it was pitch-black in the room. Something told me that this guy was dangerous. It practically seeped into the air around us.

The cigarette flickered into darkness. "Well, Remy,

since your being here makes me rather curious, I don't think I'll say anything to the others. I do, of course, have to give you the standard pat-down to make sure you're not coming in to cause trouble. No crucifixes, holy water, things like that."

"Of course." Remy's voice returned to a more neutral tone, and my heart stopped hammering in my throat. "I'll owe you one for this, Zane."

"I know you will." He sounded amused by her promise. "Now, if both of you would be so kind as to put your hands into the air?"

I obediently raised my arms in the darkness, feeling somewhat silly. "Is this really necessary?"

Two warm hands were suddenly resting on my breasts, kneading them. "Ah. She speaks." A quick brush of the fingertips across my hardening nipples, and I felt the kiss flare on my forehead as sensation rushed over my body in response. The stranger chuckled near my ear. His thumbs flicked over my breasts again, deliberately. "Nice rack."

The kiss flared, saving me from jumping the asshole's bones, and I slapped his hands away. "Forget it. I'm done here. Screw you, buddy."

"Jackie," Remy's voice warned me from a few steps away. "Don't mess this up."

"Do you know where this fucktard has his hands?" I felt them reach for my behind and sidestepped to the left. "I agreed to come here. I didn't agree to be grabbed like some two-bit hooker."

"That's right. You girls are so much classier than that,

aren't you?" Zane's smooth voice rolled across the room again, and I felt his hands encircle my waist.

I could hear Remy sigh. "Don't be such a prick, Zane. You've got us in a bind, and she's new, all right? Cut her some slack."

His hands stiffened on my waist and then pulled away. "New?" There was a pause, then a chuckle. "Interesting. Not the place I'd think you'd bring a baby Suck to, but then again, I'm not you."

"No, you're not." Remy's voice sounded strained. "So can we go in or not?"

"Depends. Who's her daddy?"

"I beg your pardon," I said, outraged.

"He means your master, Jackie. He's just being a jerk—"

"Oh. I don't know who—"

"And you don't have to tell him anything," Remy warned, cutting me off before I had a chance to spill everything. "Got it? You're not obligated to tell him squat, and Zane knows it's impolite to ask. He's trying to slip one past you because you're new."

Oh. Whoops. "Gotcha."

I felt Zane's breath against my ear as he chuckled. "That new, eh? Your secret is safe with me, Princess."

I shoved him away again, thankful that the kiss was on my forehead. It burned into my flesh, reminding me of the uncomfortable situation we were in. "You're a real prick. Can we go in or not?"

The door behind us swung open, casting light inside and letting me see Zane's face for the first time.

Dark, dangerous eyes glinted at me. Slashes of black eyebrow arched in my direction, curving upward in amusement. There was a shadow of stubble across his strong, crisp jaw, and it accentuated the most perfect, most sardonic mouth I'd ever seen. His hair was short, just brushing his ears, and cut in a fashion that I'd come to associate with Ivy League lawyers if not for the floppy lock that hung over his forehead, making him look as if he'd just rolled out of bed. He looked familiar, but I couldn't place him. Perhaps it was the familiarity that comes with being breathtakingly gorgeous, with a face that every sane woman would want on the pillow next to hers.

Sans fangs, of course.

His eyes swung up and down over my figure, assessing me, and came to rest on my face. "I do hope we'll be seeing each other again, Colette." He held the door open and gestured for me to walk through.

"It's Jackie," I reminded him, brushing past and noticing he was dressed entirely in black leather with lots of buckles and straps. Sure, it was a cliché, but it worked for him. He looked like a dark, scary cousin of James Dean.

I was fascinated despite myself.

He just gave me another lopsided smile. Remy gave me a shove in the back, hurrying me through the door and away from Zane.

As I stepped into the "vampires only" part of Midnight, I noticed three things. One, that it was decidedly less crowded than upstairs, and two, that you could barely hear the music. And three, it was filled entirely with men.

All of which, I was pretty sure, were of the fanged persuasion.

The bar itself was more ordinary than the one upstairs. Polished wood, clean bar stools—the place looked like a snappier version of Cheers. It was downright weird, given the fact that the occupants were rather intimidating. To a one, they were pale-skinned, on the intimidating side, and completely riveted by the two of us.

The heat of a hundred pairs of eyes on me was an uncomfortable feeling, and I shoved Remy ahead of me. "You go first."

She rolled her eyes at my sudden cowardice. "Don't be such a chicken. Nobody knows who you are here, got that?"

"But that Zane guy—"

Remy shook her head and leaned close to me. For a moment I thought she was going to plant one on me again. I moved back instinctively. "No, silly." She gestured for me to lean in, and I did so. "They won't figure out that you're a succubus unless you offer it up. Zane's an exception to the rule—he was the second to fall, and so he's got edgier senses. If anyone else asks, you're wearing my clothes, and they won't be able to tell the difference in the smell. Now find what you need and let's get out of here, okay?" She pushed away from me and headed toward the bar.

"Wait," I said, following after her like a lost puppy.

Remy shot me a look that could have pinned me to

the wall from ten feet away. "You're making a spectacle of yourself," she hissed. "Girls come down here to hook up with dates, if you get my drift. Go find yourself a date and I'll find me one—got it?"

Ick. Most of these men were creeping me out, not turning me on. I glanced around as I stood near the doorway, uncertain.

Behind me, Zane chuckled. "Something I can help you with, Colette? Or could it be that you're attracted to my charm?" His eyes slid to my breasts again, and he gave me a knowing smile. "At least parts of you are."

Bastard. I ignored the flaring of the kiss on my forehead and scowled at him. Like I'd let him know that he turned me on. I crossed my arms over my chest and stalked away, trailing Remy again. She'd seated herself at the far end of the bar, away from the other patrons. I'd have bet money that she wouldn't be alone for long though, judging by the way they eyed her. "Remy," I whined.

She put her hands over her face, and I thought I heard her mutter something in a foreign language. "What? What now?"

I slid in close to her and spoke low so nobody could hear—especially not that Zane, who still watched the two of us with amused eyes. "How am I supposed to get this information I'm looking for?"

Remy pinched the bridge of her nose, stemming off a headache from my ineptness. "You could put your date to sleep, for starters. Then you read his head."

I frowned. "Read his head?"

"Didn't I tell you about that?" Remy shooed away the bartender when he came over, then turned to face me fully. "That's part of your powers. You can read dreams and stuff—just don't go crazy with it. The vamps are a bit sensitive when it comes to us mucking around, since we're supposed to be neutral. If you get caught, it's very bad news."

Right. I remembered something about that from my conversation with Uriel. "Don't get caught. Got it." I glanced around, then whispered, "So how do I put them to sleep?"

Remy shrugged. "Touch him, kiss him—it's hormone induced. You'll figure it out—I don't know the exact mechanics. I just think it, and boom, it happens. The kind of sleep we induce is not the same as regular sleep. He won't remember any of it, if it makes you feel any better."

I frowned. As answers went, that kinda sucked. "And I'm supposed to get jiggy with someone in the middle of a vamp bar?" I turned to look at Zane, and sure enough, he was still watching me. I made a rude gesture and he took the hint, laughing and wandering off. "Remy, they look at us like we're appetizers."

"Darling," Remy said, patting my arm. "We are."

"Oh great. I feel so much better now. Thanks so much."

She winked at me and then gave me the same shooing motion as the bartender. "Off you go, then."

Off I go. I turned away from the bar, since that was Remy's territory. Zane was loitering by a pool table, his eyes focused on me. *Definitely* not heading over there.

A few booths lined the back of the dimly lit room, and only one was occupied. The two men watched me with hawklike interest as I wandered in their direction. One was blond, the other one dark-headed.

"Time to take the bull by the horns," I said to myself, reminded of the angel kiss on my forehead that still burned. I strode forward, sliding my hands down my skirt and tugging at the hemline as I approached the table. "Hi, boys," I said brightly, forgetting for the moment that I had to be seductive. "Want some company?"

My boobs were about eye level with the men, a fact that was lost on none of us. The blond stared at them in fascination, his bottle of beer poised halfway to his mouth. His mouth opened a bit and I could make out the tips of a pair of gleaming fangs. I wondered how long it'd take before they heard my knees start to knock together.

Blondie slid over in the booth. "Have a seat."

I contemplated it and glanced over at his dark-headed companion. He had horrible red eyes, a scarred upper lip, and a look on his face that only Charles Manson would understand. I quickly sat with Blondie, forcing my chipper smile back on my face. "Hi," I repeated, feeling like the lamest succubus ever. "I'm um, Colette." I figured since I was doing super-spy stuff, I might as well have a super-spy name.

"Well, Colette," the scary vampire across from me drawled. "Are you a natural redhead? Because that's an impressive color. Don't suppose you'd let me check the undercarriage, would you?" He leered at me.

It was on the tip of my tongue to tell him to get lost,

then I remembered where I was. "Sorry," I said, trying to remain perky and not burst into frightened tears. "The undercarriage is off limits." I glanced over at his blond friend, who was sucking down his beer, his eyes still on my boobs.

"Then why are you here?" His red eyes bored into me and I began to feel alarmed. Time for a little action.

I looped my arm around Blondie's neck, my breasts nearly falling out of my corset, and gave Ugly what I hoped was a confident smile. "Because I thought your friend here was cute. Would you mind giving us some alone-time?"

Silence descended over the three of us, and I waited for someone to respond. Kick me out, buy me a drink, kill me, whatever.

I felt a hand slide up my thigh under the table, testing the waters. I shifted, resisting the urge to sigh in delight at the sensations the simple touch sent scattering across my flesh. "Why don't you leave the two of us for a bit, Joel?" Blondie said to his friend, and his hand slid higher up my skirt, closer to my eagerly awaiting loins.

Success. I gave Blondie a faint smile and slid closer, practically shoving my cleavage under his nose. "What's your name, sweetheart?"

"Adam," Blondie said as his friend got up and stalked away from our shadowy corner. His voice was slightly hoarse, his eyes darkened to a reddish shade, and his fangs had grown longer. Part of me wanted to run away screaming, and part of me was turned on by the power I had over him. I liked that I could make him lose control.

"What brings you here tonight, Colette?" I felt his hand slide up my skirt even farther and felt the Itch begin to stir. Uncomfortable as I was at the situation, the Itch didn't give a rat's ass.

I thought about his question for a moment, then leaned in. "Boredom?" It seemed a good enough answer as any. "It's been a dull week. I needed a rush. My friend suggested we come here."

"She suggested right," he whispered against my neck. He looked like he was about to fling me down onto the table and have at me in front of all these people. He inhaled sharply, and then stiffened. "You smell like—" His eyes widened, flaring to full-blown red.

My heart hammered as I put a finger to his lips. "Shhh. Didn't I tell you who my friend is? She let me borrow her clothes." I put my fingers under his chin and tilted his gaze toward the bar, where Remy sat, surrounded by vampire admirers.

"Ah." He inhaled deeply against my neck again, licking at my skin. "You smell amazing." He sniffed again, and I remembered. *Like catnip to their kind,* I had joked, and it certainly seemed to be true. He'd forgotten all about his beer, and the friend who he'd pissed off. "Why don't you sit in my lap?"

The Itch was turning into a full-on throb despite the sizzling on my forehead, and I obligingly slid onto his lap, straddling him and pressing my breasts against his chest. I could feel the hardness in his pants against the junction of my legs under my skirt, and the realization made me smile with arch delight. "How's that?" I let my long curtain of hair fall over his face, shielding the two of us from any onlookers.

"Perfect," he said, his voice hoarse. His hands gripped my hips and ground them against his cock. "You're a smokin' little number, Colette."

"I like to think so," I bragged, and the angel kiss flared again, instantly quelling any desire my charged hormones felt for this guy. Instead, I was reminded that I was grinding down on an oversexed vampire in a public bar full of the type. And I needed to pick his brain.

He ground my hips down on his again and I took that moment to kiss him, hoping I could avoid fangs. *Sleep,* I thought, and a weird sensation flooded through me, my nerves tingling.

It worked almost too well. Adam became instantly limp, and I had to close my lips over his again to muffle a snore. Well, that was a neat trick, but now what? It wasn't like I could go up and ask Remy what to do. If someone found out what I was up to, I'd be toast. Going on instinct, I pressed my forehead to his and tried to see what was going on in there.

I was immediately thrust into a series of images in his mind, some cloudy, some distinct and fully formed. It was like wandering into someone's cluttered bedroom, seeing all their stuff spread out over their furniture. Everything I needed and more was here, if I knew where to look.

I was temporarily distracted when I noticed my dream-self straddling Adam's dream-self on the dream-bed. My head was thrown back and he was grabbing my hair like I was the pony and he was my rider. Dream-Adam was pumping into me as hard and fast as he could, and Dream-me was squealing like a stuck pig.

Real-me made a face and hands went to my hips. "Oh, that is *so* typical."

Dream-Adam opened his eyes and looked over at Real-me, standing in the middle of his psychic bedroom. Every thought he'd had this evening was scattered in random fashion around the messy bedroom—I guess Adam still hadn't grown up. Girly mags were strewn in one corner, a video game system in the far end of the room, and bouncing, red-haired succubus in the middle. Confusion settled over his lust-smeared face. "Two of you?"

Suddenly a second Dream-me popped into the room and started mauling down on him, licking his jawline.

"Oh, ew. If I sit on your face in this dream, you are in so much trouble." I made a face and began to pick my way into the room, looking at the objects there for hints. I passed a half-eaten container of chicken wings and hoped that didn't have any hidden meanings.

"What are you doing here?" He was coherent enough to ask that between moaning and slurping noises, and I tried not to look over there.

"Nothing. Go back to boinking the two of me. I'm just shopping around." I picked through a stack of magazines slopped onto the floor, wondering what I was looking for.

"You're so hot," he moaned, sounding like a brain-dead surfer, and I looked over to see Me-Two jerk his head backward and stick her tongue down his throat.

Ugh. I moved over to Adam and pushed one of the slut-puppy versions of me out of the way. "Hey, I'll turn this into a group effort if you share a little something with me."

His eyes bugged out. "Oh yeah."

I felt bad for about a nanosecond, then realized he was doing lewd and disgusting things with me in his dreams. "What's your little gang of friends up to lately that would make the angels nervous?"

"Hmm?"

I had to pry Me-Two off him again. Damn, that bitch had a tongue like a heat-seeking missile. "You guys are up to something, and it's making the other guys—you know, the ones with wings—a bit antsy."

"I'm not doing anything," Adam said, giving me a lazy smile. "You can climb on top now."

A halo flickered into existence over his head, and I flicked his nose with my fingernail. "You're a bad liar."

"Ow!"

"I'm serious here," I said, getting irritated with this man's dream. "Are you guys plotting to take over the world? Stealing something? Burning down a church?"

He rubbed his nose and glared at me. "You're mean."

Maybe I was going about this the wrong way. I trailed my finger over his lips and played with his fangs, and his eyes nearly rolled back in his head at the pleasure of it. "Why don't you just tell me what sort of super-spy stuff you're up to and I'll let you go back to playtime, hmm?"

"Ex-ex-expedishn," he said around my finger, sucking on the tip of it like some gigantic leech.

"Expi-what?" I pulled my finger out of his mouth and resisted the urge to wipe it on my dream-skirt.

"Expedition. Queen wants the halo."

Huh. I'd thought he was just trying to be clever with the halo gimmick. "Got anything more than that?" I trailed my finger across his chin, staring at the glowing circle over his head. It looked . . . like a plain old halo. "Any other tidbits to tell me?"

"I love you," he said, a dreamy look on his face as he stared up at my breasts.

Just then my corset top vanished, and I cursed as my breasts nearly bounced into his face. I'd be willing to guess that I was just about to lose control of this dream, and I jerked myself free.

I shivered back into my body, feeling the way a wet dog does when he shakes his coat free of water, and found myself straddling a horny, snoring vampire. Drool slithered down one of his cheeks and I backed away, slowly extricating myself from his lap and hoping no one noticed what we were up to.

A quick glance around the room showed that I was safe. Remy's crowd of paramours at the bar hadn't budged an inch, but I noticed her flick a look over at me. I got the hint and slid back down in my seat, trying to push my skirt back down. I poked Adam in the side, trying to look casual. "Wake up. You're drooling all over the table."

He didn't wake up.

I poked him again, harder. The first stirrings of fear swirled in my mind and I pinched his side. Adam smacked his lips, smiled, and slumped against me.

A snore erupted from his mouth and I froze, hoping nobody else heard it.

But not two seconds passed before Mr. Hideous Joel was back, scowling at me with suspicious eyes.

I tried to deflect him by cuddling up against Adam's side and looking like the happy couple. "Mind leaving us for a bit? We're just getting cozy."

Another snore punctured the silence, and my lie burst like a bubble right in my face. Damn. I forced myself to keep the fake smile pasted on.

A hand snarled in my hair and dragged me out of the booth and across the floor. The room had become deathly silent, except for the sounds of my panicked breathing and the soft snores coming from Adam. My head was a mass of pain, my eyes squeezed shut to try to take the edge off it.

"Hey," I protested, my hands clamping around his wrist to relieve the agonizing pressure on my scalp. It was a wonder my hair hadn't ripped out of my head. "What's the big idea?"

Joel hauled me to my feet and stared me in the eye. "Is there something you want to tell us, missy?"

I winced and tried to disentangle his fingers from my hair with my own. "Um, I'm a Scorpio and I like long walks on the beach?"

The next moment, I was kissing floor as my face slammed into the marble tile. It took me a moment to recover my breath, and I rolled over slowly, turning to find myself eye to heel with Remy's stilettos. I followed the shoe upward and found her staring down at me, a chagrined look on her face. Two overly muscled vampires had her by the arms.

Joel hauled me up again by the hair, and I screamed in protest. "Ow! Lay off of the hair pulling! What did I do to you?"

I struggled to pull myself free without much luck. Succubi got the short end of the stick when it came to supernatural strength, and the vamps got it all.

Joel held me pinned against him, his lip pulled up in a snarl. "What did you do to Adam?" He shot a look over at Remy. "Did you have anything to do with this?"

Remy put her hands in the air, denying his words. "We just came down here to get a drink. You're getting carried away. Is all this really necessary?"

He tilted my head back, exposing my neck, and pure panic shot through me. "Can't we talk about this?" When I saw his head disappear under my chin, I squeaked in a last-ditch effort, "I'm positive for hepatitis, you know." My eyes squeezed shut, waiting for the worst.

The feel of a warm, slimy tongue rasped against my neck and I shuddered with distaste. "I thought so," Joel rumbled, then dumped me to the floor at Remy's feet.

I rubbed my scalp, staring up at the people surrounding me, my panic threatening to turn into full-on crisis. "Thought what?"

"You're like her." He scowled at the circle of vampires standing a little too close for my comfort. "Colette here's a succubus."

"Colette?" The rich, coffee-smooth voice rolled over me and I got to my feet as the crowd parted, letting Zane in. "My my," he said, looking me over like a buffet. "This just gets more and more interesting, doesn't it? I had no idea that you were a succubus. What brings you to our little club?" The twinkle in his dark black eyes was amused. He was having fun at my expense; he knew darn good and well who and what I was.

Before I could protest, Joel broke in again. "She's put Adam to sleep," he said, the look on his face grave.

My stomach fluttered when I noticed Zane's smile fade as he turned back to me. One dark eyebrow arched. "You put him to sleep?" He flipped out his cell phone and started dialing. "Wake him up, will you? The queen's going to be mighty pissed when she hears about this."

Remy paled and struggled in the arms of her guards. "Do you really think that's necessary? We'll leave immediately."

Zane looked me up and down, his dark eyes unreadable. "No can do, my dears. The queen would have my head if I didn't let her know you two were here, nosing around. Rather poor taste, don't you think, Remy?" He gave her a half smile and walked away, sliding the cell phone to his ear. "This is Zane. Is the queen awake?"

Remy struggled forward and grabbed my arm, leaning in to hiss into my ear, "Are you crazy?"

I scowled at her panicked face. "I don't know. I'm in the basement of a club with a porn star and a bazillion vampires, and we're waiting for their queen. You tell *me* if I'm crazy."

She forced me to step into the corner of the room.

Our new friends followed us, naturally, not saying a word. The silence was more disturbing than anything they could have said. I heard the soft mumble of Zane's voice in the background as he discussed our appearance at the nightclub with someone.

"Do you realize how much shit we're in?" Remy asked.

I rubbed my forehead, glancing over at the happily sleeping Adam. "No, but I'm sure you'll tell me."

Remy made a sound of frustration, then I heard her exhale as she tried to calm herself. She whispered, "All I can tell you is to play it cool with the queen and try to avoid eye contact. Okay?"

Well, that sounded scary as all hell. "Got it," I said, hating the quaver in my voice.

Zane returned, flipping his phone shut with a click. "I'm afraid that the queen is on her way, ladies, and she has requested your presence." He smiled over at me, all charm and ease again. "It seems you'll be our guests for a bit longer, yes?"

Remy crossed her arms over her chest and tossed her ponytail. "I wasn't aware that we had a choice, Zane."

His dark eyes fixed on me. "You don't."

I was silent. Hell, I'd already ruined the evening. I didn't need to say anything else.

Zane glanced over at Adam, who was still asleep in the booth. He stilled, turning to fix his gaze on me, and his fangs extended a bit in a veiled threat. "Didn't I tell you to wake him up?"

"You did," I agreed, putting my hands on my hips.

"Well?"

I raked a strand of hair off my forehead in a nervous reaction. "Teeny problem."

He crossed his arms over his chest. A rather broad, leather-covered, delicious chest. "And what's that?"

"Well, I don't know how to wake him up." I gave him my brightest smile. "New girl on the block and all."

Zane swore.

Chapter Thirteen

The next half hour was the longest one of my life. Waiting for the vampire queen was akin to waiting in the dentist's office, without the benefit of knowing that you'd get Novocain. I sat in the booth next to my sleeping buddy Adam and twiddled my thumbs. Remy was kept separated from me by about a dozen pissed-off vampires. I could hear her repeating from across the room, "Look, I don't know how to wake him up. The only one who can do that is the succubus who put him under in the first place."

Which was me. Ignorant, ignorant me.

Zane sat across from me, an indifferent look on his face as he regarded my fidgeting.

Adam still snored peacefully. I'd attempted waking him up a few times but to no avail; I simply didn't know how to flip the switch now that I'd turned it off. Kissing him hadn't worked; poking, prodding, screaming . . . I'd tried it all without success.

When I started popping my knuckles for the ninth time, Zane reached out and placed his hands over mine. They were very warm, with a hint of manly callus, and brushed over mine with a seductive touch. My brain unfocused. "Do you mind?" The edge of a teasing grin tugged at his lips.

"No, actually," I shook off his hands and punctuated each word with an obnoxious pop. "I don't mind at all."

Zane inclined his head toward Sleeping Beauty. "The queen might be more lenient with you if you wake our little friend up." He leaned back in the booth in a casual slouch that made my hormones pitter-patter, and his teeth bared in a fanged smile, reminding me of who he was. "Or is it your plan to drive her to anger?"

"Yeah, and don't you think it's working swell? I have you just where I want you." I rolled my eyes at him. "Look, you don't think I've tried waking him up? I have, and I don't know how. New here, remember?" I lowered my voice so the other vampires wouldn't hear my dirty secret. "Remy's not exactly the best teacher to have. She forgot to tell me all the pertinent stuff—like the dreams and the constant need for sex, and a few other perks of the job." I couldn't mask the disgruntlement in my voice.

"Speaking of," Zane drawled, his accent more pronounced. "How do you feel about the urges you get? I know Remy has adapted to them quite well over the years. You must be struggling." His gaze roamed over me for longer than necessary. "From what I've heard, it takes several months for the needs to settle into a regulated pattern. The first few weeks are the worst."

"Are they?" I tried to keep my tone bright and cheerful. "It must affect everyone differently, because I'm just fine. Fine and dandy." I batted my eyelashes at him.

"You do seem to be acclimating rather well," he agreed, amusement rumbling in his throat. I felt an answering tingle down my spine and the angel kiss quelled the urge. Like it or not, there was something fascinating about the vampire seated across from me. I couldn't put my finger on it, though I suspected that it was the utter menace under the indolence of his pose. "It almost makes me wonder if you're a different sort of creature from Remy."

I crossed my arms over my chest and scowled. Was that a backhanded compliment or an insult? Unsure, I replied, "We're not much alike, she and I. Don't let the clothing fool you."

"Miss Summore is very basic in her needs," he agreed. "You seem like you want something different than her hedonistic lifestyle. It surprises me." One black brow arched as he studied me, reaching for his beer and taking a long swig.

Pigeonholed. Now that smarted. "Did it ever occur to you, Mr. Tall, Dark, and Fanged, that I might have had a job and a life I was happy with before everyone started messing with me? I liked my world safe and normal and neat. I even liked being respected for my brain and not how well I fill out a bra. That all changed when your kind started fucking with me."

I took the beer from his hand and swigged the rest of it myself. Pissed wasn't the word for how I felt at the moment. On fire with angry self-righteousness, maybe. They'd come into my life and turned it upside down, and now had the nerve to be irritated at *me*?

He laughed in my face and let me have the beer. "I can't imagine your life was so wonderful that it couldn't use a bit of improving."

Anger fired through all my synapses, and I saw red. "Where do you get off, buddy?"

"The blood bank," he said calmly, responding with another sly smile. "And judging from the noise upstairs, you have about two minutes to wake Adam up before the queen gets here."

Oh, crap.

I turned to Adam with a sudden desperation and pressed my forehead against his again. The slither of my mind leaving my body shuddered through me, and within moments all was black and dark as night as the world lost focus.

"Hey again."

I opened my eyes, staring into Adam's dream bedroom once more. My slutty clones were gone, and Adam reclined on the bed, flipping channels on the TV with the remote, his pants still down around his ankles.

"Hey," I said in automatic response. I stood awkwardly in the middle of his room and tugged at my skirt. "Um, what are you doing?" The conversation felt awkward without the horny twosome there to break the tension.

"So when are we leaving this dump?" Adam gave me

an insolent look and scratched at his naked crotch on the bed. Nice. "As much fun as it is to be here, the girls went away when you left last time, and I'm bored out of my fucking mind sitting here. Can you bring them back?"

Good question. Could I? I didn't know.

"Let's not talk about that right now," I said, switching the subject back to the current situation. "Your queen is on the way, and I need you to wake up again, so both of us aren't chewed up and spit out."

"I'm asleep?" Adam seemed surprised by this. A moment later, he paled and shot up out of his bed. "The queen? She's coming? Here?"

"Well, not *here*," I corrected. "To the club. Where your body is at, but your brain is here. Make sense?"

"You've got to wake me up! She won't like it if she sees I've been messing around with one of your type." His red eyes actually looked worried. "Bring me back."

I spread my dream-hands in a nervous gesture. "I don't know how."

He bounded across the room and grabbed me by the shoulders. "What do you mean, you don't know how? Do something! Sprinkle some magic dust, suck me off, sit on my face, whatever it is your type does to get people awake."

I jerked away. "Back off, loser. I'm trying to figure it out, all right?" I just didn't have any idea of which direction to head.

I put a fist to my brow and concentrated. *Think, Jackie, think. If you want to wake someone up, what do you do? Call their name? Throw water on their face?*

Inspiration struck, and I reached out and pinched sullen Adam. Hard. "Wakey wakey."

His mouth opened, showing his fangs, and then he vanished, popping out of the surreal reality like a soap bubble.

Before I could wonder if my method had worked, I was shaken back into my body. My spirit slithered back into my skin and my body crawled with a long, intense shudder. It was a disgusting feeling, the opposite of a snake shedding its skin.

Then I crashed to the floor as Adam shoved me off of him, my head thumping against the marble with a crack. The world went black for a moment . . .

And then I abruptly came to again, fully alert. Crap—I guess succubi couldn't be knocked unconscious. Which kinda sucked at the moment; I wouldn't have minded being out when the queen made her entrance.

"Careful," Zane's smooth voice warned. His fists were clenched and he was giving a rather sleepy (yet pissed) Adam a dangerous look. "The queen's going to want to talk to her. Don't damage her."

Damage me? Hell, if *that* was all he was worried about. Disgusted, I picked myself up and dusted off my skirt (which had crawled up over my glorious backside, exposing it to the public). "No, no, don't help me up," I jibed at the vampires who stood watching me haul my ass off the floor. "I've got it. Really. It's a piece of cake, getting up off the floor in a miniskirt and stilettos. No shit."

I heard Zane smother a half laugh, but the others were silent, their faces as stony as gargoyles. Adam was watching my ass, with a mixture of lust and anger at what I had just put him through. I had thought he wouldn't remember anything, but I guessed wrong. Big surprise there.

Across the room I heard Remy's muffled whimper, and then darkness descended on us all.

The queen had arrived.

I couldn't tell if it was a physical darkness or a mental sort of darkness; all I knew was that I was on my knees again, gasping for breath in lungs that had suddenly become too constricted with fear to pull in air. A miasma of dread covered the room, the temperature dropping several degrees to an icy chill. I could feel dark, old hunger, black malevolence, and greed as it swept over me and swarmed through the room, and I felt it approach. My eyes were squeezed shut and I didn't realize that I was biting my lip to keep from screaming until I tasted blood.

"A party?" The voice whispered across the gloom and rang in my ears, as loud as gunshots in the silence. "And I see you've invited friends, one of whom I have not met before."

I felt the full impact of the queen's focus on my body, and I nearly slithered into a boneless heap on the floor. There was something inherently *wrong* about her, something that made me want to run screaming and sleep with the lights on. This was old, old evil, and it had focused its attention on me.

"A whore-child? Unexpected. What is your name, whore-child?" I heard the clack of heels as she approached, could feel the malice rolling over me as I crouched and whimpered on the floor.

To my surprise, Zane spoke. "Her name is Colette. She's a succubus like the other one."

Oh lord, why was he lying to the queen? I wanted to babble out my most fearful secrets to her, even though I knew she'd use them against me. My mind was like a brick of ice as I stood there, paralyzed with fear and unable to function. "I—I . . ." I tried, and failed. My thick tongue wouldn't work.

The queen sighed, the sound surprisingly gentle. "Ah, yes. I do remember the other one. I have not seen her in some time, though it is always a treat to see one of her . . . ilk." The way she tasted the words made me think that it was not a treat at all, but a huge inconvenience, and both Remy and I would pay the cost. No wonder Remy had been skittish around the vampires, and I hoped I'd never have to see them again.

"It has been so long since your ilk," she paused, reminding us "ilks" that it wasn't a good thing to be, "have graced the halls of my own. There must be a reason," she said, her voice becoming soft and deadly.

"Queen Nitocris," Adam's voice babbled up from the darkness. "The red-haired one put me to sleep. She was asking me things. Asking me about what we were doing. What we were searching for. She wanted to know specifics." The words rolled out of his mouth like an awkward teenager tripping over themselves in their haste to escape his lips. "She was in my mind. I had to tell her."

That little bastard sold me out! I should have left him to rot in his filthy little mind, where he belonged. Anger surged inside me, only to be washed away by the sound of Queen Nitocris's laughter.

"What does a sex slave care about our doings?" There was mirth in the queen's voice, but it wasn't a good sort of mirth. It was more like oh-shit-you're-in-trouble-now mirth. I cringed. "Perhaps we should speak to our lovely Colette."

Icy fingers raised my chin, my eyes still squeezed tightly shut. "Look at me," she commanded, and I found I had no choice but to obey.

Queen Nitocris was hauntingly beautiful. Dark mahogany brown hair was pulled tight against her scalp, and elegant, aquiline features with a haughty, delicate edge looked back at me. She wore a thin band around her forehead that proclaimed her queenship, and was dressed simply in an elegant red sheath that accentuated her spare, willowy figure and creamy golden skin. She looked like a movie star, a throwback from Hollywood's golden days.

Except for the eyes. They were black, pupilless horrors that stared at me with malevolence hidden behind the bow of a smile. They filled me with terror, and she grinned at my fear, displaying a mouthful of razor-sharp teeth. A shark's mouth, a killing mouth, outlined by ruby red lipstick.

I turned away, unable to look at her face any longer, my gorge rising.

She laughed again, the sound tinkling through the too-silent air. "Why, Colette is scared. Very astute of her—she has much reason to be scared, does she not, my Zane?"

"Yes, my queen." Zane's voice was smooth and bland, not the teasing darkness I remembered from earlier. All darkness had been swallowed up by the queen herself; she was a black hole in a room full of supernovas.

"What does a sex slave want to know about our doings?" the queen repeated, and I realized she expected me to answer.

I couldn't tell her about my deal with Uriel. My mind wouldn't work, though, and I couldn't come up with a feasible lie. So I stood there quietly and choked on my own saliva, my eyes squeezed shut as I hoped this would all go away.

I didn't see who flung me to the floor, nor the heel of the queen's shoe that dug into my back. "She is not speaking, Zane. Make her talk, or I will."

"You'd better tell her," Zane told me quietly. "It's not wise to anger the queen."

I nodded, unable to look them in the eye. "Someone . . . asked me to find out what you are doing. Why the vampires are out on the streets lately." I heard Remy's sharp intake of breath behind me, but I didn't have much choice.

"Oh? I can guess." The queen knelt beside me and

forced my face back toward her with those icy fingers. I felt them brush against my forehead, burning when they touched my angel kiss. "My, my. Didn't your friend teach you not to pick sides, girl?"

My forehead felt like it was on fire, except where the tips of her fingers were touching my skin. It was like being caressed by evil itself. "I . . . I don't have a side. He talked me into it, and I didn't know what he was doing." It sounded lame even to my own ears.

"Mmm." The queen's fingers left my skin, and I rubbed the burning spot with my fingers. The skin felt whole, even if it hurt like a bitch. "It could be that you're too stupid and young yet to decide what you wish to do—this is true." Her heels clacked away, and I squeezed my eyes open a crack, watching her go.

Then she turned to face me again, those black eyes fixed on my face. "Of course, if you can do a favor for the Archangel Gabriel, you can do a favor for me, can you not?"

Oh shit. That was the last thing I wanted. "I'm not working for Gabriel," I protested, my words sounding weak.

"No? Then who?"

Ashamed at the compulsion I felt to respond to her words, I dropped my gaze to the floor. "Uriel."

Her low chuckle made my skin crawl. "Just as well. He's been fascinated with our doings for centuries. I just never thought he'd find someone foolish enough to do his dirty work."

Yay me, for being the biggest fool in millennia.

She took my silence as a good sign. "You may go back to your little friend Uriel and tell him what I am up to. I don't care. After all, we've been dealt the perfect hand. He's trapped in his church like a holy rat, because he refuses to possess someone to seek what he desires. So it will do him no good to know what we seek." I felt her burning gaze turn back onto me, even though I wasn't looking at her. "You do know what it is we want, do you not, child?"

"A halo," I whispered.

"Not just any halo," she corrected, her shoes moving back toward me in the low angle of my vision. I cringed. "The halo of Joachim himself. Do you know who that is, little idiot?"

"No."

"Joachim was the first angel to fall. He was the most beautiful of their kind, and he led the others down the path of sin when they chose to touch human women and know their bodies. Gabriel asked the angels to give up their lovers, but Joachim could not give up *his* mortal woman—me."

My eyes shot up to her face. She didn't look mortal, not one teeny bit.

Her mouth widened into a sharky grin at my surprise, and I flinched away. "It surprises you, little one. Back then I was the greatest queen my country had ever known, and I was a goddess to my people. I destroyed my husband and set Joachim on the throne in his place.

"But Joachim changed. Without his wings, without

Heaven, his mind became unhinged, and he descended into darkness. Long years passed, and I looked for ways to please him and make him whole again. I practiced my witchcraft and learned pleasurable things, learned to keep myself young and pretty, but it was all for nothing. Joachim was lost.

"So I struck a deal with Lucifer himself, who knew something of the despair that my beloved was going through. Give him his wings back, and I will give Lucifer whatever he desires."

Her smile became thin, brittle. "I should have guessed that Lucifer wanted something more, when he asked for nothing from me. He gave Joachim his wings, but in return, he warped and perverted the curse that Gabriel had laid upon the Serim. Gabriel's curse was not a harsh one: to make love every full moon, to remind them why they were there on earth instead of in Heaven.

"Lucifer made Joachim crave blood. He got his wings, but he must drink human blood every day." Her laughter was harsh and mocking. "Lucifer turned him into a monster. And my Joachim felt despair, even as he exulted in that which had been forbidden to him. What do you think of that, little one?"

I tried to swallow to wet my throat and failed miserably. "It must have been hard on him," I rasped.

"Wrong," she snarled, stalking over to me and slapping me across the face so hard that I felt my neck snap backward, making a cracking noise. Blackness bloomed in front of my eyes again, and receded just as fast.

"I gave him everything, and still he was not satisfied. Everything! I seduced the others to the same foul deal, so he would not feel alone. I destroyed my kingdom for him, feigned my own death and went into exile, all for *him*. I gave up everything I loved for Joachim. I even sold my own soul to Lucifer in exchange for a child of our own, thinking that would please him.

"I let Lucifer twist and manipulate me. I fornicated with his demons, let one possess my flesh, all to bring the shine back to Joachim's eyes. And do you know what happened?"

I worked my jaw slowly, hearing the bones crack with each motion, shooting pain through my entire face. It sounded like a few things had broken. Did she really expect me to answer? I stared up into her mad black eyes.

"He turned on *me*. He said that *I* had turned him into the monster he was today. He did not see the power I had given him." The wildness in her eyes was replaced by the frightening calm once more. "He took our son and left me, in search of redemption. He went to appeal to Heaven itself, to beg and plead his way back in. My strong, beautiful Joachim, reduced to sniveling, begging for another chance."

Her lip curled in disgust, making the beautiful face a macabre mockery of itself. "He returned to the first temple consecrated to God, a temple he had built as pharaoh, and entered the doors, leaving my son on the doorstep. And do you know what happened to him?"

I shook my head, ignoring the cracking sounds in my neck. I didn't trust my throat to answer.

"They destroyed him," Queen Nitocris said in that horribly toneless, bland voice. "He appealed to them, begging for mercy, and they destroyed him where he stood. My son watched him burn alive, until all that was left was a halo on the altar—the essence of who he once was."

Nitocris moved over to Zane and began to stroke her fingers through his hair in a maternal gesture, tucking the locks behind his ears. "And when my son returned to me with the news that he had failed both me and his father, I broke him as punishment."

She focused another hideous smile on me and I cringed backward. "As I do to any who fail me," she said, her words hissing between her teeth. "I stole his essence, pried it from his living form, and made it part of my own. It dwells inside me, as does the demon I gave myself to when I took what Lucifer offered."

Yikes. I totally did *not* want to mess with this woman ever again. Frightened for my life, I wondered if sucking down the soul of a succubus could augment her powers. I hoped not. I hoped we didn't give anyone anything but venereal disease.

"So what is it that you will tell Uriel, child?"

Oh, crap. On the spot again. She was gazing over at me from where she was draped all over a stiff-looking Zane, her eyes boring into me.

"Uh, I'll tell him that you're looking for your old boy-friend because you miss him and you're lonely?"

The queen laughed again, putting my nerves on edge. "Wrong, my dear." She stalked over to me and put her hands on my cheeks, as if she were staring down at a lover. "Do you know what you'll tell him?"

"No," I said, shying away from the terrible face that hovered too close. "What do I tell him?"

"You're going to tell him that I want the halo. But not because I want Joachim back. Oh, no." The rumble of a laugh started in her throat. "Not after he betrayed me. But I do want his power. And when I have his halo, I will absorb his essence into my flesh and become the most powerful creature on either side of Heaven or Hell."

It was too terrifying to even think about. "I'll tell him," I agreed, too scared to do anything else.

"Good," she purred. "And tell him that you'll be getting it for me." Nitocris pressed her lips onto my forehead, directly over the spot that Uriel had kissed me on. My forehead flared with heat once more, then settled into a dull, burning ache.

I jerked away from her, forgetting that she was the hungry shark and I was a mere minnow. "Me?" My voice came out as an angry squeak. "Why me?"

Nitocris studied me, smiling. "Don't you want to work for me, child?"

"No!" I clapped a hand over my mouth as soon as I realized what I had said. Nitocris raised an eyebrow, and I cleared my throat. "What I meant to say was that I can't work for you. I'm sorry."

"You'll work for me, whore-child. Do not doubt it." She laughed again, strolling back to where Remy was being held at one of the booths. A feeling of dread began to sweep over me. "You do value your friendship with this one, do you not?" she called over her shoulder, approaching Remy and putting her fingers under her chin.

Remy stared straight ahead, ignoring the queen, her eyes focused on me with a warning look. I couldn't tell if she was warning me not to fall for the queen's bluff, or to do what she asked.

"So pretty, isn't she? But then again, that's one of the trademarks of your kind. Pretty, and sexual. It's been a long time since my men have tasted the flesh of a succubus, and I know that they consider it a rare and wonderful delight." Her smile was turned back to me again. "I think your friend will stay with us while you go and find my halo. What do you think?"

"I think it's a bad idea?" I offered meekly, trying to be tough and failing miserably.

Nitocris's smile became thin. "Nevertheless, she'll stay with us until you bring the halo back and place it in my hands. Understand?" She released Remy and pointed at two of her men. "Take her away and chain her up."

The vampire pair immediately grabbed Remy, wide smiles creasing their faces. Dread settled in the pit of my stomach as Remy began to kick and scream, snarling obscenities at the two men. "Don't do it," she screamed over and over. "Don't do it!"

I didn't know if she was talking to me or the queen. I turned wide eyes on Nitocris, who was admiring her fingernails.

"Such a pity that she's not in a more amenable mood, isn't it?" She gave me a coy smile. "I'm sure that will change in the next twenty-four hours or so. How often do you girls have the urge? As often as my men must feed, yes?"

That *bitch*. I watched, helpless, as they dragged Remy away. "You can't do this. She hasn't done anything." Desperation tore through me.

"No, she hasn't," the queen agreed. "Which is why you'll want to free her from her prison. All you need to do is bring me a halo. Simple, isn't it?"

Remy's screams grew quieter and more muffled. Tears threatened my eyes, and I had to blink hard to force them away. I didn't want to cry in front of her.

"Well?" Nitocris regarded me with interest. "What do you have to say, Colette?"

My body was numb. I felt my lips move, but it didn't register, not even when I heard myself say, "You'll get your halo."

Queen Nitocris smiled. "I know."

CHAPTER FOURTEEN

As soon as I was released from the nightclub, I stumbled outside and threw up. Shaking, sick, and frightened out of my mind, I wiped my chin and stumbled to valet parking and retrieved Remy's car. No one seemed to think anything of me leaving by myself after entering with the famous Miss Summore, which made me wonder what kind of life she led, or what sorts of things truly went on in the club.

I got behind the wheel of Remy's BMW and buckled in, turning the A/C on high. I felt overheated and like I'd been turned inside out. Nitocris's hideous smile played through my mind over and over, as well as Remy's terrified screams.

This was all my fault.

My skin crawled, too. Not with fear or horror (though those were certainly running through my mind), but with lust. Queen Nitocris's kiss had canceled out the angel's kiss and replaced it with something far more compulsive. My overheated flesh cried out for relief, the soft fabric of my clothing chafing against my skin. The Itch had returned.

I opened the glove compartment and yanked out

Remy's cell phone as I eased the car onto the highway, then hammered my thumb on the down arrow to flip through the saved numbers. Her address book was enormous, but I found Noah's cell number and pressed the memory dial button. The phone rang once and went straight to voicemail. "This is Noah. Leave a message."

"Shit!" I screamed into the phone. "Answer the phone, you asshole. I need you!" I slammed my finger down on the Disconnect button and threw the phone into the passenger seat.

Then I smacked my hand against the steering wheel. "Oh, shit—it's night. Noah's not up yet." I winced. He wasn't going to like my voicemail.

He wouldn't be too keen on my news, either, come to think of it. The voicemail was the least of our worries.

I drove around for a while, trying to get my mind together. It was still at least an hour or two before dawn, and I wasn't tired, of course. I didn't need sleep anymore. I did, however, need a righteous shot of coffee and some headache pills.

I also needed to have a talk with my buddy Uriel, who'd sold me down a river with a smile and a kiss.

Half an hour later, I stormed into St. Anthony's cathedral with a latte in hand. If I'd thought the church was empty at 6:30 a.m., it was a wasteland at four in the morning. I sat down on the back pew and sipped my coffee. The heat between my legs was uncomfortable, so I crossed my legs back and forth, squirming as I waited.

For like, two minutes. I'm not the most patient person. So when the cathedral remained empty, I decided the time for pleasantry was over. "Uriel," I bellowed at the top of my lungs. "I know you're out there."

Still nothing. Oh, I knew he was there. The trick was making him show himself.

I lifted my coffee cup and threatened, "You'd better show yourself, or I'm going to head for the holy water."

"Jacqueline." Uriel's voice rang from behind me and I turned, watching the angel move forward, the white wings flowing down his back. "It is so good to see you again." He looked as beautiful and pure as I remembered. He also looked guilty as hell.

"Can the crap, Uriel. You used me because I didn't know what was going on. I should never have listened to you."

"I don't know what you mean, Jacqueline. I thought our bargain was straightforward. You get a little info for me, and I return the favor with one of my own. I fail to see how that's 'using you,' as you say."

I crossed my arms over my chest. "Yeah? Well, the vampires figured me out in three seconds flat, and now they know that you're checking up on them. They've taken my friend Remy hostage, too." Tears threatened and I had to blink hard, which only made things worse as I got mascara in my eyes. Dammit.

"What?" Uriel's features slid into a frown of concern.

"I know," I sniffed, trying hard not to blubber and not succeeding very well. "They've got Remy and I don't know how to get her back."

He shook his head. "What did you say about the vampires knowing I'm—that is, we're—involved? Did you find out why they are gathering?"

Irritation began to prick at me. "Oh, I'm sure Remy's just fine. Thanks for your concern," I said, my throat bitter. "And yes—when I met the queen, she figured it out pretty fast."

"The queen." It was a quiet statement, followed by a sigh. "You've stirred up quite a mess now, haven't you? Did you find out their plans?"

"Me?" I squeaked in protest, ignoring his fishing for information. "I didn't do anything except what you told me to do—*bribed* me to do. It's not my fault if they figured it out."

He sat next to me and brushed his fingertips across my forehead. As desire flared through my body, I dug my fingernails into my palms so I wouldn't jump him. "I see her mark upon you," Uriel said in his soft voice. "It has negated my own."

I bit back a "No shit, Sherlock" and opted for the stare-down instead. "So what now? How do we get Remy back?"

I didn't like the pause that followed. Instead of hitting me with a straight answer, he grimaced and looked away. "It's not quite that easy, I'm afraid."

"Sure it is. You go down there and wave your halo and make them give her back. You're the one with the power here, remember? You've still got your all-access pass too so maybe you should try stepping in and helping my friend." Desperation was starting to crawl through me. What was I going to do if I couldn't get Remy back? What was I going to do if Uriel didn't help me?

He patted me on the shoulder, then pulled away as if I were diseased. "I'm afraid I cannot step in, child. However, I am confident that you will think of something. Did you find out their plans?" His pale eyes glittered as he repeated the question, focusing on me with sudden avid intent. "You must have found out something."

"Oh, I found out something all right," I said, not liking the look in his eyes. "They're after some halo from some Joachim dude from way back when."

Uriel bit his lip, his wings quivering a touch. "Joachim?"

I nodded.

Uriel gave a high-pitched moan of delight and stood abruptly, his eyes intent and a tad insane. "Did they say where they've found it? Who has it in their possession?"

"See, that's the tricky thing." I scratched my head, a bit unwilling to part with what I'd learned so far. "I'm supposed to find it. Any brilliant ideas swimming around in that holy head of yours?"

His hand was suddenly clamped around my own, his face scant inches from mine. Pale blue eyes pinned me to the pew. "You must find that halo and bring it to me. It is of the utmost importance that I get the artifact, not the queen. Do you understand me?"

I tried to extract myself, sliding over on the pew. "Calm down for two seconds, okay? I don't even know where the stupid thing is—"

"I have friends who can help you find it for me," he immediately responded.

"—but the vamps want it in exchange for Remy, and

I already promised I'd give it to them." I eyed the door. "Maybe the next one that rolls around, I can call dibs for you. Deal?"

"No!" he screamed, the muscles in his neck tensing with the force of his shout, and my head snapped back at the force of his voice. "There will never be another halo with as much raw power infused in it as Joachim's. I must have it and no other." He gave me a wild look and gritted his teeth. "Do you understand? You must bring it to me."

If ever someone was in need of crazy pills, I'd put my money on Uriel. "Uh, I'd really like to bring it to you, seeing as how you're the good guy and all, but my friend's life is at stake here."

He shook his head. "You fail to understand me. Or perhaps you do not choose to." He slid forward on the bench again, and I scooted even farther back. "What will it take for you to bring the halo to me? Gold? Immortality? A child? A lover?" He touched my arm.

"Ick?" I gave him a disbelieving stare and shrugged off his hand. As much as I wanted to throw him down on the bench and ravish him, it felt wrong. Like seducing a priest. Times ten. "Look, I realize that you and I are from different generations, but I don't want you to be my boy toy, nor do I want you to pimp for me. You can't buy it off me—okay?"

"Perhaps I am not offering you the right things," he said, and gone was the pretty-boy angel look, in its place a rather scary, solemn expression. "I can offer you release from your succubi curse."

Okay, now he was delving into areas I didn't want to think about. I stood up and scooted down to the far end of the bench. "I've had enough. I don't even know where the thing is, so I can't promise you anything. I'm sorry."

"Wouldn't you like to be free from the Itch and have a chance to return to your normal life?"

I paused, weak creature that I was, then shook my head. Whatever he offered, the cost was too high. "Tell you what. I'll find the halo, rescue my friend, and then we'll talk, okay?" I headed for the cathedral doors, needing to get out of there.

"You're making a mistake," he boomed behind me. "Others will jump at the chance of what you are refusing. What will become of you if someone else beats you to the h—"

I shut the door while he was still speaking. I didn't even want to think about that.

CHAPTER FIFTEEN

Noah showed up before dawn. I'd been hovering by the window, anxiously waiting for the sky to lighten, which is why I was freaked out when the doorbell rang when it was still dark. I answered the door with a kitchen knife in hand, not sure who I would find on the other side.

The fallen angel raised an eyebrow. "Planning on carving a turkey?"

He looked wonderful. I don't know if it was my relief to see him that made my hormones surge, or the lack of Uriel's kiss on my brow. It could also be the way his very broad shoulders filled out the cream-colored turtleneck sweater so nicely, and how his hair swept along the collar, just waiting for my itching fingers to brush it back.

"Want to invite me in? Remy's got the place warded to the skies and back so I can't come inside unless you invite me."

"Sure." I put the knife down on a foyer table, my hands shaking. "Come on in."

He stepped past me and glanced around the huge, posh house. "Don't tell me—Remy's still fixing her hair." A line creased between his eyebrows, indicating his frustration. "We need to speak to Uriel as soon as possible before this stuff climbs upstairs, or you'll really be in hot water."

I burst into tears.

The look on Noah's face darkened. "You didn't, did you?"

I was unable to answer, as my throat was all knotted up in the loudest, noisiest sobs this side of Hollywood. "N-n-n-n-" I stammered.

Large hands clasped my shoulders with ferocious strength, and Noah squared my face toward his. "Jackie," he warned. "Where's Remy?"

I could tell he was trying to refrain from shoving me away or losing his temper.

Which of course made me cry all the harder. "I'm so sorry," I managed, trying to pull away. "You hate me now."

"Shhh, Jackie." Noah's large hands reached up to cup my wet cheeks. "It's going to be okay. Calm down."

Feeling helpless beyond words, I allowed him to enfold me in his arms as I cried out my fear and remorse. He led me toward the living room and sat on the couch, calmly stroking my back, just holding me and comforting me. I managed to leak the story onto his broad chest and he didn't say a word to judge me, just listened quietly until I was done.

Once the sobs dried up to the occasional shudder, I remained curled up in his arms, my head pressed against his chest, listening to his heartbeat.

Noah pressed a light kiss onto my brow. "Better now?" His voice was soft, comforting.

I nodded, leaning into the slight caress. My heart was pounding in my throat and I slid my hands behind his neck, caressing his nape without even thinking about what I was doing. "I'm so glad you're here, Noah." All I could think about was crawling into his lap and closing my eyes, hoping the world would go away for a time. My hands slid down his chest, pausing at his nipples, and my fingers found them instinctively. I stroked the pebble-hard flesh, feeling my own tighten in response.

He stilled at my touch. "Jackie . . ." Noah shifted against me. "Did the queen do anything to you?"

"She kissed me." I could feel my forehead blazing, feverishly hot. "I think it negated the angel kiss."

Noah sighed. "It did more than that. A vampire's kiss works in the opposite direction of an angel's, Jackie. Your 'curse,' as you like to call it, is going to be amplified tenfold in a few hours or so, unless you do something about it."

"It's already amplified," I said, fitting my body against his. The sensual rush swept through my body, now that my anxiety had been released. I laced his fingers with mine and turned to stare at him, lifting my cheek off his chest. "So what are my options?"

I would have cursed the compulsion that drove me, if it weren't for the gorgeous man wrapped around me. Damn, he looked delicious. I slid my hand out of his and ran it under his turtleneck, feeling his flat stomach tighten beneath my hand.

His eyes met mine, and I saw that they had flared to the vivid blue I knew all too well. "Let me help you,

Jackie," he said, lifting my hand from his neck and pressing a scorching kiss against the palm. His eyes watched mine.

Guilt and longing surged through me at the same time. I knew that it was my nature doing this to him, causing him to flare up with desire every time I was around. Remy had told me that the Serim needed to sate their urges only about once a month, and here I was driving Noah mad whenever I stepped into the same room. "I'm sorry," I whispered. "I know I'm a bother—"

My words cut off when he nipped at the fleshy part of my hand with his teeth, sending desire rocketing straight through my body. "Jackie," he warned, his lips brushing against my palm.

"Yes?" My voice sounded more like a moan.

"If your body needs release"—Noah brought my fingertips to his lips—"I want to be the one you come to. Understand?"

"I don't want to be a charity case," I protested.

"Oh, trust me," he chuckled. "This is far from charity." He took my fingertip into his mouth and sucked on it.

"Wow," I breathed, sliding the tip along his lips. "You're pretty good at that."

"Let me show you what else I'm good at." Within the space of a breath, he had flung me on my back and was looming over me. My legs were tossed into the air, still bare from the short skirt I'd worn to the club, and he slid his hand down the pale length of one thigh.

I shivered with anticipation. The glide of his hand felt wonderful against my skin, and I arched my back slightly with the pleasure of the simple caress. "Mmm. For artistry I'd give it a 5.8, but for technical merit, only a 5.4."

He pressed a kiss against my upraised ankle. "What are you talking about?" Another kiss against the tender skin of the inside of my knee.

"Nothing," I moaned, losing my train of thought. "Do that again."

Noah complied, sliding his delicious mouth closer toward my skirt. "You're so beautiful, Jackie . . ." His breath was hot against my skin, sending shockwaves through my body and making my brain spin.

"It's the succubus thing," I panted, trying not to writhe in anticipation and failing rather miserably. "Changes the way you look, and stuff."

". . . but you talk entirely too much," he chided, licking my thigh and then blowing gently on the overheated skin. "I don't want to hear talking," he murmured in that low, sexy voice, his smooth cheek close to my thigh. "I want you screaming my name."

The fabric of my skirt slid up, courtesy of Noah's hands, and the pulsing in the vee of my thighs increased in its crescendo, the Itch in full swing. His hands slid over my hips, looking for the zipper to my skirt and then sliding that down my hips, leaving me bare save for a skimpy thong. He hesitated for a moment, and I opened my eyes to protest, just in time to see his blond head duck down, and felt the crotch of my thong being moved aside to allow his fingers to rub up against my wetness.

I groaned loudly, my hands instinctively reaching for his head to cling to. "Oh, God, Noah. Do that again."

His fingers found that perfect, most sensitive spot and flicked against it gently, sending me into paroxysms of desire. "Like that?"

My head jerked into a rough nod and I bit my lip. My hips rose to meet him in silent appeal and were rewarded with the feel of his slick fingers rubbing up and down my folds, taunting me by just barely brushing against the spot that I wanted them most. Noah slid up over me, his mouth pressing onto my own and his tongue seeking out mine.

I returned the kiss with greedy abandon, my hips bucking against the teasing slide of his fingers, trying to guide them to just the right spot. Noah was an amazing kisser—his tongue slid against mine, then darted away, and he tugged at my lip with his teeth. "You taste better than anything." He pressed a kiss against the curve of my neck. "Like a summer storm, fresh and sultry at the same time."

"Quit with the fucking poetry and just *take* me!" I ground my hips against his hand.

He slid me up against his chest, ripping the back of my corset to get the damned thing off me. I was all too happy to help, and once my breasts were bare and free, I immediately rubbed my flesh against his and shoved him back on the couch. "My turn."

His blue eyes gleamed up at me and I slid my pelvis over his, excited by the feel of his erection straining against the front of his slacks.

Noah's hands reached up and caressed my breasts, teasing and flicking at my nipples. I nearly lost my mind from the sensations, but I forced myself to concentrate on returning the pleasure, grinding my hips against his erection, sliding forward to place my mouth against his and lick the seam of his lips.

A shudder wracked through him and I felt pleased at the reaction I stirred.

"Jackie—"

I placed a finger over his lips, nibbling on his earlobe. "The problem with you, Noah," I said between tiny, teasing bites, "is that you talk too much."

He groaned, his hands gripping my ass roughly and forcing it down on his clothed erection, as if by sheer will alone he could undress himself and plunge into me.

"Mmm," I moaned against his neck, teasing, and then sat up, straddling him and staring down. My hands splayed across his chest—still clothed—and I shook my head at him. "Why is it I'm the only naked one here?"

He stood up and dumped me onto the couch in his haste to undress. I lay among the cushions, watching him strip down to nothing. I hadn't had a chance to see his body very well in the confessional, and I didn't remember the time before, so I drank in the sight of his body now.

He was utterly gorgeous. His broad chest was carved into a series of rippling muscles, smooth and hairless, and he had a six-pack that a bodybuilder would kill for. His entire body was slightly tanned, as golden as his hair, and I was aroused to see no sign of a tan line anywhere. And his erection . . .

Enormous and thick, he had to be the most well-built

man I'd ever seen. I was fascinated by the sight of it, jutting toward me and ready to slide between my legs.

I slid one bare foot over to his cock and teased the tip of it with my toe, pleased to see it rear and buck at the touch. "What are you waiting for, Noah? An engraved invitation?"

His hands were on me again, his mouth hot on my own, and I felt his hands around the waistband of my thong. My arms wrapped around his neck as he lifted me and ripped the triangle of fabric from my hips, tossing it to the floor.

"Jackie," he breathed against my lips, laying me on the couch again. I stretched out erotically, arching against the hands that followed to tease my taut nipples.

I felt his hands slide around my ankles moments later, bringing them to his shoulders, then the tip of his cock teased me in the place that throbbed the hottest, the wettest. I moaned and writhed against him, sliding my hips in invitation. "Come inside me, Noah." My hands reached for him frantically, stroking any bare skin I could find.

His cock teased the folds of my core a moment longer, then he plunged into me. Immediately, the pleasure-pain feeling of intense fullness took over, and I forgot everything else as I jerked against him, moaning aloud.

Noah gripped my hips and withdrew slightly, then plunged into me again and again, each stroke driving me wilder. My leg muscles started to clench with the onset of orgasm, and I cried out his name with each thrust.

Sensing my nearness, Noah whispered my name and

pushed into me fully, the hard, single drive of his cock sending me over the top. My whole body tensed in the throes of an intense orgasm. It went on for what seemed like forever and then began to build once more when Noah thrust into me again, slowly, lovingly. I nearly climaxed again in that moment.

Then Noah thrust into me with all the force of his body, and I gladly received each hard, rough thrust with a cry of pleasure, spiraling back up the stairs of delight before I'd even had a chance to descend.

Just as my body locked into its second intense orgasm, Noah shouted my name and thrust one last time, orgasming too. He fell on top of me, sweaty and breathing hard, and I wrapped my arms around him in satiated pleasure.

Reality returned faster than I'd have liked. We were in the middle of Remy's living room, making stains on her expensive couch, and Ethel was probably upstairs, clucking at all the noise we were making.

My face flamed with embarrassment and I poked Noah in the shoulder. Not that I wanted to—he felt wonderful, so heavy and thick on top of me and inside me. "Um, Noah?"

He slid off me and stretched, not embarrassed in the slightest. "Yes, you're right."

"I didn't say any—"

"If we're going to fix this mess you've created, we need to start moving soon. There's less than an hour before the vamps all retire for the day." Noah moved toward the nearby windows and opened the blinds. Early-morning sunlight poured in.

I frowned, pulling my clothes back on. So much for Noah being sensitive to my feelings. I would have felt used for a minute there, except for the fact that I had used him and not the other way around. "They're probably already asleep. The sun's up by now."

He shook his head and retrieved his pants from across the room. "There's a time window where his kind interlaps with mine—just about two hours. Clean yourself up and dress quickly, and we should make it."

"You're not much for pillow.talk, are you?" I sighed after him, then hurried upstairs to change.

Twenty minutes later, I was hanging on to the chicken bar in Noah's Ford Explorer for dear life. I squeezed my eyes shut as he ran another red light (third one in a row) and honked his way into an exit-lane merge.

"My God, you're going to kill us! What is it with you and Remy and the awful driving?" I screamed as the car screeched to a halt and I slammed up against the window. I squeezed one eye open to glance at my surroundings, almost afraid of what I'd see.

Noah gave me a cross look. "Did you want to get here fast or didn't you?"

"I wanted to get here *whole,* is what I wanted," I muttered, climbing out of the car and shaking out my jittery legs. I'd changed into jean shorts, sneakers, and a black T-shirt from Remy's closet advertising Trojan Latex Condoms. Okay, so it wasn't perfect, but all my clothes were at my apartment, and everything Remy bought for me had sequins or feathers or exposed way too much skin.

Club Midnight looked very different in the cheerful morning sunlight. No crowd waiting outside, empty parking lot. "Do you think it's closed?"

"Not to the right people." Noah pocketed his keys and strode up to the front door, pushing it open.

I scrambled after him. It wasn't that I wanted to go *in*, as much as I didn't want to be left behind in the middle of vampire territory. "Wait for me!"

He didn't, but I managed to catch up to him in record time and cling to his sleeve. The entryway was deserted and stank of old cigarette smoke and weed, and empty beer bottles lined the walls. No one was around.

Noah took my hand and pulled me through the main room of the club. "Door to the back?"

"Yeah," I said, clinging to him. I admired Noah's calm as we made our way through the den of the enemy. My own heart was thudding at a rapid, frightening pace, and my body still throbbed despite Noah's loving. That meant that the Itch was going to rear itself again very soon. My hand clenched against Noah's at the thought.

I forced myself to focus on the situation, since no mean, nasty vampires were flinging themselves at us. Yet. "Gee, it seems like everybody went to bed already. Maybe we should come back later—"

"Don't chicken out on me now, Jackie," Noah warned, pushing through the door that led to the dark room where I'd met Zane last time.

It shouldn't have surprised me that Zane was still there, smoking a cigarette and leaning against a table, looking as calm as could be. Perhaps a little sleepy, but I doubted that made him less dangerous. In his dark trench coat and his sexy, tousled hair, he looked like a movie star slumming it in the bad part of town.

Until he smiled, baring his fangs. "Back with reinforcements, I see. One visit a night wasn't enough for you?" He took a long drag on the cigarette and then ground it out underneath his thick boot. "You must have a thing for fangs."

I flushed and stepped closer to Noah, letting his broad form protect me. "We're here to get Remy, so you might as well tell your queen that we want her back."

Ohpleaseohpleaseohplease, don't make me see the queen again.

Zane laughed aloud and arched a brow at Noah. "And what brings you here?"

Noah squeezed my hand to silence me, and gestured to the door that Zane was blocking. "Is the queen still in the building?"

"She is. What makes you think that she'd be interested in seeing one of your kind?" Zane crossed his arms over his chest and cocked his head at Noah, still amused by the two of us.

"I have a deal to offer her."

Huh? I jerked Noah's hand and tried to whisper quietly, "What sort of deal?"

His dark eyes focused intently on Noah, Zane acted as if he hadn't heard me. "What sort of deal?"

"I'm afraid that my business is hers alone," Noah replied stiffly, hostility radiating from his body.

They were locked in a stare-down.

Zane shrugged at last. "Suit yourself. I'll take you to her."

Noah gently touched my cheek. "Stay here, Jackie."

"Stay here? Are you on drugs?" But my feet stayed planted as he went to the other door and knocked quietly. Zane opened it, flashing a quick smirk my way.

"Noah," I protested, "don't leave me here with him." I pointed a finger at Zane. "In case you hadn't noticed, all these vampires want a bit of Suck action, and it makes for awkward conversation."

Noah laughed and returned to kiss me on the mouth possessively, no doubt trying to brand me as "his" in front of Zane. "He's going with me. You'll be here by yourself."

"Oh." So I wouldn't have to see the scary demon queen. Relieved, I went to a booth to wait. "Don't take too long, okay?"

The smile Noah sent in my direction was slightly wistful, his gaze lingering on me. "I won't."

Both men disappeared through the door that led to the lower chambers, leaving me to wonder.

Time passed with excruciating slowness.

I couldn't tell how much time had passed, and I wasn't sure I wanted to know, anyway. I felt like a huge coward for allowing Noah to go see the scary queen by himself, and tried not to think about what was going on. What sort of deal could Noah make with a vampire queen? Blood? Money? Both?

I heard footsteps coming up the stairs and jumped to my feet.

Dear lord, don't let it be the queen.

The door opened and I squeezed my eyes shut.

"Jackie?" Remy asked. "What are you doing?"

My eyes flew open in surprise. "Remy! You're free!" I leapt up from the booth to hug her.

She stood there silently, letting me hug her without moving. I pulled away questioningly. "Remy?"

She moved for the door leading out, ignoring me. As she reached for the doorknob, I glanced back and saw Zane in the doorway that led downstairs, watching us. I scowled at him and turned my back. The sooner I was out of his presence, the better. "Remy," I said again. "Where's Noah? Is he coming?"

"No," Remy said, her voice soft and exhausted. "He's not."

Fear trickled through me. I turned to Zane in disbelief. "He's not? Why not?"

"You a little slow on the uptake, Princess?" Zane looked me up and down, then gave a small shake of his head. "He offered a trade to the queen. Himself for your friend."

I went numb. "He did?" I turned to Remy, seeing Noah's protective smile in my mind. The way he held my hand to reassure me. His gentle caresses. "He *gave* himself to her?"

"I told him not to," Remy said, her normal ebullient personality vanished. "He wouldn't listen. At first she wanted you in exchange for me. Her plan was to get a new succubus under her wing to train as she liked. She knows she can't do much with me, since I have a long-standing agreement with my master. But you'd be perfect for her plans." Remy's bleached eyes met mine, and I realized what she'd been through.

The fear that had been trickling through me turned into a full-blown panic attack. "Me? Why does she want me?"

"She doesn't. At least not now." Zane strode forward, shutting the door behind him. "Once your friend Noah heard that, he offered himself in your place. Nitocris didn't waste any time—she's waited centuries to get her hands on another angel, even a fallen one."

I was going to be sick. "What do we do now?"

Remy snorted angrily. "We go find the damn halo and bring it back to her."

I put a hand to my forehead, trying to will my racing thoughts into order. "Right. Halo. Crap, we *can't* give it to her, Remy." That would be disastrous all around.

"That's why you're going to give it to me," Zane said, his mocking voice close to my ear. "I'm coming with you. Queen's orders."

CHAPTER SIXTEEN

"Excuse me?" I stared at Zane. "You're not coming *anywhere* with me, jerk-off. Got that?"

"You don't have a choice," Zane said, and I felt his hands encircle my neck.

I froze, but he only began to rub my shoulders, as if trying to relax me. Relax? Ha! I skittered away from him, shooting him a scathing glance.

"If I don't come back with the halo, the queen's going to destroy your friend. If she catches wind that you've abandoned me, left me behind, or worse, conspired with the Host rather than her, your friend bites it. Understand?" He leaned toward me, that arch smile pulling at his mouth.

"Yeah, I got it. Let me guess, the queen has spies everywhere, right? This is like a bad B-movie. I'm waiting for Bruce Campbell to come rushing through the door, trailed by zombies." I rubbed my forehead, feeling the onset of a headache.

"Your friend is very flippant, Remy. She must get that from you." Zane sounded amused. Did nothing get under this asshole's skin?

"Trust me, Jackie was like that long before we hooked up."

I would have been offended if I hadn't heard the thread of amusement in her voice. It sounded like the old Remy I knew, not the shell-shocked, exhausted one who had emerged from the dark depths.

"I can't take credit for anything except her taste in fashion," she added.

"If I were you, I wouldn't take too much credit in that," Zane murmured. His lighter flared, illuminating the hard angles of his face as he lit another cigarette. "So what's the plan, girls? Lead and I'll follow."

"Back to my place," said Remy, her jaw set grimly. "We'll get some equipment and do some research in the daylight hours, dumping you in my basement until the sun goes down."

"You sure do know how to sweet-talk a man." Zane chuckled, then took a drag on the cigarette. "I can hardly wait."

"I'll bet." Remy sounded disgusted. "Let's go."

The ride back to Remy's mansion was an interesting one. She wasn't talking to me. At all. I couldn't tell if she was mad and blaming me for what had happened to Noah, or if she was pissed that we had a vampire hitching a ride with us.

Zane had given me the passenger seat and had taken the back without asking. Which was good, because I didn't want to play second fiddle to him. He sat back there without a word the entire time, and his presence alone put me on edge.

I sat silent myself, Noah's capture still sinking in.

A soft snore punctuated the uncomfortable silence. I turned around and stared. Zane was slumped over in his seat, legs sprawled out. His mouth hung open, and another loud snore escaped.

Remy glanced in the rearview mirror and breathed a deep sigh of relief. "He's out. Daylight's finally kicked in."

I frowned. "So daylight doesn't kill them? I guess I've seen too many Dracula movies."

She fiddled with the knobs on the A/C for the millionth time, a sure signal that she was stressed. "They don't die as soon as day hits, no. Just like Noah's kind—the Serim—don't turn to dust as soon as the moon comes out. It's a gradual process that puts their bodies in hibernation until the next cycle that evening—or morning, depending on your company." Her eyes flicked to the rearview mirror again, watching Zane snore peacefully. "He's going to be out for the next twelve hours or so, which gives us plenty of time." She flashed her turn signal and exited onto an unfamiliar street.

Uh oh. "Time for what, if you don't mind me asking?"

Remy shot me a look. "To work on getting that halo for ourselves, of course."

I held my hands up in the air. "Whoa, Nelly. I don't want any freakin' part of that thing, understand? I just want to get Noah back."

The car cruised down one street and then another while I waited for Remy to respond. She said nothing, her hands tight on the wheel. We seemed to be heading steadily toward the slummy part of New City. Graffiti lined the brick walls of run-down shops, and I noticed a lot of unsavory types hanging out on street corners or by Dumpsters. A police car cruised silently past us in the other direction.

"Um," I tried again, rolling up my window like the chickenshit I was. "So why are we visiting the projects?"

She stopped at the curb by a run-down strip mall. Remy turned off the car and pulled the keys out of the ignition, handing them to me. "Meet me back here in two hours. I need to get a few things." She opened the driver's-side door and hopped out, glancing around and then crossing the street in her high heels from last night, fearless as ever as she approached a seedy pawnshop, complete with hoodlums loitering at the front door. One of them nearly fell over at the sight of Remy sashaying to the door.

"Remy!" I slid over into the driver's seat and rolled down the window. "Remy! Where am I supposed to go with a freakin' you-know-what in the backseat?"

She turned on the sidewalk and glared at me, shaking her head. She mouthed "research" and disappeared inside.

Crap. I rolled the window up again, fast, and turned to check on Zane. He snored on, apparently unable to hear how much my heart was hammering in my throat. Damn it. What was I supposed to do for the next two hours?

Inspiration struck and I started the car, heading for my old apartment. I wondered if the doorman would even recognize me.

○ ○ ○

The doorman did know my face—not surprising, I guess, since the last time he'd seen me, I nearly attacked him with the onset of the Itch.

Bobby blushed and waved me in with excitement. "Miss Brighton! I'm so glad to see you've returned. How was your vacation? You look so beautiful." He nearly fell over himself, trying to open the door for me.

"It was great, Bobby." I let him think I'd been on some sort of makeover vacation. Whatever. "How have things been here?"

"Lonely," he blurted, then turned fiery red. "I mean, we're busy of course. I've made sure that your mail is taken inside your apartment each morning, Miss Brighton. Wouldn't want the other tenants to know you've been away."

Okay, the crush had just taken a stalkerish turn. Warning bells rang in my mind, and I forced myself to reach over and pat his cheek. "You're sweet. Do me a favor and go watch my car for me in the garage? It's the blue Explorer and my, um, cousin is passed out in the backseat. Drinking binge." I shook my head and tried to look tragic. "Do you think you could watch him for me?"

"Of course, Miss Brighton," Bobby breathed, looking like he was about to blow his wad in his dress slacks. "I'll get someone to cover the door for me right away. Don't you worry about a thing, Miss Brighton!"

Oh, I wouldn't. If the car was stolen with the vampire in it, that'd solve two problems at once. I just didn't want Bobby wandering up while I was in my apartment. I smiled at him and headed for the elevator on the other side of the lobby.

Heads turned as I walked. Onlookers stared. Were they wondering who I was, or had someone recognized the old, frumpy me and now wondered who had done my amazing surgery? Either way, I was starting to get used to the overly attentive looks and I ignored them. You know you've got a weird life when the attention of an entire floor is focused on the way you walk, and you couldn't give a rat's ass.

The elevator was empty, and I made it up to my floor without event. The building was very quiet—one of the reasons I'd decided to live in such an expensive apartment complex—and it made me nervous. Given my new lifestyle, it was reasonable to be wary. After all, last night I'd rubbed elbows with angels, vampires, and a demon queen, and they all wanted to kill me right now.

I headed down the long hall to my apartment. There was nothing stacked up outside my door, which meant that any mail or packages or newspapers had indeed been thoughtfully placed inside. I put the key in the lock and turned it, pushing the door open with a flick of my wrist.

And then gasped. Wall-to-wall roses covered the living room, the cheap bouquets you'd buy at the store down the street. Some were wilted, having been here for several days. There were four sets of balloons decorated with kisses and hearts, and several cards were lined up on my table. I picked up the first one.

Miss Brighton, I think I love you. Love, Bobby.

Creepy. I put the card down and looked at the next one.

Miss Brighton, the sun rises and sets in your blue eyes. Would you be my girl?

Ew. Next card.

Miss Brighton—

I tossed it aside. Just what I needed—a stalker who knew where I lived and had the key to my apartment. How had he managed to get the key, anyway?

I didn't touch the rest of the gifts and moved to my regular mail, which had been neatly and alphabetically stacked on a coffee table. Bills, bills, bills, and lots of junk mail. Nothing personal, nothing that reminded me that I was a normal woman with a nine-to-five job. It was depressing.

My voicemail was depressing as well. Thirteen messages, and once I'd hit the sixth one from Bobby, I started deleting after the first word. Ten messages in, I recognized a different voice and rewound to listen.

"Hey, Jackie." The voice was Noah's, sleepy and a little unfocused. "I, uh, got your number the other day when we met at the bar. You probably don't remember that, right? I guess you're not home. No doubt staying with Remy again."

He chuckled, and my heart did a little flip. "She's a bit of a busybody, but she means well, so don't take any of her ways to heart. She's just excited to have another of her kind in the city. It's been a long time since she's had anyone to talk to but me."

The voice in the recording paused for so long that I thought the message was over. I moved to hit Delete when Noah began to speak again. "I just . . . I guess . . . ah, hell. I'm not good with apologies. I just wanted to say that I'm sorry—for everything that you've been through. I would have never done it intentionally. You know that." A huge sigh.

"You just looked so lost and alone that night in the bar, and so innocent, that I couldn't help but be drawn to you. I hope you won't hold it against me forever. I know it's hard right now to adjust, and I guess I just . . . I just wanted to say that I'm here for you, if you ever need me for anything."

I stood there in stunned silence.

The machine beeped. "End of message," the computerized voice warned. "To delete this message—"

I hit the Save button, sniffing hard. I would not cry. I *would* not cry.

Damn Noah for being so sweet and such an arrogant ass at the same time. I checked the rest of the messages, hoping for more from Noah, but the rest were just more of Bobby's mooning.

What now? Suddenly my excursion back to my normal life didn't seem so important. I stared at my shabby furniture, at the stalker roses, at the pictures on the wall from graduation and college roomies, and everything else. It all seemed utterly trivial, and I felt lost and alone. The life I'd led before was meaningless, and the life I had now was utterly frightening.

I wandered into my bedroom like one of the walking

dead. Worn-out sneakers under the bed, frumpy work clothes in the closet; I'd even neatly made my bed.

Who was I? I didn't know anymore.

Sitting on the bed, I contemplated my options. I couldn't go back to the way things used to be—my boss thought I was a crazy plastic surgery junkie. I couldn't stay with Remy; her lifestyle would never be mine. Noah was gone, perhaps forever, and I was stuck with a cigarette-smoking vampire hottie who was crashed out in the backseat of a car that wasn't even mine.

I buried my head in my hands. When did my life get so fucked up?

Much as I wanted to run screaming from the situation, I couldn't. I just couldn't bury my head in the sand and continue on like nothing had ever happened. Noah needed me. I had to at least try.

I gathered a few things: some comfortable old T-shirts, my briefcase full of museum paperwork, a few research books, and a few other doodads I didn't want to leave behind.

I had an odd feeling that I wouldn't see my apartment, or any trace of my old life, again.

Leaving the building behind, I got into Noah's Explorer with a half wave to Bobby, tore out of the parking garage, and coasted back onto the highway, my mind churning. A quick glance behind me confirmed that Zane was still asleep in the backseat—not that I'd expected otherwise.

There was still a good half hour until I had to pick up Remy, but I couldn't get much done in that span of time, so I headed back to the pawnshop and idled the car, flipping through radio stations.

Remy showed up shortly, a couple of bags in tow, and slid into the passenger seat. She dumped the goods on the floorboard and grinned, looking excited. "Miss me? You look like someone died. Everything okay?"

"I suppose, considering all the bullshit that's going down. What did you get?"

"I'll show you when we get home and drop off our third wheel." She thumbed a gesture at the passed-out Zane. "Deal?"

"Whatever floats your boat. Can we grab something to eat? I'm starving."

Remy laughed. "I thought you'd never ask."

Several hours later, the setting sun blazed through the miniblinds. Zane was stashed in Remy's basement on an old couch, we were stuffed with milkshakes, pizzas, and burgers, and she was surfing the internet on her laptop. The remnants of a pizza lay in a box at our feet, and every once in a while I'd reach down and have another slice.

"This sucks," I complained, gesturing at the screen with my straw. "First, we couldn't find anything at the library in five hours of searching, and now this. I can't believe that if you google 'halo' on the internet, all you get are nine million websites about a stupid video game."

Remy frowned and tried typing in a few more combinations of "Joachim" and "Halo." We'd been at this for a few hours now, and I was getting sick of finding nothing but random porn sites. Those interested Remy in a purely vain fashion—she wanted to see if she was mentioned on any of them—but for me, it was just annoying.

"How the heck am I supposed to find a halo that's been missing for the past, oh, three or four millennia?"

Remy shrugged, reaching for the last slice of pizza. "Maybe we need to find who had it last."

I sat back on the couch, nursing my shake and thinking. "Well, obviously the queen's boyfriend had it last. The question is, where was he when he died?" I rubbed my temples, trying to think. "Think that our buddy Nitocris was a queen before she was vampire queen?"

"We could always punch in her name with a few of the older kingdoms in history, and see what that pulls up," Remy suggested, tapping away on the keyboard.

"Phoenician," I guessed. "Zulu. Greek? Nah, they had city-states or something. Celtic? She doesn't seem light-complected enough. Carthaginian?"

Remy snorted and flipped the laptop in my direction. "You're trying way too hard. Check this out."

Under the search words of "Nitocris" and "Queen," I saw a few articles neatly listed on the search results.

"Bingo," I crowed. "Queen of Egypt. I guess that fits."

"No kidding." Remy clicked on the first link and began scanning the page. "Good lord. Did you read this stuff?" Her mouth set into a grim line.

"Well, seeing as how you're hogging the computer and we just pulled it up five seconds ago, no. Let me see." I angled the computer screen toward me a bit and leaned over her shoulder to read.

"First Female Pharaoh of Egypt" the top banner proclaimed.

Remy jabbed her finger directly over the line I was reading. "Did you read this stuff about Herodotus?"

I shoved her finger off the screen. "I will, if you give me a chance. From Herodotus's *Historia*," I read aloud, "Nitocris was the beautiful and virtuous wife and sister of King Metesouphis II—"

Beside me, Remy coughed in shock. "Wife and sister? That can't be right. Joachim was an angel, not an Egyptian. Maybe we don't have the right woman. Beautiful and virtuous hardly describes the woman I had a run-in with last night."

I shrugged and kept reading. "Wife of Mete-doofus, an Old Kingdom monarch who came to the throne at the end of the sixth dynasty and was savagely murdered by his subjects soon afterward." I paused, thinking. "She didn't say that he'd been murdered, though, just that she'd ruined her kingdom for him, and he was destroyed in the first temple of God. Maybe she killed her brother-husband-whatever for her angel boyfriend?"

"Keep reading," Remy urged. "Maybe it mentions something about that."

"Nitocris ordered the construction of a secret underground hall connected to the Nile by a hidden channel. When this chamber was complete, she threw a splendid banquet, inviting as guests all those whom she held personally responsible for the death of the king. While the unsuspecting guests were feasting, she commanded that the secret conduit be opened, and as the Nile waters flooded in, the traitors were drowned.'" I paused, my throat suddenly dry. "'In order to escape the vengeance of the Egyptian people, she then committed suicide by throwing herself into a great chamber filled with hot ashes and suffocating.'"

Remy's eyes were wide. "Crazy suicidal bitch. That's definitely got to be our girl."

"Yeah. I mean, maybe Herodotus glamorized this a bit, but it makes sense. She faked her own death to get out of Egypt. What kind of woman tosses herself into a room filled with hot ashes so she can suffocate?"

"The kind that doesn't need to breathe because she's already dead," Remy agreed. "Which makes it easy to leave the country without being suspected. But the queen didn't mention a water chamber along the banks of the Nile, just a church."

I popped my knuckles as I thought. "But if Joachim was an angel, maybe he was sickened by what she did and left her. The ancient world wasn't exactly great for travel, though, so maybe he didn't get far. We need to go to Egypt and start with that secret water chamber, or her tomb. Maybe we can find a reference to a Temple of God in Egypt."

Remy made a disgusted noise. "Egypt? Do we have to? It's so hot this time of year, and I hate camels. I promised myself I'd never ride on the back of another one for as long as I lived, and I've held that vow for the past four hundred years."

I saved the webpage link and snapped the laptop shut. "Just look at it this way—you can buy yourself some cute tourist clothing. Maybe something safari, or with a leopard print."

She perked up at that. "I suppose I could."

"There's a few Egyptian artifacts at the museum I work at that I want to take a closer look at before we go. Book the tickets for two on the quickest red-eye flight to Cairo, and we'll head for the airport when I get back, okay?"

"Don't forget me," came a voice from across the hallway, and I looked over to see Zane watching me with sleepy eyes. "If you're going on safari, I'm tagging along. Queen's orders, remember?"

I sighed. "Fine. Three tickets. I'm off to the museum, Remy."

"Me, too," Zane said. "Wouldn't want to miss an exciting tour of pottery fragments, would I?"

I rolled my eyes. "Whatever. If you're coming with me, hurry it up. I'm not going to wait for you." Maybe he'd want to take another nap and skip the museum.

No such luck. "Anything you say, Princess." Zane grinned at me and followed as I headed for the door.

I pulled up to the museum and groaned as I parked Noah's Explorer. Right next to it, Julianna Cliver's Miata gleamed in the moonlight. The rest of the parking lot was empty, as it should be at 9:00 p.m. on a weekday night. I sighed and told my passenger, "Looks like we're going to have company. We'll have to go with plan B."

Zane unbuckled his seat belt and opened his car door. "Plan B?"

I reached over and grabbed his door, pulling it shut. "Yes. As in, you stay here and guard the car, and I'll go inside and do some research. Understand?"

"No can do, Princess. If you go in, I must follow."

"Can't you let me go inside for ten minutes? I promise it won't take any longer than that."

"Nope." Zane grinned, showing perfect white teeth and a hint of fang. "Who's the driver of the sissy car that's making you run scared?"

I sighed. "The world's biggest pain in the ass, who also happens to be my boss. I'm *begging* here."

His eyes gleamed. "A job is a job, and besides," he opened his door with a bang, smacking it against the scarlet Miata with delight, "I haven't fed yet tonight."

"No," I choked, fumbling with my seat belt and door. I dashed across the parking lot to where he was stalking purposefully toward the museum. He ignored me, so I grabbed at his arm. "You can't go in there and eat my boss," I hissed, furious. "I'll get fired."

He shrugged his shoulders, hands deep in the pockets of his trench coat. "I'm not going to eat her, Princess. I'm just going to have a little taste." He gave me a wicked grin, and I could have sworn I saw a gleam of red in his eyes.

My heart pounded. This was very, very bad. I ran ahead of him to the glass doors of the museum, determined to buzz myself in before he could get there. The employee badges had only a fifteen-second grace period.

If I could get inside before Mr. Tall, Dark, and Hungry, I'd be in luck.

Of course, as soon as I started running, Zane started running right after me, laughing like a madman hunting his prey. No sooner had I swiped my badge and cracked the heavy glass door to slide inside than he had his hands on the door handle. I stood on the other side and tried to hold it shut, but it was like arm-wrestling with King Kong. I didn't stand a chance.

Little by little, the door slid open and Zane's confident smile grew larger as he outmaneuvered me. I let the door slide backward, nearly smacking him in the face.

"Fine, you win," I grumbled. "But if you eat my boss, I'm returning you to your owner."

Zane winked. "Bad doggy, eh? Gonna get out a newspaper and swat me?"

I thwacked him in the arm with my purse. "Behave. This is a museum. None of your hijinks in here."

He saluted me like a mischievous Boy Scout and moved to step in behind me as I strode through the museum with purpose. "Absolutely no hijinks." He paused in front of a painting—a popular Jackson Pollock—and made a noise of disgust. "Do people truly consider this art? It looks like garbage." He stared at the painting, tilting his head to the side and then the other.

I stopped in my tracks and glanced over, amused by his assessment. "Jackson Pollock was renowned for his performance art. You either get it or you don't." I didn't get it either, but I wasn't about to let him know that. "We need to head to the east wing of the museum."

The east wing housed all the BC artifacts, and luckily was the farthest from Julianna's office near the gift shop.

He shrugged. "Whatever you say. You're the boss." His devilish little grin implied that I was anything but.

"You'd better remember it," I sassed, and turned my back, hoping he'd take the hint and follow. Zane seemed to have a shorter attention span than most supernaturals, and I was hoping he wouldn't wander off at the sight of a shiny object.

To my relief, he pulled into step beside me, whistling to himself, his eyes roaming the dark, empty hallways.

"So, have we met before? Because you sure seem familiar to me." There was something about him that seemed like it was on the tip of my tongue, but I couldn't remember. "I don't suppose you hang out in dark alleys near nightclubs, looking for dorky girls to molest?"

"Huh?" He gave me a vague look.

"Never mind," I said, waving off my comments with a flick of my fingers. "I was just wondering if you were my vampire master. Forget I asked." I felt a bit dumb for bringing it up.

The cleaning crew wasn't due to come in until midnight, so if we could just avoid Julianna, I'd be happy. With luck we'd be out of here before she realized I'd made a pit stop.

"You're not asking," Zane said as we walked, looking over at me with a secretive smile, an unlit cigarette hanging from his full lips.

I reached over and plucked it out of his mouth before

he could light it. "No smoking in the museum. Now, what is it I should be asking about, Dr. Seuss?"

He grinned and paused in the midst of a series of Roman emperors' busts on loan from the Smithsonian. I held my breath, thinking for a horrible moment that he was going to reach over and topple one of the priceless objects, and I'd have to explain to the National Museum *and* my boss what had happened. To my great relief, Zane just pointed at one of the security cameras in the corner of the hall, red light flashing to indicate that it was working. "You're not asking why no one's coming out to check up on us."

My eyes narrowed as my brain absorbed that. He did have a point. I was in the museum after having called in sick for the past few days (which was odd, but not completely strange), accompanied by a dark, mysterious man covered in black leather head to toe (very strange). The security guard should have at least stopped by to say hi or do a bit of random clubbing with a nightstick. So why hadn't he?

There were a few possibilities, none of them pleasant. One: George the security guard could be dead. A long shot, but since I'd just spent the last two days with fallen angels, vampires, and succubi, I was willing to work murder into the realm of plausibility. Two: George knew we were here and was dialing 911 for backup. Or three: he and Julianna were having mad sex in the control room and were too busy to notice the odd couple in the security cameras. But since George was ninety if he was a day and Julianna had a permanent icicle up her ass, I doubted that very much.

So I shrugged, trying to look nonchalant. "I give up. Why don't you just tell me?"

"You're no fun." Zane had another cigarette between his lips and lit it before I could protest. "Come on. I'll show you." He stalked ahead of me and turned down a hall.

I trotted after him, making sure that his long, sweeping coat didn't knock over anything vital. "Where are you going? That's the wrong way. We're looking for the Egyptian wing, not the Mayan exhibit."

He ignored my stressed squawking, heading straight for the men's room.

I pulled up short as he stepped inside. Well, okay. This threw me for a loop. I didn't think vampires had bodily functi—

Zane cracked the door back open again and gave me an odd look. "You won't be able to see anything from out there."

My jaw dropped. "What exactly do you think I'd want to see in there?"

He rolled his eyes and yanked me into the bathroom with him. "You're the most paranoid sex fiend I've ever met, Princess."

"I'm not a sex fiend," I protested, as he turned me to face the mirror over the row of sinks. "I fail to see . . ." The words died in my throat. "I . . ." Failed again. "Oh."

My reflection stared back in the mirror, looking as uncannily sexy as ever. I also saw the wall behind me. And a cigarette dangling in the air.

As in, by itself.

"Er, you're not in the mirror." I pointed at where his reflection should have been.

Zane smacked a hand to his forehead. "My word, you're right." He shook his head and took a long haul on his cigarette. "It's a wonder you Suck girls aren't prized for your brains. That's some keen wit you've got there."

I slapped the cigarette out of his mouth and ground it under my shoe. "Can we go now? I realize this is all fun and frat-boy games to you, but I've got to figure out where your queen's been hiding her fashion accessories for the past four millennia before she kills my friend."

I didn't like being made fun of, and there was something about Zane that always put me on edge. His laughing sexuality? His devil-may-care attitude? Whatever it was, I didn't trust him one bit. Even worse, I didn't trust myself around him.

He really did have the most amazing lips.

"She won't kill him, you know," Zane called after me. "She'll use him for a bit to see if she can breed a child off his seed and make a divine vampire. Failing that, she'll just drain him of his powers."

"Well, don't I just feel *so* much better now," I gushed. I stormed away, determined to get to the Egyptian wing without any more distractions from the fanged menace.

Zane didn't say anything else for a good ten minutes, allowing me time to get my thoughts in order. Somewhat mollified, I shared my theory about Nitocris being an ancient queen of Egypt and he didn't laugh at me, which was surprising.

The Treasures of the Nile was my favorite collection in

the entire museum. It was our most popular wing, so I'd never been assigned to it, since I was the lowest docent on the totem pole. But I had the guided tour memorized in the hopes of one of the more prestigious docents calling in sick and me getting my chance to shine.

A full-blown sarcophagus encased in glass heralded the entrance of the Egyptian wing. The walls were painted with a scene of the banks of the Nile, and a few fluted columns topped with palm leaves added to the feel. The piped-in Eastern music that normally played here was silent, so the only noises were the swish of Zane's clothing behind me, and the sound of him inhaling on his cigarette.

"So, what are we looking for here?"

"Egyptian stuff. Duh."

He looked like he wanted to choke me for a moment, and I felt exceedingly proud of managing to get under his skin.

He leaned over a glass case and stared at a line of ushabti figurines. "No, Princess. I meant, what did you hope to find at this particular museum?"

It was a long shot, but I had remembered something that I thought might be worth a try. I brushed past him and gave him a breezy smile, heading toward the far end of the crowded exhibit. "Carrie Brown worked here last summer."

"Who?"

"She was a graduate student at Oxford in their archaeology program. She interned here last summer and worked in the Egyptian wing." Lucky bitch.

I headed to the far end of the room, behind the movie screen that played *A Day in the Life of Egypt* on an endless twenty-minute loop during business hours. "She wrote her thesis on female Egyptian pharaohs. Carrie left a copy for the museum's records, so I'm going to rummage through her papers to see if she had anything good."

I fumbled behind the screen, feeling around, and turned my finger in a small indention. The storage door slid open a few inches. The room was so crammed full of boxes of old documentation and gift shop receipts that it was impossible to open the door fully. I wedged one lean thigh in the door and forced it open, squeezing my body through the crack. There was a slight problem with the boobs, but I managed to shove my way through without damaging myself.

I flipped on the light switch and stared up at the daunting stack of boxes. I'd had to box up the crap the giggly interns had left on their desks last summer when they'd returned to college, just in case they wanted it back. Carrie Brown's documents should still be in her storage box, including her well-detailed thesis.

"Are you going to be in there long?" From outside of the claustrophobic storage closet, Zane's voice echoed in the quiet hall. "Or shall I wander off?"

Hell, no! Thinking fast, I stuck my head out to look at him. "Do you know what Nitocris's cartouche looks like?"

The vampire gave me a blank look. "I beg your pardon?"

"The cartouche?"

An offended look crossed his face. "How dare you ask me about such a thing? She is my queen, not some common slut—"

I blinked hard and resisted the urge to giggle at the pissy look on his normally blasé face. "Whoa there, stud. I meant her name. Spelled out in Egyptian hieroglyphs."

"No, I wouldn't know."

"Then do me a favor and start reading these." I pointed at one of the informative plaques next to the glass cases. They gave a small blurb of history about the object inside or sometimes a quote from a historical document. "Look for anything that mentions a hidden room or a chick pharaoh. Got that?"

Zane flicked a cigarette on the polished wood floor, no doubt to tick me off. "You're the boss."

"Shut up," I snapped. "And quit smoking in the damn museum! You'll set off the smoke detectors."

He laughed, which only irritated me more. I turned back to the mess inside, muttering about prick vampires, and tackled the first box.

An hour or two later, I discovered the box I was looking for. It reeked of cheap floral perfume and had the initials C.B. on it.

When I flipped open the box, the scent hit me like a ton of bricks. I gagged, forcing myself to pick through the box. At the bottom I found a spiral-bound copy of her thesis manuscript and silently cheered. If there was any condensed research on the vampire queen, brainy little Carrie Brown would have found it. I'd be willing to stake my life on it.

No pun intended.

Shoving the boxes into some semblance of order, I pushed my way out of the storage closet and sucked in a clean breath of air. The wing now smelled like Zane's cigarettes, but I'd take second-hand smoke over one more lungful of Tabu any day.

The exhibit hall was empty, devoid of bored vampire. I clutched the thesis to my chest and began to run, looking frantically for his long leather coat.

I didn't have to look long. As soon as I rounded a corner, I saw Zane's broad shoulders by one of the leafy pillars and just about collapsed in relief.

Until I saw that he was talking to Julianna, which caused me to nearly choke on my own tongue. At the sound of my strangled gargle, they both turned to me.

Zane's eyes were slitted in a sexy, sleepy gaze that made my body throb with immediate recognition. To my surprise, Julianna wasn't shooting me looks of hate. She seemed glazed, flushed, and slightly out of it. Julianna smiled at me and then turned back to Zane, her eyes wide and adoring. The first three buttons of her starchy white shirt were undone, and she was toying with the fourth.

Oh, shit. I rushed forward and shoved myself between them, which got a chuckle of amusement from Zane and a sound of consternation from my boss.

"Is something wrong, Princess?" Zane moved me to the side. "Didn't you find what you were looking for?"

"I found it, all right. And now that we've accomplished our goal, we can go." I forced a tight smile and directed it at Julianna. "Sorry to make a late-night pit stop at the museum. I know you don't approve, but—"

Julianna cocked her head and looked at me as if seeing me for the first time. Given my modified appearance, that probably wasn't too far off the mark. "Did you do something different with your hair? It looks nice."

Uh.

I turned to Zane suspiciously. "All right, lover boy. What did you do?"

He gave me a slow smile that caused my heart to skip a beat. "Do? Your lovely coworker found me out here and has been helpfully answering my questions about the Egypt exhibit."

"She has?" I shot another suspicious look over at Julianna. She looked more like she was about to pull her blouse off than give a lecture on the difference between Old, Middle, and New Kingdom Egypt.

Julianna wiped a stray lock of hair—the first stray lock of hair I'd ever seen in her otherwise immaculate coif— off her brow. "Mr. Hatfield was just telling me of his interest in the female pharaohs." Her voice was breathy with delight. "Isn't it wonderful that he has such an avid interest in history?"

"That's just great," I replied. Mr. Hatfield? Did that make Noah a McCoy? "So did you find anything on Nitocris?"

She shook her head, her eyes glued to Zane. "Nothing, but I did tell Mr. Hatfield that Nitocris is a rather ancient figure in history. We don't have many Old Kingdom artifacts here in our museum, mostly New

Kingdom. I suggested that he check out the Cairo Museum of Antiquities if he is looking for specific artifacts."

Zane looped an arm over my shoulders, grinning down at me. "And I told her that's just what we'd be doing."

The casual touch sent a tingling sensation through me, and Julianna's adoring look faltered into one of hate, directed my way. I slid out from under Zane's arm.

Zane reached for Julianna's hand and brushed his lips along her knuckles. "Thanks to this lovely creature's advice."

Julianna giggled and turned her adoring gaze back to Zanc. "If there's anything I can do at all, let me know. It's so wonderful to meet someone who understands the importance of . . . the Old Kingdom."

I rolled my eyes. I doubted the Old Kingdom was even on her radar at the moment. "Fascinating. Can we go now, please?"

"Of course." Zane ran the back of his hand down Julianna's cheek. "In just one moment . . ."

I watched in horror as Julianna tilted her head back, exposing her neck.

"Wait a minute!" I shrieked.

It was too late. Zane leaned in, and I heard the slurp of flesh being punctured.

Shocked, I could do nothing but turn away. "Zane!"

He ignored me. I heard Julianna's moan and wondered if it was from fear. It sounded more . . . well, sexual.

I wondered if I'd sounded like that when I'd been attacked in the alley. Had I enjoyed it? Made the same kittenish noises that Julianna was making? Pressed my body against his and begged for more? Noah had told me that being bitten by a vampire turns your sex drive on high, but I couldn't remember any details. It was difficult to equate someone sucking all the blood out of you with mind-blowing sex, but that was what Julianna sounded like she was having right now.

I heard one last slurp that sounded like a wet kiss, and then the sound of a body collapsing on the floor. Zane made a pleased noise under his breath, and despite my misgivings, I turned around to look.

Zane wiped his mouth with the edge of his sleeve and winked at me. "Couldn't help myself." His eyes blazed a brilliant red that died down as I watched. At his feet, Julianna lay collapsed in a heap, her eyes closed. I could see a small trickle of blood from her neck.

Panic bloomed through me.

"You fucking freak!" I screamed, smacking him. "Did you just kill my boss?" I knelt at her side, pressing my fingers against her throat for a pulse. "Ohmigod, I am *so* fired. Do you know how hard it is to get a job in a museum, you stupid idiot?" I threw the notebook at him and knelt over Julianna, slapping at her cheek. "Wake her up right now, dammit."

"Calm down," Zane said, the hint of a smile still in his voice. "She's not dead. I usually don't bite to kill."

"Wow, you're a real peach," I snarled. My finger caught the barest of pulses in the thick flesh of her neck and I breathed a sigh of relief. "Thank God." I stood up, wiping the sweat that had broken on my brow. "It scared the heck out of me, seeing her laid out like that. Why's she passed out?"

He shrugged. "Orgasm, I imagine. That's how it affects most women."

I shot him a scathing look. "Oh, of course. The touch of your lips is so amazing that it makes women fall over in a dead faint."

Zane chuckled. "Most human women experience an extreme reaction to a vampire's touch, to the point of dizziness or even blacking out from pleasure. See if her panties are wet, if you don't believe me. Or maybe you'd like a demonstration on yourself?" His dark eyes flickered red again, and he stepped close—almost too close. I could feel the heat pouring off him. "I'd be willing to feed twice in a night for you." He touched my arm, trailing down my sensitive skin.

I took an involuntary step backward.

He smiled at me, continuing to approach like a tiger cornering its prey. "Could it be that you're jealous?"

"Don't be ridiculous," I bluffed, scooting back nervously. My backside bumped into a glass case and I froze, then took a step to the side.

Zane's hands planted on the glass case next to my head, trapping me between him and the display. The scent of leather and cigarettes swam over me, and I looked into his smiling face. He really did have the most sensual mouth.

"Leave me alone," I said, my voice sounding weak.

"Poor Princess," Zane said slowly, leaning in closer. "Wants a taste of the big bad vampire, but she's too embarrassed to admit her own feelings." He tsked, his nose almost touching mine now. "Lucky for you, the vampire has no problem with admitting that he'd like a taste of the princess."

With that, he leaned in and kissed me.

I don't know what I was expecting; something hard and rough, with a lot of teeth. But Zane's soft lips touched mine gently, teasing, coaxing mine to open and allow him in. His tongue lightly danced along my lips and I opened up to him, closing my eyes and giving in to the forbidden taste.

His mouth was sweet, with a hint of copper and smoke to his lips. He expertly teased a response out of me, his hands sliding to my shoulders, then to my hair, pulling me against him in a tender embrace that took me completely by surprise. The Itch awoke inside me, flaring heat through my limbs, and I clutched at his jacket, pinning him against me.

This is wrong, I thought, even as I gently sucked his tongue. Even as I gasped when he licked my lower lip and pressed gentle kisses against my jawline. His hands were respectful, remaining on my head and cupping me against him like a fragile creature.

He moved lower, licking gently at my throat, his teeth nipping against my skin. God, it felt good. I wanted him to lick harder, to press those sinful lips against my pulse. To sink his teeth into my flesh and give me the same orgasm he'd given Julianna—

Reality hit me with force. I was making out with a vampire. My enemy. Noah's captor.

Ashamed, I squirmed out of his embrace. "Stop it," I said. "Don't touch me."

Zane didn't seem offended by my reaction. He only looked at me with those hooded eyes, and a lazy grin spread over his mouth, sending my pulse skyrocketing. "For someone who professes to hate vampires, you sure do like kissing them."

"You're a pig," I called back, storming away to hide the shiver of attraction I felt. "Find your own way home. You're not coming with me."

"Don't you want your purse?" he said behind me, his amusement obvious. "You left it and your notebook here."

Blast. I swore under my breath and stalked back to him, snatching them from his hands. "Do me a favor and leave me alone."

His hand clasped around my wrist, stopping me. "Don't be like that, Princess. I'm sorry I kissed you."

I'm not, I thought, and hated myself for it. "Don't touch me again," I said, wrestling my hand out of his grip. "We're not going to be able to work together if you don't follow the most simple rules. I told you not to eat my boss, and you didn't listen to me, and now you've cost me my job. How am I supposed to trust you on this treasure hunt if you won't behave for five minutes? Just go back to the queen and leave me to handle this—it's my life we're screwing around with, after all."

As I turned away, strong hands gripped my shoulders and forced me to turn around. I looked up at him breathlessly, part of me hoping that he'd give me another one of those soft kisses and part of me disgusted that I'd even look forward to it.

His expression was sober, though, and he clasped my hand in his own and brought it to his lips. "Jackie," he murmured against the flesh of my palm, and a shiver went down my spine despite myself. "You know I would never do anything to hurt you."

I was having a hard time concentrating all of a sudden. His lips danced across my skin, and my nerves shuddered with delight. I pictured those lips moving across my throat like they had on Julianna. I pictured them skimming across my breasts, teasing the tips with his sensual lips that I wanted to bite.

"You wouldn't hurt me? You just did." I had to force the words out and stared pointedly at Julianna, sprawled across the museum floor.

He shook his head and the stubble on his chin scraped against my hand. "Why do you distrust me so much, Jackie? Why is it you trust me so little and trust Noah so much?"

"Gee, I don't know," I said. "Could it be the fact that one of your kind attacked me in a bar and sent me down the path that I'm on right now?"

"I see." His voice sounded sad, so unlike the urbane, devil-may-care Zane I knew. "Perhaps someday you will learn to trust me."

I walked away.

○ ○ ○

Remy was waiting in the driveway as we pulled up to her mansion a short time later. Suitcases littered the sidewalk, and she had her cell phone clutched to her ear. "Oh good," she called as I pulled into the driveway. "I was just about to go looking for you. We need to hurry or we're not going to catch the next flight."

I'd barely put the car in park before she swung open the rear hatch and tossed a suitcase inside.

"Right now?" I sputtered. "We have to go right now? But I haven't even packed . . ." I trailed off, feeling unsettled. If we left now, it meant this whole crazy thing was green-lighted. I really was going after a halo like some sort of oversexed Indiana Jones. I mean, of course I knew this was going to happen. But right now?

Right *now*?

The thought scared me shitless. I jerked the keys out of the ignition and bolted out of the car.

"Hey," Remy called after me. "Where are you going? We need to leave if we want to make our flight."

"Be right back. Bathroom break," I called as I dashed inside and ran up to my room. I slammed the door behind me and leaned on it, my heart hammering. Somewhere out there was a halo with my name on it, and a thousand pissed-off vampires were searching for it, too. I grabbed a tote bag and stuffed a few items in it.

My bedroom door opened and I looked over.

Zane.

"Don't you knock?" I shot him an irritated look and forced the zipper shut on my bag. There were a few things left in my life that I didn't want him sticking his nose into.

"You seem a bit flustered," he observed. "Something bothering you?"

"You mean other than the fact we're on a witch hunt for a halo that the queen of all vampires wants, and if she gets it, we're screwed? But if she doesn't, Noah's screwed and me, too, because he's the only guy I'm screwing?" I gave a sharp, bitter laugh.

Zane slid over to me. "Is that what you're worried about? 'Cause I've got all the same parts as your angel, babe, and I certainly don't mind helping the needy—"

I covered his mouth before he could finish. "Such a hero. Pardon me if I pass."

He pulled away from my hand. "The offer stands for as long as you like." I could hear the laughter in his voice. "Vampires are known for their . . . endurance."

I snorted, trying to deny the mental picture that made my knees weak. "Forget it," I said. "You wouldn't understand what I mean. I'm not looking for stud service." Though he definitely fit the status of "stud."

"Suit yourself, but you'll come around . . . in about twenty-four hours, unless I miss my guess."

Asshole. I stomped back down to the car, tote bag tucked under my arm. But as soon as I hit the driveway, another disturbing sight made me pause.

Beside Remy stood a really cute unfamiliar guy, loading her bags into the back of the car. He looked like a surfer—tan, muscular, bleached blond hair. He also looked like a college kid. I'd never seen him before.

I tossed my tote into the car and strode around to the back. "Uh, Remy? Can I talk to you for a minute?"

She gave me a distracted look. "Huh? Oh, sure. Stan, can you finish loading the car? Don't forget your things." Remy batted her eyelashes at him.

I dragged her over to the far side of the car. "Who the heck is that?"

Remy looked surprised at my vehement reaction. "It's Stan."

I resisted the urge to bang my head against the windshield. Repeatedly. "And just who is Stan, and why's he coming with us?"

She patted me on the arm. "He's for the Itch, hon. I'm due in about eight hours, so I figured I'd need someone along for the Mile High Club and Stan has a passport. Besides, we don't know how long we'll be gone." She looked at Stan and a tiny sigh escaped her. "Just look at those muscles. Hard to believe I found him in a grocery store."

"Not so hard," I snapped. "He looks like he has the IQ of a cabbage."

"Jealous?" Remy grinned at me. "I notice you don't seem to have anyone along for the ride. Not exactly forward thinking, given our situation."

"I've got it covered," I snapped, embarrassed and irritated.

"Are you sure? Because—"

I held up a hand. "Trust me, I've got it covered." She didn't need to know that I'd packed a vibrator. Zane wasn't an option; I wasn't touching that man even if he was the last jerk on earth. "Does he have a ticket? Can we just get going already?"

Remy blinked in surprise. "Wow, something eating you?"

"Nothing I want to talk about, thank you." I got into the car and turned on the engine, waiting for everyone else to get ready.

Egypt. Ready or not, here we come.

CHAPTER SEVENTEEN

I was in Hell.

Remy swatted me with her boarding pass as she stood in line, waiting to hand it to the gate attendant. "Chill out, Jackie. What is your problem?"

I wasn't about to tell her; the humiliation would be too deep. I stood my ground, glaring at the security officer and clutching my tote bag under my arm. "You are *not* nosing through my carry-on. There's nothing bad in there—no bombs, no matches, no razors, all right?"

The guard wasn't budging, either. "Airline policy, ma'am. We randomly search every eighth person."

"Check number nine this time." I gestured at Zane, who stood behind me, hands tucked into the pockets of his leather trench coat. "Ten bucks says that if you search him, you'll find plenty."

The security guard glowered at me, his face turning red behind his thick white mustache. "Miss, you'll have to get out of line right now, and I insist on searching you—not your friend. So hand me the bag." He reached for my carry-on again, scowling when I moved it out of reach. "Now."

Remy groaned. "They're not going to let us board if

you keep pulling this crap, Jackie, and I'm more than ready to hit the drinks in first class." Her blue eyes stared at me impatiently, and if I looked down I'd probably see her Manolo Blahnik sandal tapping impatiently. The Itch was a lot like PMS in the beginning stages; the onflux of hormones brought on some serious mood-swing action.

"I think you should let them check your bag," Stan chirped helpfully.

"Shut up, Boy Wonder. Nobody asked you." I pointed at the ancient security guard. "I'm thinking Gramps here picked me out of the line because he wants to feel up my boobs on the pretense of hidden weaponry."

"Jackie." Zane placed his hand on my shoulder and his eyes met mine. "Let the man check your bag so we can get on the plane."

And just like that, I handed my bag to the security guard and allowed him to open it in front of the entire line. Numb with dread, I watched as he pulled my items out. Blow dryer. Curling iron. My Ziploc-bagged hairspray. Not that I was going to be spending a lot of time fixing my hair in Egypt; I'd hoped all the junk would mask the true item I was trying to smuggle in.

No sooner did I think it than the security guard pulled out a long, flesh-shaped object. "What's this?"

I heard Stan snort with laughter. Remy howled with delight.

"It's nothing," I said, wishing the ground would swallow me up. "Just put it back, all right?"

But no. The security guard was apparently curious about it and switched it on. A loud buzzing sound filled the air, and the few people in line who weren't already interested were suddenly glued to the sight of my vibrator going off in the man's hand.

"Oh," he said, straightening his glasses in surprise. "I . . . oh." Words failed him.

I covered my eyes, wondering if my day could get any worse.

Zane strolled over and looped his arm over my shoulder, his long coat blocking me, the guard, and the bag from the rest of the crowd. Gratitude rushed through me.

"You do realize," he drawled softly in my ear, "that a vibrator's not going to help the Itch? You need a willing *human* partner. Or once-human. Lucky for you I'm along for the ride." He smiled down at me, a lazy look of amusement on his face.

My gratitude dried up in an instant. Yep, my day had just gotten even worse than before.

Before I could burst into tears, the security guard crammed my things back into the bag and shoved it into my hands. "You're free to go, ma'am." He touched his hat and moved down the line as fast as he could.

I let Zane continue to drape his arm over my shoulders like we were a couple until we boarded the plane. "So," I murmured under the warmth of his large arm. He smelled like aftershave and cigars, a heavenly combination. "Why do I always end up doing whatever you tell me to, if you're not my vampire master?" I was still skeptical about that.

"I'm just enticingly persuasive and you're a closet submissive?" He flashed a white smile at me and I automatically moved closer to him. His gaze dropped and I noticed that being under his arm gave him a perfect view down the front of my shirt.

"Ugh. How did you become such a creep?" I skittered away.

He laughed. "Millennia of practice, my dear."

The flight itself was nice and relaxing. As soon as we sat down I put on headphones and ignored Zane, who sat next to me. First class was a definite improvement. Here you had room to stretch out and get comfortable, and I did just that, flipping open Carrie's thesis and starting to read.

Seven hours and one layover later, it was 5:00 a.m., and we were waiting for the plane to take off for the final leg of our trip to Cairo. I'd read every page of Carrie Brown's thesis from cover to cover, but there was nothing there, except for a brief mention of Nitocris as a "legendary" figure in history. Frustrated and cranky, I shoved the notebook into the seat back pocket and ripped my headphones off. I needed coffee. Lots and lots of coffee, and an idea of what to do next.

Depression crept into my mind, and I thought of Noah, trapped with the vampire queen and her minions. He'd made a noble sacrifice for me. *I'm failing you, Noah. I'm so sorry.* My fingers twitched, and I resisted the urge to pull the thesis back out and give it one more go.

Zane looked over and gave me a sleepy look. "Hey there. Decided to talk to me again?" The hint of a smile curved his mouth, and I found myself fascinated anew by his lips.

He looked breathtaking in the early-morning light. Maybe I was just tired of bickering with him, or maybe it was the heavy-lidded look he was casting my way. There was no ulterior motive in his gaze, just an almost sweet smile that made me want to curl up in his lap with his arms around me. My irritation at him ebbed away, replaced by the returning warmth of attraction. I knew Zane was bad for me, but I didn't care.

"I was just trying to get some coffee from the flight attendant," I explained, tucking a lock of now-flat hair behind my ear.

"I doubt they'll be serving much until the plane takes off," he said, his sleepy eyes focused on me.

"True," I admitted, glancing around the small cabin. This last flight was about nine hours long, and I wasn't looking forward to being stuck in my seat for the entire time. The plane was nearly full. An occasional straggler wandered in, and judging from their speed (or lack thereof), we still had a few minutes before the doors were shut. I glanced over at Remy's seat.

Empty.

I frowned until I realized Stan's seat was empty as well, and my eyes immediately went to the first-class bathroom. A man in a dark jacket knocked on the door, frowning. If Remy was doing what I suspected, he was in for a wait.

A low moan came from the bathroom, and the waiting man's face showed horrified surprise. I lifted the thesis higher to cover my burning cheeks. My mind pictured what they were doing inside that tiny room and I felt an answering throb inside my body.

Zane's lazy chuckle reached my ears. "Doesn't look like he'll be getting into the bathroom anytime soon."

I shot a quick glance over. He was stretched out with his long legs under the seat in front of him. His long, heavy coat trailed onto the floor, and I frowned. "Aren't you hot in that thing?"

He winked at me. "Do you think so?"

I sighed. "Not like that, you idiot. Aren't you uncomfortable? You haven't taken it off the whole time, and it's going to be a hundred degrees in Egypt."

He yawned, settling farther into his seat and closing his eyes. "I have my reasons."

"And what would those be?"

One eye cracked open. "A killer sense of style?"

Eye roll. "You're incorrigible."

"I know." He waved a hand at the rumpled thesis. "So, did you find anything useful in there?"

"Nothing," I said, sounding as miserable as I felt. "If this water-death-trap existed, nobody knows where it is except Nitocris herself, and she didn't feel like telling anyone."

"The water chamber was destroyed so that it wouldn't be used again," Zane said, closing his eyes. "You won't find it."

Huh? "What do you mean, I won't find it?" I reached

over and raised one of his eyelids. "Repeat that?"

He chuckled and pushed my hand away, closing his eyes again. "I said, it was destroyed a long time ago."

"So why are we going to Egypt?" My voice raised a decibel or three.

Zane shrugged. "I thought you might want to see her tomb. I can take you there if you like. That's why she sent me with you, after all."

Unbelievable. "You let me go on a wild-goose chase for the past day for nothing," I sputtered, "and you could have told me all along what I needed to know." Hurt, I turned my eyes to the window on my left, arms crossed over my chest. I wasn't talking to him again until he apologized.

Silence. A moment passed, then a soft snore punctuated the silence. How could he sleep at a time like this?

The flight attendant shut the plane doors, and we soon began to pull away from the jetway. As the angle of my window changed, sunlight blasted into my eyes, and I pulled the shade down.

The sun . . .

I looked over at Zane's sleeping form with horror. I hadn't even thought about the fact that he hibernated in the daytime. He didn't seem disturbed by the sunlight streaming in through the windows. His face was slack with sleep, his lips hinting at a leftover smile. I poked him tentatively. Nothing. He might as well have been dead.

The flight attendant stopped by our row. "Your husband will need to put his seat up for take-off."

I thought fast. There was no way I could raise that seat with two hundred pounds of conked-out vampire in it. "He's um, narcoleptic," I said. "The doctor says it's best to leave him undisturbed if he has one of his spells." I tried to look pained. "I hope this isn't a problem?"

She gave me a sympathetic smile. "I'll talk to the captain, but I don't think it will be."

Whew. One crisis averted.

Remy slid into a seat across the aisle, Stan dutifully following. Her lipstick was all over his face, and she had a cat-licked-the-cream smile on her lips, her eyes bleached silver.

"You have no shame, do you," I said.

"None whatsoever," she replied, wiping the corners of her mouth with a manicured fingertip. "Doesn't do a lick of good in this line of work."

I sighed and picked up the in-flight magazine. It was going to be a damn long trip.

Fourteen hours later, after three more explanations about my husband's narcolepsy, two runs with mishandled luggage, and a taxicab to the hotel, I was more than ready to call it a day. The sun was setting across the Nile as we pulled up to the hotel.

With the help of a few eager bellhops, I dumped Zane into his room across the hall. I tipped the men generously so no one would ask too many questions, then escaped to my room.

Hotel sweet hotel. The room was clean and spacious, with a king-sized bed and a window A/C unit that I cranked up to full blast. The balcony overlooked a crowded, dirty street full of tourists and locals, and white linen curtains swayed in the twilight breeze. Pretty swank. There was a full bath and shower, and a closet to hang my things, so I unpacked and tried to relax for a few hours.

My thoughts kept turning back to Noah, and I thought my heart would shatter. I wasn't in love with him, but he was the only person who made me feel safe in this new, crazy life, and he was in the clutches of the enemy a thousand miles away. And it was my fault. *I won't fail you, Noah.* Overwhelmed, tears threatened, and I tried to focus on calming myself.

Which lasted for all of five minutes, until I saw what Remy had packed for me. I pulled out a stiletto and groaned, tossing it aside. More digging revealed a silk sundress, tons of lingerie, and several pairs of fishnets. Good God, when did she think I was going to wear those here? I resisted the urge to run next door to the room she was sharing with Stan and choke her with them. Two suitcases full of clothing, most of it completely unsuitable. I sighed and headed for the shower.

The long, hot shower perked me up immensely. It felt weird to go 24/7 without even a nap, but while I was weary from travel, was I sleepy? No.

I luxuriated in the soap and hot water until my fingers began to wrinkle, then reluctantly got out, drying myself off and wrapping my hair in a towel. I slathered lotion on my arms as I walked back into my room to get dressed. There might be a good guidebook in the gift shop downstairs; I'd check it out.

A wolf whistle made me look up in shock and I saw Zane on my bed dressed, looking up at me appreciatively. "Wow, you sure did fill out. I think you've got a bigger rack than Remy."

I swallowed the scream that had bubbled in my throat and ripped the towel off my head, wrapping it around my body. "What the *hell* are you doing in my room? I thought you were asleep!"

He gave me a devilish smile. "I woke up. I was hoping you'd missed me. I guess not."

"You guessed right." I went to the bed and pulled at his leather jacket. "Please get out of here so I can get dressed."

"Why leave? I've already seen everything you've got to offer, Princess." He beamed a slow smile at me, teeth gleaming. "Modesty is misplaced in one of your kind, my dear."

I clutched the towel tighter. "You have three seconds before I call security."

He laughed. "Security won't be coming over, my dear. They all think I'm your boyfriend, and I bribed the bellhop—who's quite in love with you and your red hair—to stay away. I told him you were into kinky sex games and tended to get noisy." He traced a circle on the bed with his finger. "Speaking of which, isn't it about time for your Itch to kick in? Your eyes are blue."

"Get out! I mean it." I searched for something to throw

at him. "If you don't leave this room this instant . . ." My fingers closed around a stiletto sticking out of my suitcase, and I lobbed it at him with all my force.

It smacked him straight on the forehead. Before I could delight in my perfect aim, Zane fell back with a groan of pain.

The room was silent. I frowned and stared at his unmoving body sprawled across my bed. "Zane?"

No response.

Crap. I'd done it now. I'd gone and killed the vampire queen's premier employee. I scrambled over to the bed. He was pale, but then again, he was always pale. There was a bright red blotch on his forehead, and he was completely, utterly motionless. Worry niggled at me, and I put a finger under his nose to see if he was still breathing.

Nothing.

"Shit," I cursed, jumping onto the bed beside him and slapping his cheek. "Wake up, Zane. Wake up."

No response.

I took his chin in my hand and jiggled his head back and forth. "Come on, wake up," I pleaded. "Your queen is going to kill me if she finds out that I accidentally killed you with a shoe." I leaned over him, prying open one of his eyelids to check his pupil.

"I think I'm gonna need mouth to mouth," he said suddenly, his arms snaking around me to pull me down against his naked chest. "Wanna volunteer?"

I yelped in shock and tumbled onto him, losing my balance. My elbow slammed into his chin and he gave another groan of pain. "Let go of me," I demanded, trying to pry his arms off my waist.

"Damn, baby. This is the best view I've had all day," Zane said appreciatively when my now-bared breasts brushed against his face.

Hot desire pounded through me, immediate and horrifying. I put my hand against Zane's chest and shoved hard, but my wimpy muscles were no match for a vampire's strength.

In a blink, Zane had me flat on my back and was straddling my naked body, his heavy form pressed over mine, his knee sandwiched between my own. My struggles to get up lessened as the familiar lick of fire ignited in my body, and my pulse sped up as he leaned over me, his eyes hot on my damp flesh.

"Well, well, well," Zane breathed. I caught the glimmer of red in his eyes that told me he was feeling it, too. "Looks like I win the wrestling match, Blue Eyes. Do I get a prize?"

He stretched my arms above my head and leaned over me, his breath light and hot on my cheek. His face brushed close to mine and I heard him inhale my scent.

A tingle shot straight down my legs and I wriggled under him, but it was more of a token protest at this point. "Zane," I pleaded.

"No more begging for me to free you, Blue Eyes?" His lips nibbled across my jaw, and I sucked in my breath in sheer delight. "No more throwing things at me?" I felt the graze of his teeth against the soft flesh of my neck, just enough to excite me and make me writhe.

He ground his clothed groin against my naked flesh, and I lost track of everything in that moment.

His lips teased a trail down to my collarbone and straight to my breasts. "You like being here with me, don't you, Princess? I can see in your eyes what you really want." His tongue touched the valley between my breasts and I bit my lip, hating the moan that bubbled in my throat.

"My eyes tell you nothing," I breathed, trying not to arch my breasts straight into his lips, "except that I don't have any choice over what my body wants." A token protest at best; at this point, I didn't want to stop.

Zane paused, his form growing still atop mine. Then, a soft chuckle. "Touché, Princess." He kissed the peak of one breast gently, inflaming me, and then took my hand in his to pull me up off the bed. "Get dressed."

"Huh?" I blinked, ready to toss him down on the floor and have my way with him. Vampire or not, he was gorgeous, sensual, and I was Itching like mad. "Get *dressed*?"

He turned away, straightening his heavy coat. "You wanted to see Nitocris's tomb, right? I'll take you there tonight. Just give me a few minutes to . . . prepare myself."

I frowned. "Excuse me? Were we, or were we not just about to make out on my bed? I don't know about vampires, but I can't just shut this stuff off like it's a faucet." The blood was throbbing so hard in my nether regions that I was going to need another shower to be able to walk, if he wasn't going to help me out.

Zane turned to face me, his eyes a vivid red that turned my angry retort into a muted squeak of distress.

"On the contrary, Princess." A rueful smile curved his lips. "I can no more turn it off than you can. But I am not the monster you make me out to be, and if your heart isn't in it, neither is mine."

I gasped. "You're going to torture me like that, then hang me out to dry? You *ass*! I should find that shoe again and whack you good."

The hint of a smile returned to those disturbing red eyes. "I said I wouldn't take you against your will. You only need to ask me, Jackie."

I wouldn't ask. I'd burn in Hell first.

No doubt sensing my answer, he turned and headed for the door. "Fifteen minutes and I'll be back. I expect you to be ready to go."

That didn't give me much time. I dove for the phone. "Let me call Remy and tell her—"

"No. Just me and you tonight."

Suspicion shot through me. "This is serious stuff, and we're going to need Remy's help."

"Those are my terms. You and me alone, or not at all."

I sighed. "Fine. Fifteen minutes."

As soon as he left the room, I called Remy. "Here's the situation," I said. "Zane says he'll take me to the tomb, but you guys aren't invited."

"Mmm," Remy said, and then I heard her break into a giggle, followed by Stan's moan.

"Oh, *gross*. Please don't tell me what you're doing—I don't want to know."

Remy laughed at me. "Do you trust Zane, or do you think this is a trap?"

"I suppose I trust him," I said, thinking back to our conversation. "I don't know what he's up to, but he can't murder someone who's already dead, right?"

"Honey, you're worth more to his kind alive than dead, trust me on that. Murder's probably the furthest thing from his mind."

"Okay. If you don't hear back from me by morning, it's safe to say the vampires have carried me off for their nefarious needs, and I'm somewhere in a tomb in the middle of Egypt. That should narrow it down, right?"

She paused. "Give me five minutes and I'll be right over."

"Sure." I hung up the phone and sighed.

I dressed quickly in the only decent items in my closet. My underwear was a G-string and a ridiculous bra that was all sheer lace and push-up madness, but I covered them with a low-cut black T-shirt and khaki short shorts.

There was a knock at my door before I could find any shoes. "It's open," I called, as I dug farther into my bags. "Come on in."

"Looking for something?" Remy asked, watching as I demolished my closet.

I turned and glared at her. "Yeah, how about a pair of shoes that don't have a spike heel?" I held up a Prada sandal. "What am I supposed to wear to go hiking?"

She looked at me in consternation. "What on earth do you want to go hiking for?"

"Uh, the tomb? Maybe the halo? That crazy little thing we flew here to find?"

Remy sat on the edge of the bed. "Just wear some sandals. There's like a path, right? Those shorts will look amazing with the crocodile heels I packed, now that I think about it."

I put my head in my hands and forced myself to count to ten slowly. "Did you pack anything that doesn't have a heel?" I repeated.

"If you *must* wear something unfashionable—and judging by that outfit, I see that you must—I suppose you can borrow my shoes." She slid them off her feet and handed them to me.

They were brown leather sandals, which might have been all right, except the wedge heel rocketed up four inches. I sighed and strapped them onto my feet. They'd have to do.

She laughed. "Before you chew me out entirely, let me give you what I came over here for, before your vampire boyfriend shows up."

"He's not my boyfriend," I protested, testing out the new shoes. I just hoped I wouldn't break an ankle crossing a sand dune. "Noah's my boyfriend, if anyone is."

"Is he? Sex doesn't make a relationship, sweetie. You need to learn that to succeed as a Suck." She studied me, then gestured at my eyes, which were no doubt neon blue. "I see you haven't managed to shake your Itch yet. Want me to send Stan over?"

"Absolutely not." I headed for the bathroom, jerking my hair into a messy ponytail. At least I didn't need makeup. "If you send Stan over here, I'll send him back to you in pieces. Got that?"

Remy chuckled and waved something in my peripheral vision. "Suit yourself, but he's going to start looking pretty good in a few hours, if all you've got is that vampire and a million strangers."

"I'll worry about that later." I was worrying about it now, but I'm sure she could tell just by looking at me. The front of my T-shirt had headlights, for crying out loud, and I suspected they wouldn't go away until the blue eyes did.

From the corner of my eye, I caught a glimpse of something shiny as Remy moved to the side. "Well, at least allow me to give you this."

I turned and found myself looking at a gun.

CHAPTER EIGHTEEN

Remy grinned and waved it in the air. "Know how to shoot one of these babies?"

"No. And could you *please* not wave it around?"

She laughed and lowered it. "Oh, you big baby. This gun can't hurt you."

No? "Are succubi bulletproof?"

"No, silly." Remy flashed me a white smile. "While you can't *die* from a gunshot, you can look pretty hideous for a few days. Trust me on that." She held the gun by the barrel, extending the grip toward me. "This is a special kind of gun."

I took it from her with distaste. It was tiny, with a teeny barrel and a pearl pink grip. Count on Remy to have a fashionable gun. "That's great," I said, "but I don't think this is going to hold off a vampire. It looks like it needs to grow up first."

She rolled her eyes. "This is a Derringer, honey. It's small to fit under your clothes." Remy took the gun from me and opened it, revealing the bullets inside. "It holds two shots, and you'll want to be up close to shoot, because they don't aim worth a damn."

"And why do I need a gun? Especially one that I won't

be able to aim? And how did you get that through airport security?"

"I put one of the baggage check guards to sleep when you weren't looking." She snapped the gun shut again and pulled a holster from her purse. "We don't have a lot of time, so the pink gun is for the vamps. Remember, pink for vamps." She lifted up my shirt and put the gun holster around me, adjusting the Velcro straps so they slid down under my cargo shorts to just above my underwear. Well, that explained how nobody would see it.

"So what's the gun do if it's for vampires?"

"The bullets have been blessed by an angel. One good shot to the head should kill him. If you want to play nasty, just shoot him in the groin. It'll incapacitate him for an hour, which should give you plenty of time to get away if you need to. But if it's not a fatal shot, you'll also piss him off. So be careful. Don't use it unless you have to."

"Okay, I got it." I shoved the tiny pink gun into the holster. "Thanks for the protection."

I looked up and found myself eye to eye with a blue-handled gun.

"This one is for the Serim, in case you run into any," she said.

I took the gun with skepticism. "I don't see why I'd need to be protected from the Serim, Remy." If anything, I needed to be protected from the angels.

She put the gun in the empty holster at the small of my back. "They're not on your side any more than Zane

is, kiddo. Remember that both sides want that halo—
and if you stand in their way, they'll just mow you down
like they do everyone else. Now, remember," she said as
she tightened the straps and I felt the gun barrel slide
against my thong. "The one against your ass is for the
angels, and the one against your cooch is for the pricks.
Got it?"

"Got it," I said, tugging my shirt down. It looked like
I had a little junk in the trunk, but other than that, you
couldn't see the firearms. "I still don't see why I need
these. You said that our kind are worth more alive than
dead to them." That frightened whine was back in my
voice.

Remy put her hands on my shoulders and gave me a
comforting squeeze. "That may be, but nothing is more
important than that halo for both sides. Watch yourself—that's all I'm saying."

"Lucky me." I reached for my purse. "My allies
and my enemies both want to kill me. I'll keep that in
mind."

"I'm your only real ally, I'm afraid," she said softly.
"Just remember that."

A knock sounded at the door. Zane.

I shoved Remy into the bathroom. "Go back to your
room when we leave, okay?"

She nodded at me, crossing her fingers in the "good
luck" sign before closing the bathroom door.

I opened my door a crack. "Yes?"

Zane turned at the sound of my voice, extending a
bouquet of white and orange lilies surrounded by baby's

breath. Surprise made my throat catch, and the smile that curved his mouth shot a pulse of desire straight to my groin.

Damn the Itch. Damn damn damn.

"Hi," I said, trying not to sound too breathy and failing miserably. I stepped outside my room and took the flowers, surprised by the gesture. "Why flowers?"

"Thank you, Zane," he mimicked, grinning at me. When I blushed, he took my hand and brushed his fingertips across my knuckles before settling a kiss there. "I figured you'd be mad at me, so I brought these to make amends."

It worked; I'd forgotten completely that I was pissed at him for the seduction stunt. But it had nothing to do with flowers. One smile from him, and I'd forgotten everything but the fact that he was gorgeous. That floppy lock of hair was falling over his forehead again, touching his eyebrow.

"I'm ready when you are," I blurted. A blush touched my cheeks when I realized the double entendre.

He chuckled, a low, sensual sound that did terrible, wondrous things to my insides. "Glad to see it." He still held my hand in his, his thumb caressing my skin. The feeling was carrying straight to unmentionable places on my body, and I was losing my sanity, fast. No doubt my eyes were blazing the hottest blue this side of the Caribbean.

I frowned as I realized something, staring into his dark, laughing eyes. "The red is gone."

"Hmm?" Zane gave a gentle tug on my hand, pulling

me into his arms. I went willingly. Actually, I shouldn't
say "willingly." I should say "plastered my body against
his and wrapped my arms around his neck." All I could
smell was the dizzy scent of blood and man and leather
that made up Zane.

Zane's hand came to rest on the curve of my lower
back, reminding me that I had two guns strapped against
my flesh and he wasn't supposed to find out. I pulled
away, an embarrassed flush heating my cheeks. "Your
eyes," I repeated. "They're not red anymore."

"No, they're not. Unlike you, I have no problem with
using others to satisfy a need, whether I like and respect
them or not. Sometimes when the urge is upon you, anyone will do." He shot me an oblique look, daring me to
say something.

Offended, I stiffened and crossed my arms over my
chest. So he'd gone and slaked his needs and left me
hanging? Typical man. Typical *vampire*.

I opened my door and tossed the flowers inside. When
I remained silent, he sighed.

"Come on. Let's go."

"Why do I need this?" I complained as Zane slid the
burqa over my head and over my shoulders. The souvenir shop was hot enough without a heavy cloth covering
me from head to toe.

"It's for your own safety." He smoothed the fabric
down my body. "Nobody will look twice at you dressed

in one of these; the way you were dressed was getting too much attention if we want secrecy."

The burqa was designed to cover a woman from the prying eyes of men. This one was baby blue—a fashion choice, I assumed, since most of the others in the shop were unrelenting black. A thin mesh opening over the eyes allowed me to see out into the world. It was heavy and stifling, but I saw his point.

I sighed. "You should see the *other* stuff Remy packed."

He handed me a disposable camera. "Remy is an idiot when it comes to suitable clothing. That woman doesn't have a practical bone in her body."

As Zane paid for the clothing, I went to the shop's door to check out the Cairo nightlife. The streets were lit up despite the early hour of the evening, and still crawling with people of all shapes and sizes. Directly across the street was an antiques emporium.

Several men waited outside the shop, young, rough sorts with dirty clothing, and ugly smiles. They sat casually in front of the store, talking among themselves. One began to clean under his nails with a long knife.

As I watched, one gestured at the door of the souvenir shop and said something to one of his companions. The bearded man shrugged, then made a chopping notion across his throat. The other men laughed.

My throat suddenly dry, I swallowed hard, then said, "Um, Zane?"

He appeared at my side. "Yes?"

"Those men out there—"

"So you see them now."

I faced him. "What do you mean, 'now'? Have they been there the whole time?"

He steered me away from the door, whispering against my fabric-covered ear, "Slavers. They've been following us since the hotel, doubtlessly tipped off by someone who works there. You'd fetch a fortune with that red hair."

Slavery in this day and age? I couldn't imagine being sold into a brothel—it was too TV-movie-of-the-week.

"What do we do now?"

Zane rubbed my shoulder comfortingly. "We go out the back way."

I slid my hand into his and allowed him to lead me past the counter. "Back door?" Zane calmly asked the sales clerk.

The shopkeeper pointed one finger toward the far end of the store, saying nothing.

Zane's smile flashed across his face. "My thanks, friend." He laid a handful of bills onto the counter. "You didn't see any American women in here."

"Egyptian women only," the shopkeeper agreed, his eyes bright at the sight of the money.

Zane led me into a dirty storage room, cracked open the back door, and glanced out. "We're clear. Just an alleyway filled with garbage."

He led me through the filth-strewn alley, the burqa flapping around my legs. "How did you get that wad of money you gave him?"

"Same way I got rid of the red eyes. You want details?"

Ugh. "I'll pass, thanks."

He chuckled. "Someday you'll get over that charming squeamishness of yours, Princess—and that'll be a shame."

I snorted in disbelief. "If that means you expect me to dive into your arms at some point, forget about it." But just speaking the words aloud caused my body to throb.

Zane led me through a maze of dark alleys and back streets. I had no idea where we were and clutched his hand. If I got separated from him I'd have no idea how to get back to the hotel, and the thought of being alone and lost in a city where I could be nabbed by slavers was first and foremost in my mind.

The vampire seemed to know where he was going. We hailed a cab and took a wild ride through the streets to the outskirts of the city. There, he led me through the maze of streets until we came face to face with a pair of camels standing in a dark courtyard. One looked over at me, chewing hay with a stupid look on its face. "Here we are," Zane announced.

I hesitated. "Don't tell me—our transportation?" A nondescript man stood between the camels, holding their bridles with an expectant look.

Zane grinned in the darkness, his white teeth flashing. "How'd you guess?"

"A lucky hunch," I said, my voice muffled through the burqa.

Zane handed the man a wad of bills, took the reins of the first camel, and got it to kneel. "Ladies first."

I sighed and stepped forward. "Don't these things spit?"

Zane grabbed me under the arms and helped me into the saddle. "They do. Just don't provoke it and you'll be fine."

His hands on me caused my banked desire to burn full-blown once more. I lost track of my thoughts and clung to the blanket-covered saddle with my knees as the camel stood again. "No provoking. Gotcha."

As Zane mounted his camel with expertise, I focused hard on things other than the Itch. Kittens. Puppies. Bottled Water. Hamburgers. Ice cream. Licking ice cream off Zane's hard, flat stomach—

My mental imagery needed a little work if I was going to stay calm and cool. Though he was a jerk sometimes, he had a boyish charm. Except for the room-entering incident, I suspected Zane was being courteous in his own way. He'd stopped when I'd asked him to stop, he was concerned with my welfare, and he'd been helpful. Either he was a genuinely good guy with a bad rap, or he had something up his sleeve.

Zane turned to look at me. "Everything okay?"

"I'm fine." If confused.

He tapped the rump of his camel with a crop. The camel lurched forward and began to head out into the surrounding desert.

I thumped my legs against my camel's sides, and it trotted after Zane's mount.

Despite all his antics and issues, Zane had been someone I could count on since we got to Egypt.

"Zane?"

He turned to look back at me. "Yes?"

"Thanks. For everything."

The grin that crossed his face was devilish. "You can thank me later—preferably between the sheets."

I resisted the urge to throw my riding crop at his head. Barely.

CHAPTER NINETEEN

"We're here."

Frowning under the sweaty burqa, I gazed at the desolate landscape. "If by 'here' you mean the middle of nowhere, then I'd agree," I said, halting my camel with a tug on the reins.

We'd passed a few small villages in the middle of the night, passed a few tourist attractions, and traveled deeper into the desert. At least I assumed it was the desert, because there was sand and cliffs and rocks. The Nile glittered behind us, my only hint that we were still along the river. Somewhere. We could be on the outskirts of Cairo still, and I wouldn't have any clue.

Zane dismounted from his camel. "The tomb's just a few hundred yards ahead. You might want to walk your camel in, since the footing's a bit slippery."

I slid off the side of my beast and fell into a heap on the ground. "Can I take off the burqa now? I'm dying of heat under here." The veil was plastered to my forehead.

"That should be fine," Zane said, stroking the nose of his camel to soothe the creature.

I yanked the baby-blue fabric over my head and wadded it into a ball, sighing with relief as the night wind touched my skin. I closed my eyes and tilted my face to the breeze. "That feels wonderful." I cracked an eye and looked over at Zane. "Speaking of, it's over eighty degrees out here and you're still wearing the trench coat. What gives?"

He ignored me, leading his camel up the trail. "You wanted to see the tomb, right? It's this way."

I made a face at him. "Fine, fine. I'm coming." Taking the camel's reins in hand, I followed Zane up the sandy path—if you could call it that—between a pair of large dunes. There were no trees, no archaeological ruins, nothing to mark this spot of land as different from the rest of the desert, but Zane seemed to know where he was going.

On the other side of the dunes I saw a tall cliff wall of sandstone and granite in the distance. "Is her tomb in there?" I called.

Zane just turned and grinned at me. "Wait and see."

A million or so sand-filled steps later, we stood at the base of the cliff. It didn't look like a tomb. It didn't look like anything, in fact, but I was willing to give him the benefit of the doubt.

Zane handed me the reins to his camel. "Be a good girl and find someplace to tether these, would you?"

Before I could retort, huge yellow camel-teeth snapped at my hair. I jerked away. "It's amazing you've managed to last this long without some woman killing you, Zane."

"Like you, Princess, I'm already dead." He walked toward the rocky tumble at the foot of the cliff, scanning the ground for something.

I peered after him despite myself. Sucks really seemed to have the short end of the stick in the Afterlife; vamps had perfect night vision. Zane searched the tumble of rocks for a few minutes, taking his time. When it was obvious that we wouldn't be making progress for a while, I went off in search of a hitching post.

The soil at the base of the cliff was covered with stones worn down from the cliff face long ago. It made walking treacherous, and I stubbed my toes a few times in my sandals, cussing the whole time. When I spotted an outcropping that looked slender enough to tie a rope around, I hurried over and secured the beasts.

As I returned to Zane, I heard a soft slither on sand, then a sibilant hiss.

I froze, hardly daring to turn my head, and saw a big cobra leering at me in the darkness, its tongue flicking, less than twelve inches from my bare leg and foot. I remained as still as possible, my hands twitching against my sides. Could I draw one of my guns without having the snake attack? Would the bullets even work on a snake?

Zane's hand brushed my arm and I smothered a yelp. "Are you done playing around out here?" he said. "The tomb's this way, and I only have until dawn."

I pointed a trembling finger at the snake, which rose taller to knee height. "S-s-snake."

He sniffed dismissively. "You're afraid of that?" He squatted in front of the snake, stared at it, then stood. He took me by the elbow and steered me away from the snake, which remained frozen in place. "You're an immortal, Princess. It won't kill you."

My gaze remained glued to the immobile snake. "It'd hurt like hell though." The creature still did nothing—no tongue flicking, no biting, nothing. "What did you do to it?"

He grinned down at me like a mischievous little boy. "Charmed it. I'm an expert at charming, wouldn't you say?"

Blood throbbed through me in a heady rush, and my knees went weak. I understood how the poor snake felt. Forcing myself to pry his fingers from my heated skin, I moved away. "You're not as charming as you'd like to think."

"No?" He slid his hands around my waist. "That sounds like a challenge to me."

"Give it your best shot," I scoffed. "I'm sweaty and I smell like camel. If you want to try to seduce me now, bring it." Two could play his little game.

His hands slid upward, stroking my ticklish sides through my damp T-shirt. "Even with your hair plastered to your head, you're still achingly beautiful, Jackie." The light, feathery touches sent a flush of heat through me that had nothing to do with the temperature outside. "I like seeing you sweaty," he whispered, pulling me closer until I was pressed against his jacket, my nipples brushing the leather and visible through my shirt. "I'd love to spend all night tasting your flesh. Licking you everywhere. Making you sweaty with need."

Oh. My.

Like the cobra, I was entranced by the seductive words, helpless to pull away.

"Do you know where I'd kiss you first?" His fingertip slid to my mouth and parted my lips, seeking entrance to the hot well of my mouth. I took the tip of it between my lips and bit gently at it, entranced by the suggestion. "Not here," he said softly, his reddening eyes locked onto my blue ones. "That's where a conventional man would give his woman her first kiss. I'd want to give her something she remembers. Forever."

His fingers brushed up the front of my chest to my breast. The backs of his fingers slid over the fabric there, gently teasing the aching peak into taut hardness. "I'd kiss her here," Zane said, his mouth moving lower to follow his hand. "The skin is sensitive here, and sweet, like the most delicious of desserts." His dark eyes stared up at me, waiting for me to tell him no, to protest or push away. But I didn't.

His lips closed over my nipple, and he kissed me gently. Despite the fabric that separated my flesh from his mouth, I felt burned to my core. A low, aching gasp caught in my throat.

Zane moved across my chest to my other, neglected breast. "My second kiss would be here," he said, teasing the second peak with the barest hint of tongue.

I thought I'd burst into a spontaneous orgasm right there. Heat throbbed between my legs, and my pulse pounded so loud I could barely hear his soft words. Zane slid lower down my body, until he was kneeling on the ground. His mouth hovered near the apex of my pelvis, scant inches away from the flesh that yearned for the same treatment.

"And the third kiss?" I asked, my breath catching in my throat.

He looked up at me, that delicious smile curving his beautiful mouth. "The third kiss, she has to ask for."

I stumbled backward, breathing hard. "I'd, uh, like to see the tomb now."

"Your wish is my command, Princess." His mocking tease grated on my frayed nerves, but he got to his feet and dusted off his coat like nothing had happened between us.

I wanted to weep at the unfairness of it. "I just want to get this done so I can go back to the hotel and take a shower." A nice cold one.

Zane just laughed and took my hand. "This way, then."

Zane's lighter sparked, then flickered into a small thread of flame, illuminating the darkness around us. I sucked in my breath at the unnerving sight of his sharp features lit up in shadow. "Here we are."

"Light something bigger, would you?" I rubbed my arms and stared around me at the dark hole that was Nitocris's tomb. I clamped my jaw when it threatened to chatter; Zane would have totally made fun of me.

I'd settle for him wrapping his arms around me and chasing the fear out of me with a nice, steamy bout of sex. But a girl has standards to uphold . . . Damn Itch. I hated it and the way it messed with my mind.

The tomb was damn spooky. I wasn't scared by much; I didn't scream in horror movies, and I wasn't even afraid to skydive. But this? This small, dusty tomb in the middle of the stifling desert? This hole of choking darkness, the heart of evil as I knew it?

Yeah, the tomb scared the hell out of me.

Outside, Zane had pointed out a small, square passage in the rock wall, the edges surrounded by archaic symbols of scarabs and ankhs that I recognized as Egyptian. He'd gestured for me to crawl down inside and I had, not knowing that the descent would be a hundred feet into the earth in a small, cramped passage where I couldn't even stand upright, leading into total darkness.

I definitely hadn't thought that one through.

I sneezed as dust tickled my nose, and rubbed my hand against my face, imagining spiders and creepy-crawlies hovering in the darkness. Ahead of me, the lighter flame spread as he held it against a rag-wrapped torch. To my vast relief, the darkness retreated a bit as he held the torch out to me. "Here you go, Princess."

I took the outstretched torch, relieved. "Thanks for the light. It's a bit creepy in here."

Zane laughed at the expression on my face. "I can't imagine why. The tomb of the most ancient and evil of all vampires? Not nearly as scary as Remy at a shoe sale."

I gave him a wry smile and held the torch up to get a better look around. The walls were smooth, the room narrow enough to be well-lit by my torch but long enough that the far end lurked in shadows. The ceiling was low, with lotus columns between the carved-out floor and the ton of rock above our heads.

The tomb was empty save for some rat droppings in the corner and a few heaps of scattered, rotted fabric. Like every other Old Kingdom tomb, it had been ransacked millennia ago.

"It's odd," I said, stepping forward and staring around me. "Most funerary dwellings in the Old Kingdom were either pyramids or mastabas. Your queen doesn't seem like the type to want to be hidden away in the middle of nowhere in a cliff-face tomb." I shot him a questioning look.

Ever easygoing, Zane shrugged carelessly, his arms crossed in a stance of boredom. "Nitocris decided to end her mortal reign with a bit of a bang. Killing all of your closest advisors and then destroying your mortal form doesn't exactly earn you legions of followers. She had a few priests who were devoted enough to entomb her here."

I continued my hesitant exploration of the room. A large blocky shape—a sarcophagus, I assumed—dominated the shadowy far end, and I decided to leave exploring that for later, concentrating on the wall paintings instead. "They must have liked her a lot if they came to decorate the place ahead of time."

"They didn't. Most of the tomb paintings were done after Nitocris was entombed and had risen again."

The hairs on my neck prickled. *Spooky.* I stared at the large figure painted on the column in front of me. It was your typical Egyptian tomb mural, a woman in a sideways pose, her hands upraised. Closer inspection revealed a black cloak flowing down the woman's back. Her upraised hands were covered in red, which I assumed was blood. "That's odd." I pointed at the woman's cloak. "I've never seen that in all the archaeology texts I've studied."

"There's a lot down here you won't see in books, Princess. Now finish your exploring so we can leave already." His tone was curt.

I turned in surprise and looked at him. "Don't tell me this place gives you the willies, too?" It made me feel a bit better to know I wasn't the only one freaked out.

"Not exactly," he said dryly. "More along the line of bad memories."

"Do I want to ask?"

"Probably not." He leaned against one of the beautifully painted pillars and gave me a lazy look. "So find what you need and let's leave."

I gave him a one-finger salute and moved to the next series of pictures. More Egyptian scenes of the Afterlife, sprinkled with some rather disturbing elements. I turned away from a depiction of Nitocris holding aloft the severed head of an enemy and looked back at Zane. "I'm not going to find anything here, am I?"

"Depends on what you're looking for."

"Thanks for the cryptic answer. You know exactly what I'm looking for: clues to where this damn halo might be."

He shrugged his shoulders and lit up a cigarette. "Don't ask me. I'm just here to enjoy the scenery and to make sure that you pass our lovely prize over to the queen." His eyes rested on my breasts, outlined by the sweaty black T-shirt that clung to me. "Nice scenery, by the way."

"Fuck off. When I'm interested, you'll know." I turned away from him so he couldn't see the hardening of my nipples. Oh God, was I interested. One more of those sexy, full-lipped smiles, and I'd be lost. *Be strong*, I reminded myself. *Be strong for Noah*.

If I didn't have sex for another day, would I spontaneously combust? It was starting to feel that way; I was way overdue.

My torch sputtered and flickered, reminding me that I didn't have time to study the paintings at my leisure. I fumbled for the disposable camera hidden in my pocket, clicking the flash on and holding it up to the walls.

Snap.

A bright flare of light illuminated the tomb, momentarily blinding me. Spots swimming in front of my eyes, I moved to the next section of wall and took another picture.

Zane hissed in distress. "Woman, are you trying to blind me?"

He was shielding his eyes with the thick sleeve of his jacket, a scowl on his pale face. Perversely, I moved to the other side of the tomb, taking several photos without really paying attention to what I was capturing. "Quit being such a baby, vampire. As much as I love to spend time in your company, I'm taking pictures so we can get out of here quickly."

Snap, snap, snap. I flitted around the tomb, taking

photos with haste. Just when I was reaching the end of the film, I heard a moaning gurgle from behind me. Irritated that Zane was trying to make me feel guilty, I shoved the camera back in my pocket. "Would you cut it out? That's really getting on my nerves."

Zane grabbed me by the arm, causing me to drop my torch, and began dragging me away from the mural I had just taken a picture of. "That wasn't me," he murmured in my ear. "And we need to leave. Now."

A chill shivered down my spine and I froze up. "If that wasn't you—"

The moan sounded again, filling the tomb. "What is that?" I whispered, clutching Zane's upper arm. My other hand fumbled for one of the guns, then paused. Which one should I use? The wrong one would be useless and might get us killed—or worse.

A shuffling noise came from the far end of the tomb. Red eyes blinked into the darkness, then focused on me.

Zane cursed, and he tensed under my hand. "I should have guessed."

"Guessed what?" I slid behind him, peeking out from around his shoulder.

His sigh sounded more exasperated than anything else. "That she'd have one incubating down here."

"One what?" It couldn't be the answer that popped into my mind. Surely not. Surely we weren't that unlucky.

A hiss in the darkness, and the creature took a few steps forward into the light cast by the torch that now flickered on the ground.

It was a man or a Serim. Once. Red, unholy eyes

glared into the thick blackness, and the sound of sniffing filled the silence. Then his eyes focused on me. "Blood," the man growled, his mouth opening to reveal an enormous set of white fangs.

Yikes!

I slid a shaking hand under my shirt, reaching for the vamp derringer. Before I could whip the gun out of its holster, Zane was stepping forward, arms spread wide in a protective gesture as he blocked me from the creature's view. "That one belongs to me, friend," Zane said, his voice taking on an urbane, smooth quality that I was learning to recognize as his "charmer" voice. "You'll have to look elsewhere for your first meal."

First meal? My mind flashed back to Zane's previous comment about incubating, and it hit me like a ton of bricks. The red-eyed monster was a newly made vampire, and he was hungry as hell and looking to me for dinner.

I slid the derringer into my hand and cocked it. The click echoed in the silence, but neither vampire turned to look at me. They were locked in a showdown, circling each other like a fanged version of *West Side Story.*

Zane's eyes flared red and he bared his fangs. "She is *mine,*" he repeated.

At that moment, the torch sputtered and went out, leaving me in darkness save for the red eyes that reminded me that I was alone in a tomb with two vampires, one of which was very, very hungry.

The stupid Itch was aroused by the fact that the two men were fighting over me, and my body throbbed with a mixture of fear and excitement. Would Zane win? What would happen if he didn't?

I backed up against the wall, gun clutched in my hand as I waited.

One set of red eyes leapt at the other, then there was a terrible orgy of sounds as the two vampires launched into an epic fight in the dark. Snarling, hissing, and the sound of flesh tearing filled the air. I cringed with each new sound, wondering if Zane was winning, or if I'd have to run for my life. The hot tang of blood filled me with fear, and I clutched the gun with shaking fingers, hoping I wouldn't have to shoot.

After a few tense minutes there was a cry of pain and the sound of fabric tearing, and the next thing I knew, rough hands were grabbing me by the arms.

It was now or never—I closed my eyes and pulled the trigger.

Chapter Twenty

The boom was deafening, and the explosion of light illuminated a bloody and battle-torn Zane.

Whom I'd just shot.

"Zane," I cried as he began to curse long and fluently.

The gun was wrestled out of my hand. "Where did you get this?" His angry voice pounded in my ear, and I shrank against the tomb wall.

"Remy gave it to me."

"You've nearly shot my hand off," he said, barely leashed fury in his voice.

I bit my lip. "I wasn't sure if it was you or not. How was I supposed to know?"

"You could have fucking asked! How many shots are in this ridiculous little gun?"

"Um, two."

Zane stormed away, his footsteps echoing in the silence, punctuated by a faint groan from the vampire he'd just defeated. There was another click, and another gunshot rocked the tomb.

The moaning stopped.

"Our friend's taken care of now," Zane said, his voice cold.

A shudder racked through me and I slid along the wall, frightened of what Zane might do to me, trying to feel my way to the exit. My fingers discovered air—the doorway. I crouched low and scrambled back through the long tunnel, panting with fear.

The wind cooled my clammy, sticky face as I emerged on trembling legs. The camels whuffed at the sight of me and I ran straight for the first mount in full-blown panic mode. Untying him, I slapped his rump to send him off into the desert, stranding Zane out here. All I wanted was to get away from angry vampires, friend or foe.

I managed to shimmy up into my kneeling camel's saddle and slapped at the creature's rump. The beast tried to bite me, but when I slapped its rump again it began to trot away at a rapid pace.

I didn't start to breathe until my camel crested a dune and the tomb was out of sight. I checked to see if Zane was running after us, but the desert was empty. Part of me felt strangely disappointed that he wasn't bothering to pursue, but I quelled the feeling, concentrating on staying atop my camel. I'd find my way back to Cairo somehow.

Suddenly rough hands encircled my waist, and before I had the time to think, I was plucked off the camel's back and hoisted straight into the air. A scream tore from my throat and I struggled, totally disoriented and confused as to what was going on.

"Stop fidgeting," Zane admonished from above me. "You just about killed my hand with your damned gun, and my grip's not so good. It'll be your fault if I drop you on the sand, and that'll be a long, painful recovery."

I stilled in his arms, not quite willing to believe my senses. The smell of cigarettes and sand and another smell I couldn't quite place filled my nostrils. "Z-Zane?"

"Put your arms around me, Princess, and it'll make the flight a lot easier on both of us." His voice sounded strained.

I turned over to wrap my arms around his neck, and wonder and disbelief struck me as I watched his long, beautiful ebony wings flap in the night sky—wings that stretched from Zane's corded, muscular back.

"Your trench coat," I murmured, realizing that my hands were knotted against his bare skin and not his leather trench coat. "It's gone."

"Lost it in the fight," he agreed, his gaze focused on the ground below us. "Do me a favor and save the small talk for later, all right? I'm not in the mood."

I huddled against his neck and watched his gorgeous wings flap above me. *Wings. All this time, and he never told me. This is what he traded for when he became a vampire.*

It was a sobering thought, one that kept me quiet until we reached the hotel several hours later, when dawn was beginning to color the skies with pink.

Zane landed on the roof with a slight thump and released me. "Do you still have your burqa?" he asked, his massive wings folding against his back like a neat, black-feathered cloak. His face was shuttered as he stared at me, his eyes cold slits.

"I lost it in the desert," I said, feeling slightly ashamed. Why the hell did I feel guilty? I had no reason to, but somehow he managed to make me feel like a misbehaving child.

He strode past me and headed for the door that led down into the hotel, pulled it open, and gestured for me to enter before him.

I stepped past him and descended the utility stairs.

"If we meet anyone on the way to your room, I want you to distract them, understand me?" His dark eyes blazed with anger. Definitely furious at me.

I nodded in silence and headed for our hall.

A busboy pushed a room service cart down the hall as we turned the final corner to our rooms, and I froze at the sight of him.

He stilled at the sight of me as well, noticing my stained, sweaty T-shirt and the blood on my shorts. (Zane's blood, not mine.)

Zane coughed behind me, reminding me of my task, and I strode forward toward the busboy.

"Hi, there," I said, sidling up to the cart and leaning over it to smile at him. "You must be room service. What've you got for me?"

His jaw dropped slightly as I leaned forward, and his eyes focused on my double-Ds. "M-miss Brighton," he stammered. "It is a pleasure to meet you."

I frowned. "How do you know my name?"

"We all know your name and your room number, Miss Brighton. Everyone in the hotel does." He continued to stare at my breasts, a look of wonder on his face.

I was getting a little turned on by the attention, thanks to the Itch. I slipped an arm around his neck and pressed myself against his torso. It felt so good to my starved body that I wanted to cry, but I forced myself to remain on-task. "Were you coming up to visit me?" My voice dropped an octave, husky and seductive.

Good and distracted, the busboy planted his hands on my behind and rubbed it, his eyes wide and unbelieving. "You smell like camels, Miss Brighton," he whispered, dipping his face down for a kiss.

I averted my mouth at the last moment, noticing his very bad teeth and even worse breath. "Is that going to be a problem?"

"No, miss," he said reverently, and buried his face in my cleavage.

Zane stalked past me down the hall and turned the knob to my room, shutting the door behind him.

The busboy bit the side of my breast, jerking my attention back to him with a gasp. The feeling was pleasurable, and I could tell from the look on his face that he was willing to go at it right here, right now in the middle of the hallway.

My body wanted it *badly*, but the rest of me was repelled. I pried him off my breasts and forced him to look into my eyes. "What's your name, honey?"

"Kasib, miss."

"Well, Kasib," I said, sliding one of the hot breakfast plates off his cart. "What time do you get off work?" I touched the tip of my finger in the pat of butter sliding off a pancake and licked it suggestively.

His jaw dropped at what I was implying, and I must admit, it sent a thrill straight through me as well. The fact that I had so much power over a man went straight to my head at times. No wonder Remy was such a slut.

Kasib began to stammer. "I . . . I . . . I am free after seven tonight, miss."

Making a note to be long gone before then, I smiled seductively. "Come to my room then, Kasib, and we'll finish what we started here."

"Yes, miss!" He adjusted his crotch and raced back down the hallway with his cart.

I ran to my room, heading straight for Zane, who was seated on the far side of the bed, bent over. His injured hand was splayed out before him, his good one clutching his wrist.

"Oh my God," I said, dropping beside him as I stared at his injuries. Shriveled and blackened as if scorched in a fire, his fingers were curled into his palm against the pain. The skin of his hand was charred black and looked like it had been melted by intense heat. Blisters covered every inch of skin up to his elbow.

"My gun did that?" I put my fist to my mouth and bit down hard, determined not to cry. "Oh Zane, I'm so sorry. I didn't mean to."

"I know you didn't," he said, his voice tight with pain as he slowly uncurled his fingers. "Get me something to wrap this up."

I quickly brought him a cool, wet towel, and he carefully wrapped it around his hand. As he did, I caught a glimpse of a small tattoo—a symbol I had never seen before—on his inner wrist. An angelic symbol, just like Noah had. It was a stark reminder of what he had once been.

"I'm so sorry that I shot you," I apologized again. "Remy told me to use the gun if I got into trouble and I, uh, jumped the gun. No pun intended."

He snorted. "Count on Remy to buy an outdated gun with terrible accuracy and only two shots. No doubt it was stylish, or something idiotic like that."

"Pink," I agreed, feeling like a moron. "I didn't know it was that bad of a gun."

"All guns are shit in the wrong hands."

I couldn't disagree. "Will it heal?"

He gave me a wry look, a return to the old, familiar Zane. "In about two to three days; faster if I get a few good feedings in to rejuvenate my system." He cast a meaningful look at me.

Desire shot through me and I swallowed hard. When he'd asked me a few hours ago, I'd turned him down. But I'd seen some aspects of Zane recently that confused me, and some that charmed me, as well. He was human underneath his tough vampire exterior, underneath the wings. He'd saved me, kept me safe when he could have abandoned me. He'd carried me back to Cairo with an injured hand, when he could have left me to wander in the desert.

Underneath it all was a man who I could have fallen in love with when I was human.

But things changed. I had changed. And he wasn't a man I could ever, ever fall in love with.

He was the enemy, an agent for the Queen of Vampires.

I sighed and moved away from him to try to ease the fierce longing throbbing through my body. My vision was hazy at the edges, my hands unsteady, and I knew it'd only get progressively worse as I continued to fight the Itch. "I can't, Zane."

"Your eyes are so blue," he said, catching my hand with his good one, pulling me back down close to him. "You must be in terrible distress."

A good, if old-fashioned, way to put it. My clothes were chafing my ultra-sensitive skin, and I had to resist the urge to fling them off and jump on him. "You're wounded, I'm dirty, and we're both worn out," I reasoned, trying to remain strong in the face of opposition.

His fingers skimmed my cheek, brushing away sand. "Liar. You don't get tired."

I looked into his eyes, seeing the rim of red slowly flaring into the black irises. He was interested, all right, wounded or not. I averted my eyes, my gaze landing on the black waterfall of feathers edging gracefully over the bed. "Your wings are so beautiful," I said, enthralled by the sight of them. "Can I touch them?"

His eyes flared red and he gave a jerky nod.

My hand stretched out, gingerly touching the feathers. The interior feathers were extremely soft and downy, the ones on the edges harder and longer. My fingers trailed over the smooth, shining fall with wonder. "They're incredible."

He remained silent, and I looked over at him. His eyes

were bloodred, watching my every move with unnerving intensity. His fangs grazed his lower lip, and his hands were curled into fists that shook ever so slightly.

"Don't," he said softly.

I pulled my hands away from his wings. "Does it hurt when I touch them?"

Zane's voice was a low growl. "If you touch them again, I'm going to throw you back on this bed, throw your legs over my shoulders, and fuck you. And not gently, like I want to. Because I won't be able to control myself."

The images flashed through my mind with breathtaking intensity. "Oh," I said, feeling a twinge of disappointment that he was so controlled. I clasped my hands on my lap. "You . . . you wanted them back?" I wasn't sure how to phrase my question. "The wings?"

"I fell for the love of a woman, just like every other Serim," he said, his hot eyes intent on me. "I left Heaven behind for her, and when she was taken from me, I had nothing left but an eternity without her." He looked away, and the room filled with silence. "When Nitocris offered, I took the chance, hoping for . . . well, never mind that. I was young and foolish, and I didn't know everything that her bargain entailed." He gave me the lopsided, self-incriminating grin that was becoming so familiar, and my heart flipped in my chest. "We all do things we regret at some point."

I had to have him. Vampire or not, enemy or not, I was drawn to his tortured soul. I wanted to pull him to my breast and make him forget all about her. I wanted to kiss him so hard that he'd never remember her and think of me. I wanted to be the only woman he thought about.

"Zane," I breathed, putting my hand on his knee and leaning into him. Mindful of his injured hand, I gently tilted him back on the bed, those marvelous wings tucked underneath him and almost out of sight. His few simple, sweet words had wormed into my heart, and I wondered if this was the real Zane, the one who hid behind the brash, laughing exterior.

It nearly drove me mad with desire.

I straddled him, pressing my hips against his erection and sliding my hands under his black shirt, wanting to feel his skin against mine.

"Zane," I murmured. "I can't hold out for much longer." I slid my wrist against his mouth, and felt his teeth scrape against it. "Use my blood to heal your hand."

"Are you sure?" His question was a warning, even as his lips nuzzled the soft skin of my inner wrist.

Hell no, I wasn't sure. My feelings for Zane conflicted with my loyalty to Noah, and I didn't know what I wanted—except that I wanted to climb on top of him and let him take me to the longest, slowest, hardest climax I'd ever had.

"You use me," I said, sliding my hand down his chest, "and I'll use you." His hips fit just right under my own, rubbing against the juncture of my thighs in the most sinful way.

His teeth broke the skin of my wrist, and he was unable to hold back any longer. I felt a soft, gentle pull as he sucked on my skin. Desire flared through me white-hot, and I moaned and rubbed my hips against his harder. His tongue moved against my wrist, and just the barest of sensations drove me wild.

"Zane," I begged, "I *want* you."

No response.

"I *need* you," I pleaded.

Still no response.

I pulled my wrist away and leaned in for a fierce kiss . . .

And a gentle snore came from his lips.

"What the—" I shook Zane slightly, in total disbelief that he'd fall asleep at such a crucial moment. As anger cleared my fog of passion, I realized that sunlight was streaming through the panes.

"*Goddamn* it! This no-daylight shit is pissing me *off*."

I stared at his beautiful face with longing. Something inside him was noble, even if he didn't like to show it, and that part of him called to me like nothing I'd ever felt before.

I finally hauled myself off him and headed for the bathroom and a cold shower. On the way, I grabbed the breakfast plate.

If I couldn't have the man, pancakes and bacon was the next best thing—right?

CHAPTER TWENTY-ONE

Several long, agonizing hours later, I sat with Remy in the hotel restaurant, clutching my coffee cup in shaking hands. "I don't know what to do with myself. My whole body aches; it feels like I've been beaten with a stick. I'm exhausted, frazzled, and tense, and I know it all has to do with the Itch."

Shrugging, Remy licked her fingertip and ran it along the empty baklava tray, catching a few crumbs and bringing them to her mouth. "I don't see what the big deal is. It's just sex."

"It's not just sex," I protested. The waiter came to refill our water glasses, and I whispered, "It's the principle of being enslaved to your loins." The waiter smiled at me, his eyes clearly interested, and my mouth began to water. I forced myself to avert my eyes and gulp the liquid down.

Remy shook her head. "Consider it self-preservation, then."

"What do you mean?"

"I mean you're on a one-way ticket to Hell if you keep this up." She paused, waiting for the waiter to leave.

He slid a napkin under my water glass, and I noticed

he had a room number written on there. Cute. Real cute. He bowed and left.

Remy leaned in. "So tell me, what do you think destroys a succubus?"

My Itch-induced squirming ceased immediately, and I stared at her. "Destroyed? Why are we talking about being destroyed?" This roller coaster of an Afterlife might suck, but that didn't mean I wanted it to be over.

Remy licked her fingertips languidly. "I've seen it happen two different ways. One," she flicked a finger up, admiring her shell-pink fingernail. "Both of your masters bite it. They go, you go. It's the rules of the game I'm afraid."

"Well, I don't plan on destroying Noah—we're on this whole sorry trip to save his ass. And since I don't know who my vamp master is, there's not much chance in destroying him."

"Oh, he's around, if I don't miss my guess. Vamps wouldn't miss out on the opportunity to have a succubus at their beck and call, trust me. Enough succubus blood, and even they get immunity to our powers—so I'm sure the queen's itching to get you back in hand." There was a note of pain in her voice, and she cleared her throat. "Anyhow, the second way for a Suck to die is by starvation."

"You mean . . . ?"

She nodded, all seriousness. "You're just hurting yourself with this hold-out, kiddo. If you plan on seeing this abstinence thing through, it's all downhill from here. Your hair will get dull and fall out, your skin will wrinkle up, and you'll crack under the pressure. Pretty soon your body's going to be in intense pain, too, if I don't miss my guess."

My throat went dry. "How . . . how long does that take?"

"A couple of weeks," Remy said.

A few weeks? I cringed at the thought. I was going stark, raving nuts after being overdue a day and a half. "I'd go mad," I admitted, hating myself for conceding to the Itch.

"Yeah, that's usually one of the first things to happen," Remy agreed cheerfully.

So I was truly trapped in this lifestyle for *eternity*. I forced my shaking fingers around my coffee cup and tried to breathe like a normal woman. "How long have you gone without?"

"Five days," Remy said flatly. "Not by choice, and trust me when I say it's not something you want to go through."

Numb with misery, I felt unable to focus my brain. "I miss Noah." I thought of his warm smile and his protectiveness of me. His ass that wouldn't quit. "I didn't realize how good I had it with him. So right now basically I'm stuck with Zane, then."

She snorted at me. "Not hardly, girl. If I were you, I'd avoid the fanged persuasion and find yourself a little piece of Egyptian tail. Like this one." She pushed the napkin with the phone number toward me. "Or Stan. He's damn good in the sack, and I'm not the jealous type. You're welcome to borrow him for a few hours."

The thought left me slightly nauseous. "I'll pass, thanks. Where is he anyhow?"

Remy waggled her eyebrows. "He's catching up on some much-needed rest."

I raised a hand in the air. "Spare me the details, thanks."

She lifted her coffee mug with a grin. "The offer's on the table if you want it, and I'd recommend this afternoon." Remy sipped, then continued. "But since I'm sure you won't take me up on it, what do you plan to do this afternoon to kill some time?"

The first real enthusiasm I'd felt for this excursion bubbled over. "My boss at the museum mentioned that the Museum of Antiquities here has one of the best Old Kingdom collections to be found. She suggested that we look here for stuff about Queen Nitocris." My hands clasped together eagerly. "I can't wait to go spend the day there among the treasures. I thought I'd head there after I picked up my film."

Remy looked like I'd suggested going to the dentist. "Riiiight. Boy, that sure sounds like fun." She checked her watch. "Wow, is it noon already? I—"

I laughed. "Nobody said you have to come with me, Remy. I don't mind going by myself."

Relief showed on her face. "Are you sure? With those slavers you were telling me about . . ."

"That's why I've got this." I reached into the tote bag at my side and pulled out a new black burqa I'd bribed a bellhop into buying for me. Boobs were sometimes a good thing. "This is the best disguise a girl could ask for."

Remy raised her coffee mug. "Cheers to that, then."

I clinked my mug against hers, my smile forced. "So what are you going to do while I'm gone?"

A wicked smile curved her lips. "I think I'll see if Stan's awake."

"We'll take a quick break before proceeding to the next portion of our tour, the Amarna period and Akhenaten, the heretic king." The tour guide's voice was monotone with boredom.

I dog-eared the page on my guidebook and sat on a nearby bench. No one sat next to me. I expected as much; the museum was filled with American and Canadian tourists, all of whom gave me a wide berth at the sight of my burqa.

It was nice to fade back to invisibility, even if just for an afternoon.

While the tourists milled around me, I reached into my purse and pulled out my newly developed photos and began flipping through them.

The images from the tomb were backlit with blackness, courtesy of the cheap flash camera. I stared at the painted figures in each photo, wondering if I had missed a clue. There were several of what must have been Nitocris, her hands upraised to the heavens. Her face looked just like every other Egyptian queen, but I now recognized her black cloak as a stylized image of wings. The next photo was a larger shot of the queen's wig-covered head, the Double Crown and Uraeus on her brow. Her thin mouth curved up in a half smile, which creeped me out a little. In the other pictures she was unsmiling and grim. The elongated hands were raised to the sun, and in the center of the sun there was a faded symbol that reminded me of the one on Noah's wrist. The angelic alphabet—how curious.

"If everyone is ready, we can proceed to the next room," the tour guide announced.

I slid the eerie smiling photo into my guidebook and quickly pocketed the rest of them, nearly tripping on my long burqa as I rushed to join the group.

The tour guide cleared her throat. "Akhenaten was the most hated pharaoh in all of Egypt. He took the happily polytheistic society and tried to convert everyone to the religion of the one god, the Aten, who was symbolized by the sun."

The docent launched into a long, droned spiel about Akhenaten's reign in the New Kingdom. It was amazing how one person could make an interesting subject so damn dull. Restless and bored with her presentation, I flipped through my guidebook, looking for objects of interest. I wanted to get away from the New Kingdom stuff and head to the second floor, where the Old Kingdom artifacts were kept.

I looped around the tour group to the back of the room, browsing through the artifacts. The sun was due to set soon, and I was anxious to get back to the hotel. Just the thought of Zane sleeping in my bed made my breath catch, and I fanned myself with the guidebook. Idly, I paused near a broken, wigless bust and glanced down at the plaquard. Nefertiti. I'd never been a big fan of hers; she looked cold and arrogant in all of the sculptures and paintings I'd seen, and this one was certainly no different. The beautifully sculpted lips were curved at the edges in a thin, almost bitter smile.

I paused. I'd seen that look somewhere before. Crouching low, I circled the glass case and peered at the bust from all angles. Where had I seen that regal, go-to-Hell look before?

". . . built a temple to the one god, the Aten," the docent droned.

Something clicked in my mind.

I whipped out the photo tucked into my guidebook and stared at the picture. On a hunch, I headed to the back of the exhibit, looking for tomb paintings from the Amarna period. Sure enough, there was one along the wall, and I held up the photo next to a picture of the Akhenaten's queen.

Hands upraised, she appeared to be supplicating, a thick black cloak covering the shoulders of her followers.

Wings.

"Of *course*," I muttered to myself, as I made my way out of the crowded museum. "The first church wasn't a church to God at all, but Nitocris's worming her way back into Egyptian history."

This certainly threw a kink into things. I raced out of the building and headed for the nearest taxi, burqa flying.

I needed to talk to Zane.

◦ ◦ ◦

"It's Amarna!" I entered into my hotel room with a triumphant smile, a stack of travel brochures clutched in my free hand, burqa tucked under my arm. "I figured it out."

Zane sat up in my bed and rubbed his face with his good hand, his hair tousled and falling over his forehead. His bad hand looked nearly healed, the skin merely reddened now. He gave me a sleepy look, a hint of red peeping out from heavy-lidded eyes. "Evening, Jackie. You're in a good mood."

His voice caused me to come to a screeching halt. My muscles seized up at the sight of him looking so sexy in my bed, and I had difficulty breathing. The air around me became heavy and uncomfortable, and I moved as if in a fog. "Zane," I breathed, my voice taking on a seductive timbre that caused his eyes to flick bright red with interest.

"Itch bothering you much?" He kept his voice light, though his eyes blazed red, betraying his interest. I could see the gleam of fangs against his lips.

"Not at all," I lied, slinking over to the bed and staring down at him. Blood pounded in my ears. "I'm not sleeping with you." My hands trembled from the sheer force of my body's response to his proximity. It was taking all my effort just to remain upright.

Zane stood and came to my side. He took the brochures from my clenched hand and tossed the burqa into a nearby chair. "You're torturing yourself over nothing, Jackie. Don't you realize that?" His hand went to my shoulders and he began to knead the tense flesh at the base of my neck.

Weak at his touch, I sat on the bed, my head rolling forward to allow him free access. "Sex is not 'nothing' to me. And I don't like being forced into doing anything."

"Don't do it because you have to, then. Do it because you *want* to." His fingers trailed over the sensitive flesh of my neck, and I nearly came unglued at the gentle touch. "I like you; you like me. What's wrong with sating our mutual urges?"

"Everything. It's all messed up."

His hand slid away from my neck. "Do you want me to find you someone to take care of your needs? I guarantee any sane man would be willing." His voice was solicitous, neutral.

I pulled my legs up and hugged them against my chest, feeling miserable at the desire that raged through my body. "I don't want a stranger."

"Noah, then?" His voice was decidedly cold.

I glanced over at Zane in surprise and saw anger in his eyes. He was jealous of Noah? The thought was baffling.

Zane abruptly turned. I watched the sweep of his wings as he walked away, graceful and beautiful, so at odds with my conceptions of vampires. He picked up his trench coat and shrugged it onto his back, covering his wings and heading for the door.

"Wait," I said, getting up and following him. "What's wrong with you?"

He opened the door, ignoring me.

I grabbed it and slammed it shut before he could leave. "What's eating you? *I'm* the one with the compulsion."

Zane's red glare met my blue one. "Do you think I don't care about your feelings?"

I hadn't given it much thought, to be honest. He was one of the bad guys, right? "I didn't . . ."

"Didn't what?"

In agony at this point, I just grabbed him by the front of his shirt. "I'm tired of all this crap." My mouth planted on top of his, and flashes of light sparked in my brain.

Oh *yes*. This was nice. His mouth moved under mine, tasting my lips, his tongue touching my own.

Then he pulled away from me, prying my hands off him. "No, Jackie."

"What?" I tried to wrap my hands in his hair.

He shook his head. "I don't want this."

I fell back a little, staring up at him in confusion. "Your eyes are red and you kissed me back. How can you say that you don't want this?"

"I want you willing, Jackie. I don't want it to just be the product of the Itch. I want you to be with me because you"—he touched my breastbone and gave me a soft smile—"want to be with me. Not because you feel compelled to sate an urge with the closest man around."

The man was impossible. Frustrated, I clenched my fists. "I don't know *what* I feel anymore, okay? None of this is my choosing. Do you think I really want to be stuck in a hotel room in Egypt, hoping that I can steal some halo back from an archaeologica! site before the Queen of Vampires kills a fallen angel? Because you know, it's really not high on my list of things to do before I die."

I jerked away from him and gave him a bitter smile. "Oh, that's right. I can't die, can I? I'm stuck like this forever. So pardon me for trying to make a go of things. I sucked at relationships in my normal life. I'm not surprised that they're not any easier now."

I collapsed on the edge of the bed, burying my head in my hands. "Oh lord, what is *wrong* with me?" Tears welled up as I huddled on the edge of the bed, feeling miserable, alone, and stupid.

A strong hand smoothed my hair back, and I felt the mattress give as Zane sat next to me. Heat traveled over my skin at the touch.

"Jackie," he said, and his fingers tilted my face up to meet his. "I'm sorry."

"For what?"

Fingers stroked gently down my cheek. "For forgetting that you are human, or were not too long ago. This is a lot for you to take in, isn't it?"

I managed a watery smile. "You have no idea."

He leaned in and brushed his lips against mine. A thrill shot through me at the touch, then I froze as I felt his fangs brush against the soft skin of my lips. "So . . . uh . . . can you . . . ?"

Zane gave me a wicked grin full of long, sharp teeth. "We do it better than anybody else, my dear. Shall I show you?"

My muscles would never unknot at this point. *"Please."*

His coat slid off his shoulders, and the next thing I

knew, dark wings were enfolding me, brushing against my body. "Mind if I undress you?"

"No," I breathed, unable to move. His hands slid over my shoulders, caressing my skin as if it were fragile. He peeled my T-shirt off and tossed it on the floor, his eyes resting on the swell of my breasts encased in the satin and lace bra.

"So beautiful," Zane murmured, his hand skimming along my flesh and leaving a trail of fire behind.

"It comes with the job," I said, my hands sliding to his T-shirt and seeking the hot skin underneath. "I was nothing special before."

"You have *always* been special." Before I could wonder at his words, his mouth preyed upon mine and all coherent thought escaped me.

When his mouth pulled away, I gave a little whimper of distress. Two seconds later I was flat on my back on the bed, and the distress was replaced by the thrill that shot through my body as I looked up to see my lover looming over me, his wings spread as he wrestled out of his T-shirt and tossed it onto the ground. It fluttered to the floor in one long band of fabric, specially cut to accommodate his wings.

Zane's chest was pale but exquisitely muscled, and my hands reached up to touch that marvelous flesh once more. Within moments his pants were gone as well, and Zane stood before me, as naked as when he fell from Heaven. No chest hair marred the smooth perfection of his flesh, no tan lines disturbed the cool marble of his skin. The sight of his erection surprised me for some reason, large and thick and ready, and I felt my own body's response at the sight of it.

Then his skin was pressing against my own as he covered me on the bed, his mouth touching my neck, my throat, my breasts, his teeth nipping at my flesh between kisses. "Your body is delicious, Jackie."

I felt the scrape of his fangs against my nipple, still covered by the thin fabric of my bra, then gasped as his mouth closed over the tight peak, sucking and licking through the fabric. A moan escaped me and I clutched at him, my eyes closed as the sensation washed over me. My frantic hand reached for his cock, only to be stopped midway.

"No, Jackie." Zane pressed a kiss to the soaked tip of my bra. "Let me love you. Just relax." He pulled my hands over my head in a submissive pose, stretching me across the bed and making my breasts rise against his cheek. "Can you keep your hands there for me, or shall I get a rope?"

"I'll behave," I promised, my breath escaping in sharp little pants as I obligingly clasped my hands together.

He chuckled against my flesh, his mouth skimming against my bra again. "Somehow I doubt that."

His teeth ripped into my bra, shredding the flimsy material just beneath the little pink bow between my breasts. The fabric fell open, exposing more of my breast, and within a moment both of them lay open to the air, nipples puckered, as Zane looked down hungrily. "You have the most *amazing* breasts." His mouth fastened on the tip of one once more, tongue swirling against the sensitive nipple.

I squirmed underneath him, unable to remain silent or passive. The feelings coursing through me were too strong, too violent. My fingers tangled in his hair and I hauled his face to mine for a passionate kiss, my clothed hips bucking against his hardness, suggesting to him that I didn't want slow or sweet. I wanted hot and fast and *now*.

Zane pulled away, looming over me and shaking his head. "Didn't I say 'no hands'? Could it be that you want to be tied up, after all?" The cascade of black wings shuddered as he moved, and I watched in fascination as he went to my suitcase and began rummaging through it.

I crawled over to the edge of the bed, resisting the urge to shimmy out of my shorts and get totally naked. "We're not done, are we? Tell me we're not done." My hands slid down my body encouragingly.

He looked over at me on the bed, and his wings gave a tense shudder again. "No, not done," he said, his voice hoarse. "Lie back on the bed, Jackie." He wrapped a silk scarf around his forearm, his eyes glued to me.

"I will if you'll kiss me again," I said, sitting up and cupping my breasts suggestively.

I was flat on my back again within seconds, of course. Zane's chest pressed against mine, his flat abdomen scraping against my hard nipples. It felt so good to have his weight on top of mine.

His fingers linked in mine, guiding my hand up to the

railing of the bed and pinning it there. "Do you trust me, Jackie?"

I looked into his blazing red eyes, searching for an indication that he was going to screw me over, but the only thing I could see was him wanting to screw *me*, just as badly as I wanted him. And I did trust him. Zane the arrogant jerk at the club was a very different man than the Zane I'd gotten to know.

"I trust you," I said, raising my head and biting at his lower lip.

His eyes darkened and he caught my mouth in a kiss, sucking on my tongue. I winced when his sharp incisors scraped against my tongue and I tasted blood, but that only increased the excitement and I pressed my mouth harder against his, our teeth clashing. He tied my first hand to the bedpost, and I obediently laid my other against the railing so he could tie it as well.

I tested my bonds, shivering with anticipation and hesitation, rolled in with fiery desire. My body was so hot it felt as if the sheets were going to melt. I closed my eyes and leaned my head against the headboard, relishing the feelings that were coursing over me.

I felt Zane's mouth against the button of my shorts, and he ripped the fabric with his sharp teeth. Then his mouth was on my belly button, licking and sucking the tender skin.

My hips rose to him, pushing against him suggestively. Zane chuckled against my damp skin and grazed his fangs down my flesh, sending desire pulsing through my body. Large, strong hands slid my shorts down my legs and I lifted each one to help, my efforts rewarded with a scorching kiss pressed to my inner thigh.

Nothing covered my skin now but a tiny pair of panties and the cool sweep of his wings.

His teeth nipped at my hipbones, the sharp scrape reminding me of his true nature. "Any regrets yet, Jackie?" Zane's husky voice had a note of clinical detachment to it, as if he were holding back. "Say the word and we'll quit now—because if we go any further, I'm not going to be able to stop."

He paused to press soft, fluttery kisses across my flat belly. "If you tell me no, I'll walk away right now. But if you don't, I'm going to sink my teeth"—he nipped lower, his mouth grazing the underwear covering the curls at the juncture of my thighs—"into your sweet flesh, and then I'm going to spread your legs and sink my cock between them."

He lifted my legs wide into the air, laying me out before him, open and exposed. My ribbon of underwear was a pitiful barrier against the blazing heat of his body. "So tell me now, Jackie, what you want." His teeth scraped against the triangle of silk.

His words started a fire deep inside my belly and I clenched my thighs, tightening them around his face, letting him know he was exactly where I wanted him.

He groaned against my hot flesh, then he gently spred my legs again. "I won't make you do anything you don't want to do, Jackie. Ever."

"I want to do this," I finally admitted, squirming in his hands.

His hands gripped my damp panties, pulling them taut against my skin, outlining my most sensitive parts. His tongue stroked my nub through the material, hard—

And I came off the bed with the force of my orgasm.

Before my body even unclenched in relief, Zane ripped my panties off, the head of his cock thrust into my tingling flesh, and the world shattered again.

Bliss swam through me and I wrapped my legs around his waist, careful of the wings that shuddered above us like a dark canopy. Zane ground his hips against mine and I felt pleasure rise again, the tension building as he slowly began to piston me.

My eyes slid open to watch him over me, my hands clenched in helpless fists in the bonds that were so very exciting and not at all frightening. As he stroked into me Zane leaned forward, his lips almost touching one of my breasts as they bounced from the force of his pumping. I arched my back, teasing my nipple against his lips.

His hands slid along my back, arching me up higher against his mouth, and I felt like a cat being stroked. Zane's mouth closed around my nipple and sucked hard, sending a bolt of startled pleasure through my body. My soft cry turned into a surprised gasp when I felt his fangs break through the skin, and a sear of pain mingled with the pleasure as he began to suck.

It was the most erotic thing I'd ever felt, having him suck at my breast as he drove into me relentlessly, and my third orgasm rolled hard over my body. Zane's body clenched hard over mine, and I felt the hot spill of his seed deep inside me as he reached his own climax with a groan.

My mind spinning with delirious pleasure, I looked at Zane, his mouth still fastened to my breast. When my eyes met his and I watched him suck, his tongue rasping against my sensitive nipple, it didn't disgust or revolt me. A sleepy smile slid over my face.

He lifted his face and grinned at me. "What's that look for?"

I yawned, flexing my hands in the bonds. "Just that I didn't expect this. Sleeping with a vampire and all." I blinked a few times, feeling exhausted. My body must have been tired from the constant stress of repressing the Itch. I was glad I wouldn't have to worry about that anymore.

"I wonder," I mused, replete.

"Wonder what?" Zane slid up the bed to press a kiss on my mouth.

Momentarily distracted, it took a moment for my thoughts to reschedule themselves. "I wonder why I was chosen. Out of all the girls in New City—heck, in the world—someone picked *me* to turn to the dark side. Or whatever you call it."

Zane chuckled and propped up on one elbow, regarding me. "Why do you say that?"

I tried to shrug, but the scarves binding my wrists prevented it. "I looked like a dork. I was dumpy, I had these huge, thick glasses, and I worked in a museum. Nothing that I'd think would attract a vampire."

His hand slid down my naked torso, stroking my skin, a warm reminder of what we'd just shared. "Maybe . . . maybe he liked girls with glasses. Maybe he liked your innocence." He brushed a sweaty red lock off my forehead. "Maybe he saw the potential inside of you and thought you deserved more than wasting away in a bland mortal life."

How very romanticized. "Or maybe I just looked like an easy, desperate lay."

"And maybe you looked really cute with a bean burrito hanging out of your mouth."

My brow wrinkled. "What are you talking about?"

Zane just smiled, waiting, and it took a minute before it clicked. "That was you at the mall?" I said, incredulous. How long had he been following me? "You must be really hard up for a date."

He laughed. "You're amazing, you know that?"

"Yeah, that's what I hear," I agreed, yawning again. I couldn't seem to keep my eyes open.

"I hope you can look past my nature to see the real me someday, Jackie." His finger traced my jawline softly.

I kinda liked the Zane I'd seen so far, despite my first impressions. I leaned into his touch sleepily, my thoughts becoming disjointed. "You're not like the other vampires."

"No, I'm not."

All this talk of vampires reminded me of my daunting task. I sighed, sadness overwhelming me for a moment. "I don't know if I can do it, Zane. I don't know if I can give her that halo. It'll be really bad if she gets it, won't it?"

His thumb rubbed against my lips. "Yeah." There was a long pause in which neither of us said anything. Then Zane leaned in and kissed my mouth. "I won't make you do anything you don't want to do, Jackie. Ever. Remember that."

My eyes slid shut again, and my last conscious thought was that I should have asked him to untie me.

CHAPTER TWENTY-TWO

*H*oly shit, I'm asleep.

At least, I was pretty sure I was asleep. Since I hadn't gone to sleep in at least a week, the concept was a difficult one.

It wasn't a normal sleep, but I must have had a few moments of true REM action because the scene in my dream wasn't the one I'd just left.

Zane stood over the bed in my dream, shrugging on his jacket. He was fully clothed again, much to my disappointment—the man had a sweet body—but his hair was still tousled from sex, his mouth still as thrillingly moist as when I'd last kissed it. His eyes had cooled back to their normal dark shade, and as I watched, he stuffed my gun into his waistband.

That made my dream-self pause. What was he doing with my gun? The blue one?

He stared down at the bed, remorse flicking across his face. "Sorry, Jackie. I imagine you'll be quite mad when you wake up." His hand reached down to brush my cheek.

Hell, I was already getting pretty steamed. Nobody had to wait for me to wake up.

Zane left, solicitously hung the "Do Not Disturb" sign on the doorknob, and shut the door behind him. To my surprise, my mind's-eye followed him as he walked down the hall of the hotel, whistling.

He paused outside of Remy's door and knocked, still whistling a cheerful little tune. He wiggled his fingers at the peephole, and then the door slid open.

It was Stan, his hair tousled, dressed only in pajama bottoms. He looked at Zane with irritation. "What do you want?"

The stolen derringer pointed at Stan's forehead, and the human froze. A cocky smile crossed Zane's face. "You're coming with me."

I struggled to wake up from the bizarre dream, not liking the avenue that this was turning down. But for some reason I couldn't rouse myself enough to return to consciousness. I was forced to watch helplessly as the scene unrolled before me.

Remy was at Stan's side, both of their eyes trained on the ridiculously small blue derringer. She cursed fluently, staring up at Zane with hatred. "Where did you get that gun?"

He cocked it, the heartbreakingly mischievous grin on his face tearing my soul into shreds. "I took it. Nice of you to arm your friend, Remy. The good thing about these guns is that they kill humans same as any other weapon, don't they?"

The mutinous look on her face told Zane everything he needed to know.

"What do you want?" Remy's voice was weary, her hand slowly reaching up.

"Uh uh, naughty succubus," Zane corrected, dragging Stan out of the hotel room, gun still trained on his forehead. "No touching. I'm not falling for your dream-tricks today."

Remy lunged, her hand brushing down his arm, and I tensed, wondering what would happen.

Nothing happened, except Zane sideswiped the worst of her lunge and she fell to the floor. His hand wrapped around Stan's throat and he lifted him in the air as Stan began to make choking noises. "Not nice, Remy. Now your little friend is going to suffer."

Remy stared up at him in a mix of hatred and shock. "I don't understand."

Zane grinned down at her. "Don't you?"

"Oh shit," she said, getting up off the floor. "You fucked her, didn't you? God, that girl is so stupid sometimes. You took her blood, too, didn't you? All so you could be immune to Suck powers. I should have guessed that you'd use her like that."

I should have guessed it, too.

Zane tsked, his hand tightening about Stan's throat. The human was turning an unbecoming shade of purple at this point. "That's not nice, Remy. What I do in my personal life is my own business, and I'd prefer if you didn't say unflattering things about Jackie."

He was defending me and betraying me at the same time? Part of me was flattered, but the horrified part of me squashed that thought down.

"I did it because the queen needs a halo, and I don't plan on forcing Jackie to do anything she doesn't want to do." The look in his eyes was possessive.

Oh no.

Remy smirked. "Then you're at an impasse, I'm afraid. I'm not going to do anything for you."

Even I could tell Remy was lying. Her eyes were glued to Stan's purple face.

Zane laughed and shook his head, giving Stan's limp body a little shake. "Won't you?"

Silence.

For about two seconds. Then Remy blurted, "Okay! Just stop hurting him!"

Zane let go of Stan's throat, and he clapped the human on the shoulder as he wheezed for breath. "Of course, Remy." The derringer wiggled against Stan's temple encouragingly. "But you two are coming with me."

"Where to?" Remy's voice was flat. She'd given up the argument by this point.

"I believe Jackie mentioned Amarna. It seems that she's all but found the halo for us." Again, the bladelike smile.

"Is she coming with us?"

He shook his head, the dark lock of hair falling over his brow. Even in villainy Zane was stunningly beautiful, and my heart broke all over again. "I'm afraid she's indisposed at the moment."

"If you've hurt her—"

Aww, how nice that Remy was finally concerned for me.

"Why would I hurt her?" Zane seemed puzzled. "She'll

understand what I'm doing, once she's had time to cool down." He gestured for Stan to walk forward. "Now come on—we've got a boat to catch. I've got people waiting on me."

That bastard! I recalled our conversation just before I'd nodded off into my unnatural sleep.

"I don't know if I can do it, Zane. I don't know if I can give her that halo. It'll be really bad if she gets it, won't it?"

His thumb rubbed against my lips. "Yeah." There was a long pause in which neither of us said anything. Then Zane kissed my mouth. "I won't make you do anything you don't want to do, Jackie. Ever."

In his own misguided way, Zane was saving me from a decision—and in doing so, destroying us all. I struggled again to awaken, but it was useless. I recognized the feeling of deep, unconscious sleep just moments before it swept over me, drowning out the rest of my vision.

I'm not sure when I woke up. It was more of a gradual return to consciousness, and my eyes fluttered open. My hands tingled in their bonds, and my head throbbed with an enormous headache that didn't help my mood any.

I tested my wrists. Jerking on the scarf only caused the material to cut into my skin. Damn it.

The dream was still spinning in my mind, fresh and ugly. Part of me wanted to think it was nothing more than a bizarre dream, but the realistic part of me put the pieces together. Succubi don't normally sleep, and the fact that my erstwhile lover was nowhere to be seen told me that I'd somehow glimpsed what was truly going on while I lay asleep.

The bastard just had to go and tie me up, didn't he? I jerked at my wrists again and winced when pain shot through my arms.

I pondered my options as I lay there, nude. Call for help? Wait it out? Chew my own wrists off?

"Heeelp!" I screamed at the top of my lungs. "I need help in room 214!"

After five minutes of screaming, my voice started to go hoarse. I was about to give up when I heard a hesitant knock at the door.

"Miss?"

Delighted, I jerked at my bonds again. "Yes! Please come help me! I'm stuck!" I tried to kick one of the blankets crumpled at my feet over my body, with little success.

The door opened and two bellhops entered, their eyes bugging out at the sight of me, naked and sprawled and tied down to the bed.

Uh oh. I was starting to rethink my plan. Probably not the smartest thing I'd ever done, I thought as I watched their eyes glaze over from startled to lustful. "Hi, guys," I said, trying to maintain a casual tone despite the fact that their eyes were fixed on my breasts. "Care to untie me?"

I watched them exchange a look, and my hope turned to fear. Those didn't look like the expressions of people who were going to help me. Both wore smiles that made my skin crawl and regarded me with slitted eyes.

The first one came closer, and I recognized him from my ill-fated trip down the hallway. Oh crap. It was the same busboy as before. Kasib trailed a hand across my stomach, and to my dismay, my skin began to burn with a feeling of desire.

I hated being a succubus sometimes.

Okay, most of the time.

"Look, buddy, you don't want to do that," I said, trying to keep my voice reasonable.

His friend looked hesitant, but the look in the eyes of the guy touching me didn't change. Drastic measures were going to be needed. The only question was, what would I do? I couldn't do anything special.

Or could I?

As he bent over—to kiss me, I'm sure—my leg reached up and whacked him square on the forehead. I felt my mind connect with his at the same moment that my big toe touched his brow, and his eyes rolled back in his head and he went down like a light as I sent him into dreamland.

I glared at the companion, who was staring at his downed friend in shocked horror. "He's going to be unconscious until I bring him back—and if you want that to happen, you'll untie me *now.*"

"Yes, madam." He hurried forward to undo my bonds.

Pleased, I began to plot out my next move. "Hurry it up," I demanded, "and tell me where I can rent a speedboat at this time of night."

CHAPTER TWENTY-THREE

The speedboat pulled up on the shore of the Nile, the sandy wasteland of Amarna glittering before us through the reeds of the Nile. As I spied the boats parked farther up the banks, I wondered what I was about to get into.

"Are you sure this is it?" I questioned my guide, who stood beside me in the small boat. Though a born and bred Egyptian with black hair and smiling eyes, he'd insisted that I call him "Smith." It was an alias, of course. What we were doing was highly illegal and frowned upon by the government, who protected their national treasures.

But money talks, and I had stolen a big chunk of it from Remy's room. With it, I was able to find myself a guide and a speedboat within a short time.

The trip to Amarna had been a long one. I'd sat in the back of the speedboat, lost in my thoughts. Guilt over Noah had obsessed me for the first few hours, and all I could think about was how I was failing him, and how wonderful he'd been to me. As the miles flew past, my thoughts turned darker as they led to Zane. He'd betrayed me, and now he was going to get the halo for the queen before I could save Noah, and we'd all be in deep doodoo—Remy, Stan, Noah, and me.

I was determined not to let that happen.

"Yes, this is Amarna," Smith agreed in heavily accented English, breaking my train of thought. "There is not much left of the ruins today."

"I'll say." I stared over the edge of the boat. "It doesn't look like anything." I was disappointed in my first sights of the fabled ancient city. A few tourist traps were visible over the tall reeds of the Nile, but other than a ferry ramp, it all seemed unimpressive. Where was the Temple?

I pulled out my guidebook and flipped to the bookmarked pages, looking for photos or a map. "So if this is Amarna, is the Temple to the Aten nearby?" The guidebook had listed it as the oldest monotheistic temple in the world, so I figured that was my best bet for halo finding, and no doubt where I'd find Zane and the others.

"You want the temple?" Smith asked. "I can take you there for two hundred euros."

I frowned. "There's going to be some vampires out there. I'm not sure you want to go. It's dangerous. If you could just point me the way—"

Smith shook his head. "I will take you. Two hundred euros."

I tossed the guidebook aside. "Suit yourself, buddy. Just don't say I didn't warn you." I pulled out my purse and handed him the last of the bills in my wallet. Remy had loaded us with cash for the trip, and I was just about broke by now, which was another depressing thought. Money made things happen in Egypt, and without it, I was going to be sunk.

"So the driver of the boat is going to wait here for us, right?" I looked over at our "driver" who seemed more like Smith's teenage kid than a certified, licensed tour guide. He'd driven like a bat out of Hell, though, so I had no complaints. We'd gotten to Amarna before the sun came up, and even though dawn was peeking over the horizon, I figured we still had about an hour before all the vamps dropped off the face of the earth for another twelve hours.

"Yes, the driver will wait," Smith assured me, giving me a toothy white smile. "He will wait for one hundred euros."

"Sure," I echoed, trying not to wince. "Pay you when we get back on the boat after you take me to the temple?"

Smith shook his head, frowning. "Pay now."

"Not so fast," I said, glaring at him and clutching my purse close. "How do I know that you won't just take my money and leave me here? You guide me to the temple, and then we'll talk about paying Junior here. Got it?" I thought it was a pretty good bluff, considering I didn't have the hundred.

"Fine, I will take you," Smith agreed reluctantly, and my heart eased a little in its frantic pounding.

The boat pulled up against the dock, bobbing on the waves. I scanned up and down the river before I got out. Two white specks bobbed in the distance—the boats Zane and his crew had used to get here before us. I hoped that they were empty, or Smith Junior might be in for a nasty surprise.

Don't think about that, Jackie. Just get out of the boat. One thing at a time, I told myself.

Smith and I headed into the flat, brown ruins in the distance. We didn't carry flashlights; the sky had lightened to a murky twilight, the smooth desert becoming more visible with each moment. We cut through a few of the sandy hills and, to my surprise, they weren't all necessarily dunes—crumbled bricks and neat lines were drawn in the sands.

There was a city here, after all.

We followed the tourist path deeper and deeper into the ruins. Smith didn't need my map, heading directly for one area as if he had radar. I began to suspect this was not the first illegal run he'd made to off-limit sites. The path was rocky and hazardous, thanks to my ridiculous sandals, and I had to keep my eyes glued to the path.

"Almost there," Smith announced, and I breathed a sigh of relief. Hiking sucked when I was living, and wasn't any better in the Afterlife.

Smith suddenly stopped and hunched down beside a crumbling half wall.

I nearly plowed into his backside, and instead went stumbling to the ground, wrenching my ankle with a "pop" that only I heard. I hoped that was my shoe and not the bones of my foot. If I had to make a break for it, I'd be toast.

"Someone is out in the temple ruins," Smith whispered, shivering against the stone wall and clutching his hat like a shield. "A man with a gun."

Hmm. "Does he have black hair and a long coat? Two other people with him?"

Smith just gave me a terrified look, unable to speak.

"You're a big help," I muttered, crawling a few feet away and peering over the wall.

The ruins of the Temple of the Aten lay before me in all their unamazing glory. I'd read that there was pretty much nothing left of the Aten Temple except for a few fake fiberglass columns, so I'd expected that. Only the flat lines of stone indicated that once there had been a beautiful temple here.

Zane stood outside those lines, casually pacing behind his two prisoners, gun in hand as the dawn rose behind him. On the ground at his feet, Remy and Stan sat back to back, their hands and feet tied.

They were alone, which surprised me. I'd expected a few more of the queen's lackeys to show up to ensure that this thing was done right, but nope. It was just Zane, who looked rather bored and kept checking his watch as if he were waiting for something.

Like me.

I won't make you do anything you don't want to do, Jackie, he'd whispered against my skin.

All a bunch of big fat tricks. Anger burned in my mind, searing out all the tender thoughts I'd had of him. I *hated* liars.

Furious, my hands clenched the crumbling brick wall. That asshole had used me from day one. Well, no longer. I pondered the distance between here and the boundaries of the Aten Temple. It didn't look like anything was in there, but maybe it wasn't obvious to those who weren't within its lines. Zane scrupulously avoided even sweeping his coat over the bricks. I imagined it was warded from both angel and vampire, which was why they needed a succubus to do their dirty work.

Why hadn't he used Remy to retrieve it?

I crouched back behind the wall. "Smith," I said, turning to him.

But the wall next to me was empty. He'd run out on me. Couldn't blame him. I sighed, rubbing my face. "Great. I guess I have to go at this alone."

"Wasn't that the plan all along, my dear?" The queen's eerie, purring voice sounded behind me, and I froze in place. Oh, God.

I turned slowly to face her. "I can explain . . ."

Nitocris crossed elegant arms over her chest, her red eyes burning into me. She was dressed in a dark red pantsuit that looked painted onto her, highlighting the menacing bloodred of her eyes and lips. Behind her stood several vampire goons dressed in black suits and long, dark trench coats. One of them clutched a comatose Noah, hands and feet bound, his face badly cut.

Oh, Noah. My heart ached just looking at him.

The queen smiled down at me, showing rows and rows of sharklike teeth. "An explanation? I think I should like that."

CHAPTER TWENTY-FOUR

Hands shoved me toward the ruins of the Aten Temple and I stumbled, trying desperately to keep my balance with my hands tied behind my back.

"Hey, not so rough," I protested. "If you want this halo so bad, you're going to have to treat me with a bit of respect."

A hand jabbed me in the back, knocking me down. My cheek slammed into the dirt and the world exploded in black and red.

That one was gonna hurt in the morning.

Someone hauled me up from behind and I spat sand out of my mouth, mentally cussing out my captors. "Real classy," I retorted, though due to my swelling lip, it came out sounding more brain-damaged than tough. *Way to keep your cool, dumbass.*

A hand brushed the dirt off my sleeve, and I turned . . . only to stare into Zane's eyes. I shrugged violently, trying to fling his hand off my shoulder, hurt betrayal coursing through my veins. My chin lifted, daring him to say something.

His thumb brushed under my lip, wiping away the blood from my split lip. "You shouldn't have come,

Jackie," he whispered, his gaze darting over to Nitocris. "I have this handled."

"Handled?" I screeched, jerking away from him and stumbling away a few steps. "You left me tied to the bed in our hotel and kidnapped my friends. How is that 'handling' anything? You totally screwed me!"

"In more ways than one," Remy quipped dryly from her place on the ground.

I resisted the urge to kick sand at her, focusing my hate on Zane. How had I ever trusted him?

"Touching little scene," Nitocris purred, interrupting my anger as she stepped forward to wrap her hand around Zane's throat. He stiffened at her touch, the look in his eyes growing shuttered. "Now tell me, my sweet . . . when were you planning on telling me that you were here to retrieve the halo?"

Zane's cocky, teasing smile brushed across his face. "What, you didn't get my memo?"

The queen's hand tightened around his throat, and he wheezed for breath. Nitocris's face was furious.

What was going on?

I shot a confused look at Remy, who shrugged. She didn't know either.

"You think to subvert me?" The queen hissed at Zane, lifting him into the air with one hand. Her fingers gouged into his throat. "You think to take power from me when it is so close?"

Zane's pale face was turning an alarming shade of purple, and the idiot inside me that was still charmed by him couldn't do anything. "You're hurting him," I yelled, fists clenched in frustration. "Let him go or I'm not doing this for you."

Eyes the color of blood focused in on me, and Zane collapsed to the ground as the queen's interest turned to me. "You think to tell me what to do, little one?" Her voice rumbled low, dangerous.

"Uh," I said, backing away in fear. My hands jerked in their bonds behind my back, and I could feel blood snaking over my wrists, rubbed raw through my frantic motions. "I don't know what you're talking about. Zane's on your side." I forced a fake smile to my face.

"Is he, now?" Her eyes narrowed. "Did he fuck you?"

My eyebrows raised at her vehement question and my gaze flicked over to the nearly comatose Noah. Awkward. "Well, that's a bit personal, don't you think—"

"Don't say anything, Jackie," Zane called hoarsely as he picked himself up. "It's a trap, no matter what you say."

"Touching," the queen sneered. "Your answer does not matter. I can smell the stink of your blood—blood I expressly forbade him to take—all over him. He has not obeyed one of my orders since joining you on this little trip. Not that that should surprise me," the queen said, her tone cold. "Zane has never followed instructions well. This is why I followed him." Again, I caught a flash of razor-sharp teeth.

She had told him *not* to sleep with me? Confused, I stared at Zane. His eyes met mine, and I saw a softness there. Weakness, the queen would say.

I remembered lying in bed with Zane after we had just

made love. He kissed my mouth. *"I won't make you do anything you don't want to do, Jackie. Ever."*

Oh . . .

Oh, hell. Was Zane breaking the rules for me? Was he in love with me?

The enormity of the situation crashed down on me and I slumped to the ground. What a mess. I wanted to bury my head in my hands, but they were still tied behind me.

Queen Nitocris gave a cold laugh. "I think you see the problem as I do, my little slut. What does one do with a vampire who's lost his killing edge, other than put him out of his misery? What does one do with a minion that won't obey, other than destroy him?"

My eyes squeezed shut. I was angry at Zane, furious even, but I didn't want that to happen. "Don't hurt him," I said, hating the way that it sounded like begging. "I'll do whatever you want."

"No, Jackie," Zane said, trying to get to me. "It's a trick."

"Fuck you, Zane," I said, sick and tired of it all. "It's all a trap anyhow. Does it matter what I pick?" I glared at him, shaking my head. "There's no way out of this except her way."

Nitocris held all the pieces. Her goons loomed over Noah, who had yet to speak. I saw him twitching, which told me that he was conscious or heading there. Remy and Stan were tied and bound near the queen's feet, and Zane—well . . .

I couldn't trust Zane. I didn't know what he was up to.

I lifted my chin and tilted my head. "If you want me to get this halo for you, you'll need to untie me."

"Of course," the queen said, her tone accommodating once more. She arched a brow meaningfully at Zane.

Indecision warred across his handsome face, then he slowly headed over to me. His fingers brushed against mine as his hands moved to undo the knots.

"Whatever you do, Jackie, don't give her the halo." Zane's soft words murmured against my back as he worked to free my hands. "It'll be the end of the world as we know it. If you thought the world was bad before, it'll be Hell on earth if she gets the halo."

I forced my face to remain carefully neutral. The queen was watching me, her body tense with impatience, arms crossed over her bloodred pantsuit.

I tried to think of a plan, any plan, but couldn't. My hands were free in moments and I brought them in front of me, rubbing my wrists. "What now?"

The queen glanced at the dawn-lit sky. "You don't have much time." She extended a long fingernail at the flat ruin that remained of the temple. "Go to the heart of the temple itself and speak his name, and it will come to you." The evil smile split her face again. "Then you will bring it to me."

"On the contrary," A strange voice came out of nowhere, ringing through the dusty ruin. The sound of a gun being cocked echoed in the stillness. "You're going to bring the halo to *me*."

CHAPTER TWENTY-FIVE

I stared over the barrel of the gun at the new face on the scene. A priest held the gun aimed at my chest from twenty feet away. Behind him were several rough locals who seemed familiar, but I didn't have time—or the interest—to think further on it.

Not a lot of deep thought goes through your mind when you're face to face with a gun barrel.

Behind me, Nitocris hissed and took a few steps backward. "So you have come at last, Uriel."

I frowned, examining the priest. He was an old man with thinning gray hair and a bad comb-over. Thick, dirty glasses covered most of his lined face, and he was dressed in the suit and white collar of a priest, just barely buttoned over his gut.

I almost laughed. "Dude, that is *not* Uriel. I've seen the man, and he's a lot prettier." When the gun cocked back toward me, I raised my hands in the air and added, "No offense."

"Possession," Zane muttered off to my side.

"Huh?"

"Demons can possess a person, and so can angels. They just usually choose not to."

That didn't sound too pleasant. I didn't care if it was for the good guys or not; I didn't want anyone taking over my body. I eyed the priest with horror.

He simply smiled at me. "Hello, Jacqueline." His voice sounded hollow, as if it were coming from far away. "It would not be in your best interest to go for the halo at this time, or I would be forced to shoot you."

The queen spoke up, her voice mocking. "Stop and ask yourself why an angel would defy his superiors and possess a human to chase after a halo, foolish girl."

"Gee, I give up," I said. "Why don't you just go ahead and tell me?"

"Your Uriel," she spat, "has been waging a war against the Serim ever since they fell from the Heavens. He, above all the angels, despises those who were weak, and he would like nothing more than to destroy every last one of them—starting with your friend Noah."

Well, at least they weren't trying to make this hard or anything.

I studied the group Uriel had arrived with, trying to figure out an angle, since it was obvious nobody else was going to help me. Actually, there was something about a few of them that struck me as familiar . . .

"Slavers," I said suddenly. "You've brought the slavers with you, Uriel? I thought you were one of the good guys!"

One of the priest's brows quirked. "I do not employ slavers, young woman. These men are my disciples. I instructed them to follow you through the city, so that I might keep an eye on your journey."

Scowling, I turned to Zane. "They weren't slavers?"

Zane shrugged, a hint of a grin tugging at his lips. "You bought it, didn't you?"

"Unbelievable," I said with disgust. "You are such a creep." He had lied to me over and over again. It was beyond comprehension. My heart felt frozen in my breast. I couldn't even trust the guy in love with me.

"Enough of this," the queen snapped behind me. "Either destroy Uriel's host, or retrieve the halo for me. I care not which you do."

I turned to her and thumbed a gesture at Uriel. "In case you hadn't noticed, he's holding a gun."

The queen's look darkened. "I cannot see him."

My eyes widened. "He's right there." I even pointed helpfully.

The queen shot a scathing look at Zane. "Is this ignorance a game?"

"No, I'm afraid she's really that ignorant," Zane said, wry amusement on his face again.

Both of us scowled at him.

Zane explained, "Once you've crossed over to one side, Jackie, your vision becomes distorted against the opposition." He gestured at the priest. "All I see there is a white blur. Likewise, all he can see of the queen is a dark blur. It's like that part is missing from your vision entirely. It's to prevent a war of the Heavens."

"And it's working so well," I said sarcastically. "So basically you have to use us peons as pawns to get what you want, because you can't go after each other directly."

"In a nutshell, yes."

I studied the two sides, one on each side of me. Both looked ready to attack, and frankly, I didn't care if they all destroyed each other. But the bodies of Remy, Stan, and Noah were still in the hot ground in the middle, and I dared not pull anything funny.

Besides—like it or not—I still cared about what happened to Zane. I couldn't separate sex from emotion yet, it seemed.

Which sucked.

"Well?" The queen snapped, and Uriel's gun trained on me again.

"Well what?" I snapped back. "You guys need to decide who gets the toys before I make a move."

"Neither of us can retrieve the halo ourselves, Jacqueline," Uriel explained, his voice taking on an endlessly annoyed tone. Yep, it was definitely supercilious Uriel. "It is up to you to get it and do what you think is best."

"So let me get this straight," I said, putting my hands on my hips. "If I give the halo to Uriel, he'll bring the war in Heaven down here on earth and destroy all the Serim that fell. But if I give it to the queen"—I turned and pointed at her—"she'll destroy Heaven and bring the world into total darkness."

"Something along those lines," Zane murmured.

I rolled my eyes. "Well, I'm just royally screwed either way, aren't I?" I glared at Uriel and gestured at his gun. "In the scheme of things, how much do you think that peashooter matters at this point? You don't have much leverage."

The gun flared to life, and the next thing I knew, I'd

been blown six feet backward and was choking for breath on the floor of the temple ruins. My torso screamed with agony, and waves of surging pain rode through me.

"It still hurts, doesn't it?" Uriel's mild voice sneered at me. "You can't die, but I can make living rather painful for you."

I propped myself up on my elbows slowly. A crater the size of my fist had been blown straight through my stomach, and blood was pumping everywhere.

Nobody batted an eye. I guess people had holes blown through their middles all the time in their world. I, on the other hand, was not so used to this sort of thing, and I lost it. My hands touched the edge of the gigantic hole in my middle, and pain cascaded through me. Blood ran over my hands, and I could feel the wind whistle against my internal organs.

"You fucking bastard! That hurts like hell!" Pain racked my body and I bent double with it. It was so bad that I wanted to cry, but I didn't want to give Uriel the satisfaction. How long did it take for our kind to heal?

"Bullets blessed with holy water." Uriel stroked the gun with his free hand. "One to the head and one to the heart should destroy any vampire here, including your sire."

The vampires hissed, baring their fangs. Bluff or not, they didn't like hearing that.

"And once I get rid of your sires, I'm afraid it's the end of you, as well. Unless you bring me that halo."

"Joke's on you. My vamp sire isn't here."

"Isn't he?" Uriel smiled coldly. "Are you certain?"

I stared at the crowd of fanged denizens around me and my gaze settled on Zane. I'd sometimes wondered, but never found, any proof. He shrugged, avoiding eye contact, sending a shiver down my spine. Was he playing me again?

I sat up slowly, pain my new constant friend as I struggled to stand. It was odd to feel the wind whistle through my wound—and rather revolting. My blood was soaking into the sandy desert floor, but between the red lines, I could make out the ancient flagstones.

Uriel had blown me straight into the temple, out of everyone's reach.

I smiled, an idea forming in my head. "What will you do if I just sit here and wait you all out?"

Uriel smiled. "When dawn is fully upon us, the denizens of the night must return to their holes or risk being at our mercy. They do not have long. Then you will be free to give the halo to me."

"Gee." I rubbed what used to be my stomach and winced at the pain. "And if I don't want to give it to you?"

"Then when the vampires leave, I will execute your friends."

Pfft. A hollow threat. He couldn't kill Remy, Zane would be long gone, and Noah—well, I didn't know that he could kill Noah, since he was a Serim.

But Stan was there, mucking up the works. I didn't want the blood of an innocent on my hands. I turned and examined the captives, as if debating my choices. Stan was seated next to Remy, and the front of his pale shorts was wet. No doubt he'd pissed himself at the sight of the gun, the vampires, or the queen. I didn't blame him one bit. Remy was crouched next to him, an odd look on her face. As I glanced at her, she kept her head down but I saw her mouth moving as she attempted to tell me something. Noah lay collapsed next to her, his body pressed up against hers.

I squinted, raising a hand to my eyes as if shielding them from the early-morning sun, concentrating on Remy's lips and hoping nobody else noticed my sudden interest.

Hands free, she was mouthing. Her fingers wiggled slightly behind her back. *Hands free.* She gestured ever so slightly at Noah. His eyes shone with alertness, and I realized he'd fooled me as much as he had them. A smart trick; he could do more if they thought of him as no threat.

Time to get this show on the road.

"Okay. One halo, coming up."

CHAPTER TWENTY-SIX

I stood in the Temple of the Aten, the sun cresting above my head, a big hole in my torso, and wondered why I'd ever thought this was a good idea.

"Hurry," came the imperious demand from Queen Nitocris. "Bring me the halo, or your vampire lover will die in excruciating agony."

Don't remind me, I thought as I walked through the broken flagstones of the temple.

Seek the heart of the temple, the queen had said. *Call him there, and you will find his halo.*

I studied the vast emptiness around me. It had been grand at the height of its glory; now there were just a few fake columns and a lot of nothing separating the desert from it.

I took a few tentative steps forward, and froze. Whispers began to fill my mind, soft whispers that spoke in a language that I didn't understand. The air around me grew cold and the wind began to pick up, whipping my hair around my face. Unnerved, I took a step backward, and the effects lessened. Testing, I took a step to the side. Nothing.

Following the whispers would lead me to the heart

of the temple. My heart thudded in my breast. I took a hesitant step forward again, clutching my wild hair against my neck to keep it out of my face. The whispers assailed me again, thicker and more ferocious with each step that I took.

The intensity of the wind increased and the voices in my ears began to form words, soft and hollow and sad.

My heart grows weary. My flesh is weak, as it always was. I was wrong. Save me from this eternal damnation. Forgive me.

Forgive me.

With those words ringing in my ears, I stopped near a series of nearly perfect flagstones, a broken crumble of rock ahead of me that looked like it had once been an altar. I lay a hand on the broken surface and found it to be warm to the touch, pulsing like a heartbeat.

Forgive me, the sad voice intoned. *I was weak, foolish. Let me return to Your glory. Oh please, God, forgive me.*

"Jackie," Zane called behind me, a note of frantic worry in his voice. "Jackie! Be careful!"

I barely registered his voice, lost in the sad sighs and endless whispers of the temple.

Call his name, Nitocris had said.

"Joachim," I called, my voice breaking through the tornado of whispers. "Come to me, Joachim."

The intensity of the whispers increased, now screaming and shouting their words. The winds around me became gale force, and the rest of the world was drowned out in a sea of sandy wind and shouting, unholy voices.

Forgive me! I was weak and foolish. Heaven above, take me back!

Forgive me!

"Joachim," I called again.

The intensity of the shouting turned to violent screaming, and I covered my ears. What did he *want*?

Then it clicked in my mind, and I whispered to the tempest around me.

"I forgive you, Joachim."

The shrieking died; the wind ceased. My eyes slid open once more. Grit covered everything, and I stared down at my feet, where the sand lay in a perfect circle before me on the flagstones. As I watched, the circle of sand seemed to melt into itself, turning liquid and glowing bright. The circle raised into the air, circling around me, a singing hum replacing the whispers.

"The halo!" the queen cried behind me, rapturous.

It spun above my head, a flashing circle of pulsing light and humming air. I reached one hand up to grab it and the halo fell onto my fingers, pulsing and cool. It felt like smooth glass, glowed like amber, and I could hear Joachim's sighs of sadness emanating from within. Clutching the halo in my hands filled me with sadness that so much pain and misery was going to be devoured by the queen or Uriel simply for the power it could give them. They didn't care about the man himself, only what he could do for them.

I wondered if Joachim's whole mortal life had been like that. It made me sad.

I turned and regarded my distant audience. All eyes

were trained on me, from the angel's lackeys to the vampire goons. The queen was rapt, her hand outstretched as if she could snatch the halo from my hands. Even Uriel seemed dazed by what he was seeing, his mouth hanging open.

I took a few steps forward, the halo clutched tightly in my hands. As I watched all those eyes on me, I wondered—what now? Who do I give it to?

I hesitated, and all hell broke loose.

The queen grabbed Zane and dragged him against her body, her fangs extended a scant inch from his neck. "Give me the halo," she hissed, "or I will drain your lover dry of every last ounce of blood. His flesh will wither and his soul will become mine to command."

By the way that Zane blanched, I knew her threat wasn't idle.

The sound of a gun being cocked brought my attention the other way. I looked over to see Uriel's gun now aimed directly at Stan. "Bring me the halo, or you will have the murder of this young man on your eternal soul."

"You can't kill him," I bluffed. "You're an angel." No way was he going to face eternity stuck down here with the rest of us.

A gun cocked behind him, and I saw one of his crew aim his gun at Stan.

"No," Uriel agreed. "But one of my disciples will kill him instead."

"No!" Remy shouted, shaking her head and trying to maneuver herself in front of Stan. "Leave him alone. He knows nothing about this. Take me instead."

The priest laughed. "Why should I, when I have all the leverage I need?"

"Jackie, give up the halo to Uriel. Let him destroy me—I don't care." Noah's voice was calm as he sat up. Cuts and bruises covered his handsome face, his blond hair was matted against the side of his cheek, but he was still inhumanly beautiful, his chiseled mouth stern as he looked at me. "It's the only logical thing you can do."

Compelled by the sound of his voice, I took a few steps toward Uriel. I didn't want to, but I couldn't refuse a direct order from my master.

"Do something," I heard the queen hiss to Zane.

"Jackie, stop," Zane insisted.

I halted just inches inside the boundaries of the temple. Huh?

"Don't give it to him," Zane said, his voice strained. "Give it to the queen."

I turned and headed away from Uriel, my hand outstretching to give the halo to Queen Nitocris. Damn—he *was* my—

"Stop, Jackie!"

Noah's voice caused me to stop again. Frustrated, I turned to stare at him, my mind hazy with the conflicting orders.

"Jackie, bring the halo to me . . . and the queen," Zane added at the last moment.

I started forward again.

"Stop!" Noah demanded once more.

I complied, extremely irritated now. "Will the two of you make up your freaking minds?" I shouted.

I heard Remy's gasp of shock. "Zane— he's her other master. Her vampire master."

She was even slower than me, but she got there. Suddenly I remembered . . .

A dark-haired man kissing me on my cheek as he lay me down in a Dumpster. "Sweet dreams, Princess."

Zane standing over me when I first met the vampire queen. "You'd better tell her." And I'd blabbed my story despite my fear.

"You have always been special," he'd argued with me, bending down to kiss my flesh as we lay in bed together.

I'd been such a fool. He'd been so subtle about it that I'd never even imagined, never even dreamed . . .

"You asshole!" My eyes welled up with unwanted tears. "Did you ever *not* lie to me?"

"I never lied to you about that, Jackie." Zane's expression was solemn as he met my eyes. "You never asked."

"Yes, I did," I protested, thinking back to our conversation in the museum.

"So, have we met before? Because you sure seem familiar to me." I couldn't help but ask him. "I don't suppose you hang out in dark alleys near nightclubs, looking for dorky girls to molest?"

"Huh?"

"Never mind. I was just wondering if you were my vampire master, or something. Forget I asked."

He'd never responded directly any time I'd asked. My questions had been met with a smile and a subtle topic change, and I'd been too flustered to notice.

"I *did* ask," I protested, glaring at him. "You never answered."

"I gave you an answer. Just not the one you were looking for."

"That is totally beside the point, and you know it," I yelled, my hands tightening around the halo. "How could you do this to me?"

"I have never lied to you, Jackie," Zane repeated.

I thought hard. "And the slavers thing?"

Zane visibly deflated and his mouth softened as he regarded me. "That was the only thing, Jackie. I swear. Think back. Have I ever forced you to do anything that you didn't want to do?"

"You mean, besides this whole Red-Light Green-Light game that you and Noah are forcing me to play?"

His head cocked to the side and he gave me an exasperated look. "Have I, Jackie?"

Oddly enough, his repeated words calmed me from the fury that was overtaking my mind. I remembered Zane kissing my flesh, looking up at me moments before I'd drifted off to sleep after we'd made love. *I'll never make you do anything you don't want to, Jackie.*

I believed him, of all bizarre things. And I relaxed.

"Unfair advantage," Uriel shouted off to the side of me. "Don't make me do something we'll both regret, Jacqueline!" He sounded furious, frantic, on edge.

"Jackie," both Zane and Noah began at the same time, and I backed up, stepping away from the temple's edge.

I thumped into something solid. Turning, I looked into Remy's drawn, beautiful face.

"I need that," she said, pointing at the halo. "Give it to me."

Confused, I held it closer to my side, the sad whispers echoing through my mind. When had she entered the temple? "Remy, what are you doing?"

"He's going to hurt Stan, and I can't let him do that. We're screwed either way—at least let me save Stan." She took a step toward me. "I can't live with an innocent human's death on my conscience."

Remy was deadly serious. I took a step backward, glancing over at Zane. His face was drawn, pale, his eyes glued to us. He shook his head and closed his eyes, bracing for the worst. He wouldn't try to influence me anymore.

It broke my heart. I clutched the halo tighter to me and shook my head vehemently. "No, Remy. I can't let you give it to him."

"You can't give it to Nitocris," Remy argued. "She'll turn us all into her underlings. Now give me the halo and let me save Stan!"

"He's just a human boy," Nitocris purred behind me, sensing my weakness. "Wouldn't you rather save your vampire lover? Your master? Your fate is tied to his, after all."

I hesitated when I heard Zane's muffled groan of pain. I had no doubt that the queen would torture him to try to get me to hand the precious halo over to her, and even though I had no choice but to ignore it, I still paused.

Remy's hands slapped at mine, and she made her

play for the halo. It flipped in my hands, flying into the air. The world stood still for a moment as the beautiful, shining object became airborne. My fingertips brushed against it and I grasped it once more, only to find Remy's hand clasping the opposite side of the small band of amber light.

She gave it a fierce tug, trying to yank it from my hands. "Give it to me!" she cried.

"I can't," I said, nearly sobbing. "We can't give it to either of them."

"I have to save Stan," Remy said between gritted teeth. "Uriel will save Noah if we give him the halo; I know it."

"*How* do you know that?" I screamed.

"What other choice do we have?" Again Remy yanked on the halo, and I concentrated on keeping my fingers locked around the slender band.

What about Zane? my brain insisted. *You trusted him and he betrayed you, over and over again. How can you save him now?*

I weakened for a moment, and Remy gave a fierce tug. My sweaty hands slipped from the halo and she went tumbling backward, falling against the thick temple flagstones.

The world seemed to slow down. I watched, helpless to move, as Remy tumbled to the earth. The halo lifted from her hands for a moment, then crashed against the stones near her head.

It shattered with a thousand points of light. The golden fragments gleamed for a moment, spilling over her body, then sank into her skin, disappearing forever.

Remy stared up at me in surprise.

The whispers grew loud for a moment, then vanished in the wind.

Twin anguished cries of pain drew my attention. I looked over and saw Nitocris and Uriel screaming in agony at the loss of the halo. The body of the priest shuddered with convulsions, then dropped to the ground, the gun dropping with him.

The queen released Zane and buried her head in her hands, shaking violently. "You dare to thwart me?" she hissed, raising her bloodred eyes to mine. "You have earned my undying vengeance."

"Hey," I protested weakly. "It wasn't me who broke it." I pointed at Remy. "She's your girl."

The queen hissed at me, revealing the largest set of fangs I'd ever seen, then gave an unholy scream. "This is not over!"

As I watched, black wings tore out of the flesh of her back and erupted in a wet coil of leathery flesh and sinew. They weren't the beautiful, feathered fall that Zane had; her wings were monstrous, leathery creations that unfurled over her head. She flung Zane to the ground and launched herself into the air, followed by the mass exodus of her goons. Black wings filled the sky for a moment, blotting out the sun.

They left nothing behind but a flood of silk suit jackets and one lone vampire. Noah and Stan watched me from the sidelines, untying each other and rubbing their wrists.

I looked down at Remy, who still lay on the flagstones. "You okay, Remy?" I offered her my hand.

"Who?"

The voice that answered me was deep, masculine and hollow, and definitely *not* Remy.

"Er . . . Remy?" My blood froze as I stared into her eyes. They were clear as glass, and I saw flashes of blue and red warring in them. "Are you okay?"

I watched her face contort for a moment, then her eyes swam blue. "Jackie?" Her voice was confused, and she took my hand as I helped her up.

"Is something wrong? You didn't sound like yourself for a minute there." Fear was clenching at my insides, but I forced my voice to remain casual.

"I'm only half me," she said, extending her hands in front of her and staring at them as if she'd never seen them before. Her eyes flicked red as she felt her own breasts, then slapped her hands away. "Hey! Quit touching me!"

I glanced over at Noah with a puzzled look. "Do you know what is going on?"

Remy touched her hair, felt her breasts again, then gave me a frustrated look. "*I* can tell you what's going on. He's inside me, hogging my space!"

"*Who's* inside you?"

"Joachim," she said flatly. "The halo absorbed into my body when it broke. I've got his powers—and his mind—inside my own." Her hand snaked up to touch her face, as if feeling out unfamiliar territory. Her mouth trembled a bit at the touch of her fingers.

"Oh lord," I said, my hands covering my mouth in shock. "Are you okay?"

Remy snorted, forcing a grim smile. "As long as I don't get the urge to watch football and scratch my crotch, I'll be just fine." She stomped across the temple boundaries and over to Stan's side, dusting him off.

I shook my head, wondering. My guess was that Remy would explain later, when she'd had more time to adjust. For now, we had to get out of here.

But—rush to Zane? Rush to Noah? I eyed the two men for a heartbeat. Noah sat up in the sand, his hand pressed to his forehead as he looked around.

Zane was still crumpled in the sand.

Guilt warred with my anger and my concern for Zane. I raced to his side, lifting his cheek gently off the sand. Blood covered his neck from the gouges Nitocris had bitten into his flesh. She'd chewed on him like he was nothing to her, and the sight chilled me.

His face rolled toward mine and his sleepy eyes focused on my face, his hand reaching up to brush my cheek. "I'm cast out, Jackie. A renegade."

"We'll figure something out, Zane," I said, the words sounding empty in my own mind. Guilt threaded through me. What was he going to do? A liar and a cheat he may be, but I couldn't abandon him now. Not when he'd risked everything for me.

A sexy half smile touched his face and then he went limp in my arms. My pulse hammered for a moment as panic struck me, until I realized that he'd fallen into the day slumber of the vampires.

I clutched him close to me and watched the others scrambling about. With Uriel's "possession" ended, his reinforcements seemed a bit lost. They milled around, chattering with each other in confusion. The priest sat nearby, hands on his head as if he had a migraine.

Remy held Stan to her chest, stroking his hair as he sobbed against her breast. I suspected their relationship wasn't going to survive the trip home. Our world was a little too weird for the common Joe. Not to mention the fact that Remy looked irritated as hell that he was crying on her.

A shadow fell over me, and a hand touched my shoulder. I looked up into Noah's face, the light haloing around his head with purity. He smiled down at me, a bit worse for the wear, but the same solid, dependable Noah that I could count on. "Are you all right, Jackie?"

"Shouldn't I be asking you that?" I gave him a watery smile.

He chuckled, a familiar, heartwarming sound. "I'll manage."

I looked down at Zane in my arms, then up at Noah. "Noah, I . . ." Guilt coursed through me. While he'd been tortured by the vampires, I'd been fraternizing with one.

"Hush. Time enough for that later." He kissed my brow. "We've had a rough week."

"I'll say," I agreed, fighting the urge to laugh. With a hole in my middle, "rough week" was an understatement. "What now?"

He shrugged off his shirt and handed it to me. "Well," he said as I put it on, concealing my wound, "right now I suggest we get out of the way of the tour group." He gestured over his shoulder.

I looked and saw a line of tourists on the horizon, cameras in hand, staring down at us in shock.

Thinking fast, I pointed at Zane, cradled against me, and called, "Can I get a little help here? My boyfriend's narcoleptic, and he's having another episode. Anybody got a phone?"

Sixteen phones were immediately handed my way.

EPILOGUE

"I really do appreciate the offer, Remy, but I like having my own apartment," I said into the phone. "It's not anything you did, I just like being independent."

"Come on, it's the Joachim thing, isn't it? Look, I told you that I wasn't trying to watch you shower. He took over in a weak moment, and I didn't know it was you in there."

I snorted, flipping through my stack of mail as I cradled the phone against my cheek. A lot of bills had stacked up in the past few weeks, and I needed to go through what needed to be paid with the rest of my savings, and what didn't. "Well, I can't say that it wasn't a little unnerving, but it's not that." *Not entirely.* "I just like having my own place. And since I'm applying for that job with the archaeology team at the university, it might seem a tad weird to be living with a porn star—no offense."

"None taken," she said, ever cheerful. "Speaking of showers, do I hear it running in the background?"

"Could be." I grinned and glanced at the bathroom door. Steam rose from underneath it, along with the sound of masculine humming. "You never know."

"It's seven a.m., so it could be either of your boy toys. I don't suppose you'll tell me which one it is?"

"Nope."

"You have to make up your mind between the two of them sometime, babe," she said, laughing. "Actually, you don't—but I don't imagine they like each other much."

"You'd imagine right." I heard the shower turn off and the whistling start. "Listen, I'd better go now, all right?"

"Fine, but we're still doing lunch tomorrow, right? We need to talk about the 'Jo' situation and how to fix it, before I go stark raving mad. He keeps trying to feel me up."

"I hear you," I agreed, feeling a twinge of guilt. "There's bound to be a way to fix it, and I won't rest until we find it. I'm here for you."

"Thanks, Jackie," Remy said, relief in her voice. "It's good to have someone on my side who isn't in my head and interested in seeing me naked."

I laughed. "I'll see you at lunch, then."

"Later."

Life had been pretty good in the week that we'd been back from Egypt. Sure, I'd lost my job, but it was due to excessive unexcused absences. Julianna had accused me of hiding out to recover from tons of plastic surgery, and I couldn't refute her claims. Not looking the way I did.

Besides, the truth was much, much weirder than anything she could have come up with.

I'd been sent packing with my last paycheck. I hadn't made it two feet out the door before I'd gotten a call from a local university, asking if I was still working at the museum. A position had opened up in their archaeology department, if I was interested.

Was I ever!

"Did I just hear the phone?" Zane's head poked out from the bathroom door, his black hair still dripping from the shower. One of my purple bath towels hung low on his hips, and he stifled a yawn.

"You did," I agreed, moving toward him. That towel hung deliciously low, and I was irresistibly drawn to it. That was the kind of girl I was now, after all. I pulled it aside and slid my hand over his flesh, leaning in for a kiss. "Room in that shower for two?"

His wet hands slid over my body, resting on my ass. "Who says we have to get back in the shower?"

Then the doorbell rang. Damn!

"Don't answer it," he said, pressing kisses along my jawline. "Let's hit the floor, and I'll show you where that third kiss goes."

A quiver of desire shot through me.

The doorbell rang again, and I sighed. "That might be Noah," I said, sliding away from him playfully.

He gave me an irritated look and pulled the towel back around his waist. "All the more reason not to answer it."

I ignored his snide comment and headed for the door, unlocking it.

Noah stood in the doorway in a freshly pressed suit. He smiled at me, holding up two coffees and a bag of doughnuts. The man knew my weak spots. "Good morning, Jackie. May I come in?"

"Of course," I said with a smile.

He stepped in past me, stiffening when he saw Zane on my couch, clad in nothing but a towel. "I see you have company."

"Well, he doesn't have a place to stay, what with being exiled and all," I pointed out, a blush rising on my cheeks.

Remy had been right. The constant bickering between the two men was pretty darn irritating, since each one was surprised to see the other at any given time. I scowled as Noah grabbed my chin and tilted my head up to his, searching my eyes for blue.

They were bleached silver, of course. I'm not crazy, and Zane's damn hot.

"I see you haven't been missing me much." There was a rigid set in his tone, and I noticed how blue his eyes were. He'd definitely been missing me.

Zane stretched out on the couch, looking rather pleased with himself. "Maybe you should leave."

"Maybe you should let Jackie decide on her own," Noah said in a deadly voice. Then he flicked a glance back to me and my silver eyes. "Though it seems as if you've already decided."

I took the doughnuts from Noah's hand and gave him a kiss on the cheek. "I'm a normal, red-blooded succubus who's trying to repair the hole in her middle. Your turn will come in about two hours."

Since I'd been wounded, my body had responded by trying to refuel itself more frequently. Like every eight hours. With two very sexy men at my beck and call, though, I wasn't complaining.

"I don't like him being here," Noah said, his teeth gritted. He crossed his arms and glared at Zane, looking like an angry dog defending his territory.

"Goes double for me, Angel Boy." Zane glowered at him from the couch. "She's my girl."

I rolled my eyes. "Will the two of you leave it be? I'm *nobody's* girl."

But both men had gotten their hackles in a rise.

"I think you should decide who you want to be with, Jackie," Noah said. "Decide which one you want to choose."

"Yeah, Jackie. Put this loser in his place and let me get to sleep." Zane got up from the couch and stood next to Noah, glaring at him. His towel threatened to fall from his waist, if not for the hand holding it there.

My hand.

"Choose, Jackie," they both said.

Good lord—that was like asking someone to pick which hand or leg they liked better.

"I can't choose. You both annoy me in completely different ways."

Two sets of astonished eyes focused on me.

"Noah, you're a bit too stuffy and set in your ways," I began. "You want me to be obedient, proper, and lady-like."

"That's not true," he began, a scowl darkening his face.

I raised my hand. "I'm not finished. You're a bit stuffy, but I like you. You're always there for me when I need you. You're my rock, and you're practical and reasonable even when I'm not. I need you in my life."

Zane's face had taken on a shuttered look, and he

grabbed a cigarette from the nearby table and lit it. "So this is it for us?"

"No. I like you, too, Zane. You're impetuous and slick, and you make me do crazy things—things that I like doing. You take my breath away." He smiled. "But I don't know you, and I can't trust you.

"Hence, my problem," I told them. "I simply can't choose."

"Well, you have to," Noah said, his voice unyielding.

"Pick one," Zane agreed.

Annoyed, I snapped, "Fine! I pick neither of you."

"What?" they said jointly.

I shrugged. "If I can't have both of you, I'll just have to go with option C: none of the above."

Two scowls focused on me and I raised my hand, stopping their arguments before they could start. "I've actually given this a lot of thought. My new life flows between both of your worlds, so it only makes sense to have both of you in my life, helping me where you can. Your paths will only intersect for a few hours each day, and if you can manage to avoid each other, so much the better. I can't pick a favorite, and I don't think you should try to make me choose. We have unusual circumstances, and I believe they call for an unusual solution. So what's it going to be?"

Zane grinned and winked at me. "You know my answer."

Noah was silent, then grudgingly said, "I can share."

"Ditto," said Zane. "Just not at the same time."

My eyes glazed over at the thought of being sand-wiched between two delicious men. Hmm—if they could come around to the relationship I was propos-ing, maybe I could get them to come around to that, as well.

A girl's got to have a goal, right?

AFTERWORD

I've always been a bit of an armchair Egyptologist, and a lot of scattershot, offhand research went into some of the historical elements of this book. The Temple of the Aten is generally believed to be one of the first—if not the first—monotheistic temples known in history. I thought this might be a pretty perfect setting for the back story of my fallen angels and Queen Nitocris. Not much of current-day Amarna is left standing, and no stonework, as it was likely cannibalized for other projects during later reigns.

The passage about Herodotus's *The Histories* that Jackie and Remy read off the internet is more or less paraphrased from the original. It was too awesome and bizarre not to use.

To make my story flow, I also adjusted a few other bits. The most famous bust of Nefertiti is actually in a museum in Berlin. That didn't suit my story, so Jackie viewed a similar one in the Cairo Museum. The wings/black cloaks mentioned on the wall paintings are as completely imaginary as my Serim and vampires are. The real Nitocris and real Nefertiti existed over 800 years apart—impossible if you're a mortal, but not such a stretch if you're immortal.

Also, visitors to the Amarna site today must ferry in across the Nile, but I've no idea if you can actually take a speedboat from Cairo to the site. In all my research, this was the most difficult piece to find out. I found nothing that said you could, but nothing that said you could *not*, either. Given that and the distance between the two cities (about 200 miles), I made the artistic decision to make such travel possible in the boundaries of the story.

Turn the page
for a sneak peek
at the next fun and sexy novel in
the Succubus Diaries series

Succubi Like It Hot

by Jill Myles

Coming soon from Pocket Star Books

S ince turning succubi a short few weeks ago, my Saturday nights were never dull. When I wasn't having sex with a vampire or a fallen angel, I was trotting after the only other succubus in town on yet another of her harebrained schemes.

As I watched, one of her tall red heels sank into the moist earth of the graveyard. She flung her hands up in the air with a horrified look. "Oh ew! I think I just stabbed someone in the forehead."

I flipped on my flashlight, watching Remy as she struggled to shake the mud off her expensive shoe. "I sincerely doubt that they're burying people two inches deep nowadays."

She gave me a wary look and shook her pump again to dislodge the dirt.

"Speaking of, why couldn't you wear normal shoes?" I was wearing a pair of grubby sneakers myself.

"I didn't bring any other shoes with me. When you called me, I didn't think we'd be spending Saturday night in a graveyard." Remy eyed our surroundings with distaste.

That made two of us. "You could have borrowed a pair

of mine," I argued, following behind her as she wobbled through the grassy turf.

She gave a haughty sniff. "Yours are ugly."

I shone my flashlight around, ignoring the prickle on the back of my neck when an owl hooted nearby. The full moon was out and shining high, and the squeamish girl in me was screaming in terror inside my head, even though I knew full well that there was nothing to be scared of. I mean, I regularly slept with the things that go bump in the night. I was immortal unless both of my sires were destroyed. Nothing could harm me in the middle of a creepy graveyard in the dead of night. Right?

"Now where do we want to do this?" Remy put her hands on her hips and surveyed the quiet graveyard.

It looked very well-kept. This was the nice part of town; I'd absolutely refused to go to the other side. If we rose from the dead, I'd rather have little old rich ladies than dead junkies and street rats. The tombstones here were pale white marble, with small bouquets of flowers placed on each marker. Some didn't even have gravestones, heading for the more fashionable "plaque in the grass" look. In the distance, there was a row of mausoleums for the truly rich.

Directly to our right? A nice, freshly dug open grave. No one was in it, but the sight of it still made me clutch Remy's arm and stand a little closer to her. "Let's go wherever this will be done the quickest."

I let her drag me after her, my sneakers squeaking on the wet grass. "I'm not sure—"

My voice died when a horrible, smoky smell touched

my nostrils. I pinched my nose and looked around, my insides quivering uncomfortably.

A woman with red eyes leaned against a nearby tombstone, her tweed suit shadowed by the marble angel that looked ready to attack her from overhead. The suit looked like something more appropriate for an office than a graveyard in the middle of the night. Her long, lean frame shifted. "Hello, ladies," she said in a cool tone, tilting her head to look at us over the rims of her glasses. "Enjoying the night?"

Remy swore. "Of all the luck. A friggin' demon."

I stared at the woman, unable to take my eyes off her. "How do you know she's a demon?" I whispered.

"She's female. Other than demons, succubi are the only female immortals."

Oh. Another tidbit of knowledge no one had bothered to share with me. I'd only seen males so far (other than Remy), but I hadn't realized that was a hard and fast rule.

The woman smiled, revealing a set of razor-sharp teeth beneath the demure exterior. "Hello, darling. So nice to see you again."

Remy snorted and took a step backward. "Which one are you?"

The woman waved her hand in an airy gesture. "Very small-time demon, I assure you. The big leaguers are too busy to hang out in graveyards tonight, no matter who may show." Her red eyes flashed in the darkness. "You may call me Mae."

I leaned over to Remy to whisper in her ear. "I thought we were here looking for an angel?"

"Not all the ground in a graveyard is consecrated by above," Mae said, arching an eyebrow at me. "And I can hear everything you say." The unnerving flash of teeth closed and she gave me a tight, close-lipped smile, seemingly human again. "So what brings you ladies in search of angels tonight?"

"None of your damn business," Remy said, squeezing my hand to keep me silent.

"Damned business is my specialty," Mae purred. "I can offer the same kind of assistance as any angel, and I assure you that I won't cloak my meanings with fake platitudes and prayers." She leaned back against the marble angel perched on the head of the tombstone, and touched the cheek of the cherub in an almost obscene fashion. "So how about it, ladies?"

I looked over at Remy. "What do you think?"

She turned to me, then glanced back at Mae, hesitating. "It's not ideal. Not ideal at all." Before I could ask her what that meant, she gave a small sigh. "I think it's just as safe as making a deal with an angel, provided you're extremely specific about everything."

There's a ringing endorsement.

"Should we wait for an angel to show?" I asked. If angels showed up, would it be some sort of celestial showdown? An immortal duke-out?

Remy shook her head, disappointed. "Won't happen now. Not with a demon so close nearby."

Over against the gravestone, Mae smiled at that. "I'm afraid it's me or nothing, sweetcakes. Make up your mind."

I mulled that over, looking at Mae's attempting-to-be-harmless-and-failing form. I could decline Mae's offer of help and leave the graveyard, and try another night. Or I could try a church and take my licks with Uriel, such as they were.

One of the demon's hands reached up to caress the marble cheek of the angel again, and my body throbbed in response at the sight, reminding me that I didn't have a lot of time if I was truly cursed.

"I need your help," I blurted. Remy patted me on the shoulder, as if approving my decision, or sympathizing that I had to make one. "I might be cursed and I need to know for sure."

"You've come to the right demoness," Mae purred, taking a step forward, her red eyes lighting with interest. "I can help you with that."

"You can remove it?"

She shook her head. "Removing the curse is an entirely different matter. But I can help you identify it." She smiled again, the demure, close-mouthed smile. "For a small favor, of course."

My spirits plummeted. "Of course," I replied. I hated favors, especially favors for the Infernal Host.

"Name your favor first," Remy said. "Then she can opt whether or not she will do business with you."

Smart Remy. I could have kissed her in that moment.

Mae's tiny smile remained undimmed. "I just need you to carry a message for me."

I eyed the demoness. "What sort of message?"

"A simple greeting, that's all. A tiny reminder for an old

friend to invite me over sometime." Mae took another step forward, and the air around her flashed, and the smell of sulfur rode thick in the air again. Mae froze in place. "As you can see, I am bound to this small piece of earth." She gestured to the edges of the particular grave she was standing on. "I can't leave these boundaries except to return to Hell itself."

Thank goodness for that. "A message? And that's it?"

She spread her hands. "That's all. I assure you that you will not be in the slightest bit of danger."

Yeah, sure. I gave her a skeptical look. "Who is this message going to?"

"A woman who resides in New Orleans." Again that tiny smile, hiding the wicked dagger-teeth. "Just tell her that Mae can come over. She'll know what that means."

Some sort of unholy RSVP? I tried to puzzle it out, knowing that she was trying to catch me. There had to be a secret meaning to the message—I just couldn't figure out what it was. Sure that I was missing something obvious, I glanced over at Remy, who shrugged.

"All right," I said, even though it felt like a bad idea. "I accept the offer. I'll go to New Orleans and tell this woman that you're coming to her party, and you'll help me out?"

Mae inclined her head in a gesture of acquiescence. The smell of sulfur grew thicker. "That is correct. But you must deliver the message in person."

"All right," I said grudgingly. I was sure I was going to regret the agreement later. "Now, can you help me with my curse?"

"The agreement," Mae said, her voice suddenly all business, "was for me to tell you if you were, in fact, cursed."

Touchy, touchy. I crossed my arms over my chest. "So, can you tell me if I'm cursed or not?" My heart began to pound in my breast.

"Come forward," she said, beckoning me with her hand. "I have to touch your skin to be able to tell if you are or not."

Ugh. I hated the thought of that. Swallowing, I took a few steps forward, standing just outside of Mae's reach.

"Just a bit closer," Mae said, the smile still in her voice. "I assure you that I don't bite."

Mae reminded me a little too much of the vampire queen for me to take that comment at face value. But I stepped forward again. The desire to know if I was cursed or not overrode common sense.

She placed her hands on my arms, her flesh scalding hot. Then she leaned in and brushed her mouth against mine.

An instant tingle shot through my body, and the Itch exploded in my head. My body felt like it was on fire, a volcano of intense longing and desire coursing through me. My hands wrapped around Mae's head of their own accord, and I pulled her mouth to mine again, seeking that warm tongue and the lick of heat that it brought. I needed more of her, more of that delicious burning flame deep down inside of me—

Remy's hands jerked me backward, and I slammed into the wet, cold earth, and back to reality.

My head spun for a minute, the air sucked back into my lungs, and I panted, coughing brimstone. I struggled to refocus on the too-sharp world around me, the Itch blazing through my body. My face scalded, and I touched it, feeling the blisters on my skin where I'd made contact with Mae's flesh. I glanced back up at her with shock.

The demon stood there, her red eyes burning bright as she looked down at me. Longing filled my body at the sight of her—a deep, desperate reminder of the Itch. I needed sex. Had to have sex. Would not be able to function until I had sex. I wanted to be back in Mae's arms caressing that living inferno. I whimpered.

"Snap out of it!" Remy's hard voice broke through my daze, and her hand cracked across my face.

"Ow!" I shook awake, then stared in horror at Mae. "That wasn't part of our agreement." I rubbed my face again, feeling the blisters. Already they disappeared under my fingertips—Sucks heal fast—but the memory of it still repelled me as much as it made the Itch run wild under my skin.

"I don't know why you're so upset." The demoness gave me an innocent look. "You did agree to let me touch you."

"I thought you meant on the arm!"

Mae's lips curled into a smug smile. "You know what they say about 'assuming.'"

The more time I spent around Mae, the less I liked her. "So just tell me, am I cursed or not?"

Her coy, teasing look slid away, and she was all business once more. "It's interesting," she said. "When you entered the graveyard, the power signatures that the pair of you were throwing off were off the charts. Much stronger than any normal succubus. It's what drew me here tonight." She glanced over at Remy, who still hovered protectively over me. "But after kissing the red-haired one, I've determined that the power isn't coming from *her* body after all." Blatant interest showed in Mae's face as she watched my dark-haired companion. "Care to tell me your little secret?"

A month or so ago—in my first disastrous run-in with the Infernal Host—Remy had become possessed by the spirit of Joachim, one of the first and strongest Serim to fall from the Heavens. I thought she was overcoming her problem, but when her eyes flashed bright red to match Mae's at the question, I knew that wasn't the case.

Remy looked furious. Mae simply looked fascinated.

I cleared my throat before things got out of hand. "Hello? Remember me? The girl with the curse?"

"What? Oh, yes." Mae turned back to me, reluctantly drawing her gaze away from Remy. "You asked if you were cursed. My answer is 'not directly.'"

I pulled myself to my feet with Remy's help, making sure to keep away from the edges of Mae's circle of unhallowed ground. "What do you mean, 'not directly'?"

"Curses can work in many different ways," she said. "You can force someone to ingest a cursed item, or trick them into accepting the curse. Or you can imbue an object that the owner will use on a regular basis. Another way is to curse someone else directly, and they in turn pass it on to the true recipient."

I frowned. "So which one is it?"

Mae grinned. "That would be another question, and that would require another deal. I'm game if you are." She pursed her lips in a mockery of a kiss and winked at me.

"No thanks," I blurted, taking an involuntary step backward. "So you can't tell me anything more than that?"

Remy shook her head and pulled at my arm. "Forget it. She's not going to play fair." Her eyes had returned to their normal blueish-gray hue, no traces of red remaining. Remy was back in control. "This was a bad idea, and I'm sorry I suggested it. But the good news is that I have a new idea."

I stared at Remy. "You couldn't have had this wonderful new idea a few hours ago, before we came here?"

"I didn't think of it until she mentioned New Orleans," Remy said, turning me away until I didn't face Mae any longer. She leaned in and said, "I think we should visit Delilah. She'll know the answer to your questions."

"That's great," I said, giving her a frustrated look. "But who exactly is Delilah?"

"Delilah's the oldest succubus in America," Remy said, squeezing my arm to encourage me. "She came over to escape the French Revolution and settled in New Orleans. If there's anything that a succubus has run across, Delilah's bound to know about it." She smiled. "She's also a part-time voodoo priestess, which should help."

"Oh, sure," I scoffed. "I was just thinking that we

needed a big helping of voodoo to go with our curses and demons tonight."

"What a coincidence," came Mae's smooth voice from across the graveyard. "Delilah is just the person that I need you to take my message to."

I poked at my stack of pancakes, unable to muster the enthusiasm to eat more than three of them. "So I guess we're flying out to New Orleans, huh?"

Across the table from me, Remy gave me a puzzled look and shoved a forkful of strawberry blintz into her mouth. "Why would we fly there?"

"Uh, hello? Did you forget that little interlude with the demoness tonight? You know, where I agreed to bring a message to her friend in person?" The fact that Delilah was the demoness's friend as well as Remy's still bugged me, but I didn't say it aloud.

I trusted Remy. We bickered like siblings, but she was one of the best things in my Afterlife—sister, mentor, and buddy rolled into one. We might not always see eye to eye on things like who one should sleep with (and how many), but she had never let me down yet.

Remy wrinkled her nose and shrugged, forking another mouthful of blintz toward her mouth. "Yeah, but why do we have to fly? I have a better idea: a road trip!"

"There's a flaw in your logic," I said. "If I've got to have sex every day now, I'm going to have to bring along some-one for the ride. No pun intended."

"Bring Noah," she said. "I love him."

I fiddled with my pancake, stabbing it down the middle. "We're taking a time-out on our relationship."

She sighed. "Bring Zane, then." Remy wasn't exactly his biggest fan, ever since he'd held a gun to her head. "I'll bring someone, too, so we don't have to share." She shoved the last bite into her mouth and grabbed the tab for our late-night breakfast. "Sun rises in a few hours, doesn't it? Plenty of time to pack."

And enough time for me to track down my vampire lover and screw his brains out. I was Itching like crazy and I needed him, bad.

For the hundredth time that night, I cursed Mae and her damned kiss.

By the time Zane got home, the sun was just cresting the horizon and I'd set my washing machine on spin cycle (again) in the hope that the low rotation would ease me toward an orgasm and relieve the Itching that threatened to drive me insane.

I heard the door slam from the other room and leapt up, intending to rip into Zane. I was cranky, horny, and irritable, and the sun was almost up. If I knew my vampire timing (and I did), I'd only have a matter of minutes before he'd pass out, taking up his hibernation for the daylight hours.

"Where have you been?" I stalked into the living room of my small apartment and scowled, intending to blast Zane with a few scathing comments before I allowed him to grovel and we could have blistering hot make-up sex.

The sight of him stopped me dead in my tracks. It wasn't the angry snarl on his face or the retort that he bit off to me that passed, unheard, by my ears. It wasn't the sexy leather trench coat or the messy fall of black hair over his forehead that made my burning body turn from a 6.5 on the Richter scale to an 11.

It was the burning red in his eyes as they met mine.

He was in need, just as badly as me.

"Oh . . . hey," I breathed, all the argument whooshing out of my lungs as the flesh between my legs grew instantly wet. I took a step forward, toward him. "I'm pissed at you."

It didn't sound like I was pissed. It sounded more like *Take Me Now, Baby.*

He threw his car keys down on the table and glared at me. "I'm not in the mood, Jackie. I've had a shit night and all I want to do is lie down and sleep until tomorrow."

Liar. He might not be in the mood for sex, but his eyes told me what he was in the mood for.

And I didn't care if he was in the mood for sex or not. I was.

I grabbed him by the collar of his coat, noticing that he smelled heavily like alcohol and cigarettes. He'd been to a club, but at least there was no lipstick on his collar. He had not fed. I tugged him to me, his mouth angling toward mine reluctantly. I could see the barest hint of his fangs brushing against his full mouth, and lord, I liked the look of that.

I bit down on his lower lip, hard. The taste of cigarettes and rum touched my lips, and I swirled my tongue against his mouth, all the while pulling on his coat to bring his body closer to mine.

He groaned like a dying man. "Jackie, no. I can't do this." His breath was ragged and he tried to push me away, feebly. "Not tonight, not right now unless you want me to feed from you."

"I have to have sex tonight, Zane. I can't wait."

Zane stared down into the intense blue of my eyes, his hands sliding over my back and ass as if he couldn't help himself. "You're in a bad way."

"Very bad," I agreed, my voice sounding like a sultry purr as his hands slid over me.

A slow, devilish smile spread over his mouth and he raised one hand to cup my cheek, grazing his thumb across my mouth. His eyes were locked into mine, fascinated by the intensity of color. "Been thinking of me all night? So much for Prince Charming, eh?"

A subtle dig at Noah. I nipped Zane's thumb, distracting him. I moved my hands down the front of his pants, sliding against the hard length waiting there.

"Jackie," he warned, but his hands dug into my hips, dragging me closer to him. Not much of a protest, and I knew I'd won.

Pushing backward, I edged him to the corner of the bed and knocked him onto it. Hooray for a bed. Most of the time we never made it to the bed before we had wild monkey sex.

He fell backward, and I felt Zane adjust under me, shifting to take the pressure off the long black sweep of vampire wings under his leather trench coat and crossing his back. I grabbed the front of his button-up shirt and ripped it apart, feeling a bit like an extremely horny She-Hulk. Zane wasn't protesting any longer, though, and I straddled him, rotating my hips on top of his as I leaned over him to give him a long kiss.

There was nothing slow and easy about our lovemaking. It was a mutual takeover. His hands jerked at the waistband of my jeans, and I shifted along with him, helping him rip them off my body.

Even as I slid my naked flesh over his body, he strained. I could feel the wings ripple under him, trapped by layers of half-discarded clothing and his own body weight. "Need blood," he said, his red eyes flaring as he guided my hips over his thick length and settled me over it.

My entire body quivered with anticipation at the long-sought relief, so damn close. "No blood," I said, rotating my hips and pressing him deeper into me. "Just sex."

He groaned again, throwing his head back as I squeezed my internal muscles around him and lifted, then lowered again. "Jackie," he warned.

I was past warnings. I didn't care. All I knew was that I had what I needed and I was taking it.

My body clenched around him, fueling my rocking hips faster and faster toward the orgasm that spelled relief. His fingers dug into my hips as I rolled them over him, hard and fast.

It didn't take long—a matter of moments, really. One moment I was shivering and tensing up, feeling the build as my body sped toward the orgasm, breath catching in my throat as he slammed my hips down over his. The next? Lights exploded behind my eyes, and my body quaked into a rough, ecstatic orgasm.

I breathed a long, low sigh of relief, wiggling my toes.

"Glad one of us got what we needed out of this," Zane growled under me, his fingers clenching against the soft roundness of my buttocks. He rammed into me again, his eyes piercing red as he thrust upward into my slick flesh.

Okay, so I felt a little guilty at that, and rocked my hips against his as he continued to pump inside me, fueling my body back toward another slow, delicious orgasm. Damn, I loved Zane's body against mine. I was even feeling a little generous, now that all the urgent, yearning need had seeped back out of my body for a few hours at least. I reached out and twirled one of his nipples with my finger. "Problem?"

I gasped when he thrust hard and deep inside me, growling again. His fangs glinted against his full lower lip, and he stared at my throat. "You know what I need," he rasped.

Blood—he needed to drink from me. Vampire eyes turned red like mine turned blue—a meter of how badly we needed to feed our urges—and his eyes were a stark, vivid red. But letting Zane drink from me meant putting my body in his control—totally and completely—once more. It meant giving him a taste of my powers, and succumbing to the mind-blanking numbness of sleep. A scary thing for one of my kind, seeing as how we didn't sleep. Normally I would have said hell no, and slid off him like yesterday's pony ride. But I was feeling unsettled and even a bit guilty.

I needed him for more than just sex—with Noah leaving me, I had no choice but to ask Zane to come on the road trip with me.

A compromise occurred to me and I leaned back over Zane, letting my breasts brush against the front of his chest as I reached down to kiss those pearly fangs. My carefully thought-out words died into an unplanned kittenish whimper of delight when he ground into me with one long, delicious stroke.

But I forced myself to concentrate (a difficult thing considering the sweet torment he was putting my body through) and kissed his mouth. "I need something from you too, Zane. Will you do me a small favor?"

His lips caught mine, and I felt the scrape of fangs against my lip, biting into me. The mixture of pleasure and pain and the taste of my own blood in my mouth left me coiling with excitement once more. "Ask," he rasped, his lips trailing across my chin and down my jawline, hinting at my throat.

"I need a vacation," I said. "A road trip. And I need you to come with me. Please," I added, sliding my fingers behind his neck and pressing his mouth against the soft skin of my collarbone. If he bit, I knew I had him—and my trip.

"Whatever you want," he growled against my throat, and I felt his fangs puncture my flesh. It was a sharp sting, followed by the most delicious feeling of warmth as he began to feed from my throat. Heat rolled through my body and coaxed me into another orgasm, hard and fast. His came moments after mine.

He clasped me to him, drinking from my throat and stroking my body until the aftershocks left me, his thrusts slowing. My eyelids began to flutter closed, my body drifting into the feeding-induced sleep brought on by a vampire's bite. I wrapped my arms around my lover and held him close as my body shut down, and I felt his tongue rasp against my skin, closing the bite marks with tender care.

"It's not like you to make deals, Princess," he said, his voice sleepy. "Next thing you know, you'll be working for the queen herself."

I was *nothing* like the queen, or any of the other deal-makers who used people to get their way. But the thought disturbed me as I drifted away.

Passion
THAT'S OUT OF this world.